IF IT HAPPENS WITH THE WILL OF GOD:

THE CONVERSION

KENT RISHAUG

Paperback: 978-1-961438-66-8
eBook: 978-1-961438-67-5
Library of Congress Control Number: 2023915164

This Book is a work of non-fiction.

Ordering Information:

Prime Seven Media
518 Landmann St.
Tomah City, WI 54660

Printed in the United States of America

TABLE OF CONTENTS

The Färingsö Institution is a closed prison for women found on the island of Färingsö in Ekerö municipality. The prison was previously part of the then open prison Svartsjö. Färingsö was opened in 1985 and since 1989 has only female inmates. Färingsö Prison is one of two treatment facilities in the country for incarcerated women with drug problems. The prison has fifty-five beds, forty-three closed and twelve open, and together with the prison Svartsjö constitutes the Stockholm West operating area. All inmates in Färingsö's closed part are drug users with some form of motivation to stop their addiction. All activities should stimulate a life free from drugs and crime. Efforts are being made to encourage the inmates' own responsibility and require a high degree of participation from the inmates in the planning of the execution.

INSHA'ALLAH — GOD WILLING,

Chapter 1

15 MAY 2018

THE CLOCK HAD passed twenty past seven on Monday morning on the light of the sun began to illuminate the prison grounds. At ward four in Färingsö Women's Prison, head of department Margaret Nilsson had finished the planning meeting for the week together with colleagues.

"Great, then we have the week's planning done," she said with a smile and drank the last sip of coffee from her mug. She was about to choke on the coffee when she looked at the clock on her arm. "Oops! We have to hurry to open, we are late."

Margaret rose from the table with her colleagues. She looked at the clock again to make sure she had seen correctly.

Out in the corridor of the ward, protests could be heard from inside the cells while the correctional officers began unlocking door after door. The sound of key rattling and locking pistons sounded through the corridor. It was time for breakfast, but it was a little delayed this morning.

Margaret walked with determined steps to cell number two closest to the guard room, or Plitrummet, which was the general verbal designation from the inmates. There sat a young, overly sweet,

Iraqi girl of 15 years. Her name was Nassiva, according to what was known. The identity was not clear either at the Migration Agency or at the police because it Were Some ambiguities in the case. It was not just Her youthful age that required some extra supervision from the staff of the ward, she was also nine months pregnant.

Margaret, of her sixty-two years, was one of the seasoned veterans of the penitentiary and soon gained sympathy for Nassiva once she had arrived in the ward. Largely because the girl was young, the youngest in the department, but also pregnant. Her medical records did not supply much information in comparison to the other inmates. What had appeared was personal information about the girl that came from her own statement, according to the Migration Agency's report. Little was known about the young girl or her origin, hence the investigation. Not only at the Migration Board, but also at the National Crimea and SAPO.

However, the following information was noted: Nassiva was granted refugee status when she suddenly appeared at the Migration Agency's office in Stockholm two years ago. Her passport showed that she had arrived first in Malmö together with a larger group of refugees, the majority of whom were from Syria and Iraq. After that she travelled to Stockholm. Due to the high workload, her asylum case was routinely left in the pile that steadily grew while waiting to be reviewed individually by case officers. In view of the extensive refugee crisis in Europe, the Finnish Immigration Service had busy times.

Nassiva was placed at a refugee facility for unaccompanied children at Arlanda. After a month of stay, the girl suddenly absconded and disappeared. Six months later, she was found inside the Defense

Staff in Stockholm and arrested by the police for trespassing on protected objects. After a DNA test, it turned out that it was not only the Migration Board that was looking for the girl, but also Riks Krim in connection with two brutal murders of young neo-Nazis who were found floating near the Reichstag building. Nassiva was sentenced in the District Court to fourteen years in prison and deportation, a sentence that the Court of Appeal then upheld after an appeal. The reason she did not receive a life sentence was partly her youthful age and that her background as a war refugee was considered, and partly because she was considered a first-time offender.

Margaret did not perceive Nassiva as either evil or mean, quite the opposite. The girl had always behaved correctly, shyly, and warm-heartedly in front of the staff, but not everyone agreed. Among the inmates in the ward there were divided opinions about her, especially among a Syrian woman convicted of aggravated assault and attempted murder of a taxi driver. There were obvious signs that the Syrian woman Yasmin and Nassiva did not get along and Nassiva requested to and from P37, that is, voluntary locking in her cell, so as not to be disturbed. In addition, a written request from Nassiva for transfer to Hinseberg Prison was on Margaret's desk, something she thought, with all good intentions, was a little premature and therefore left the application without any action.

The ominous rumor of the young evil Nassiva was further worsened when an elderly Finnish-speaking Roman woman named Ritva exclaimed: "That girl is the devil himself!"

Margaret had ignored it because Ritva was a well-known self-proclaimed fortune teller in the department.

She was one of those who usually had clip cards to the prison.

From inside cell number two, Margaret heard a familiar song. It was with high volume the piano notes and the voice of John Lennon sang: *Let it be.* Margaret smiled as she for a Moment recalled back to the time in the seventies when she was young and took part in the demonstrations against the Vietnam War and then-President Richard Nixon outside the U.S. Embassy.

She gently knocked on the steel door with the bunch of keys and waited a bit, then opened the inspection hatch and peeked inside.

"Good morning little friend. Have you slept well? How loud you..." she managed to say before the smile in an instant turned into a grinning expression of disgust and her face turned completely pale. The red-painted lips faded as the lower lip began to show a tendency to tremble. Seconds later, John Lennon's third verse and all the noise from the corridor were drowned out by a terrible scream. Margaret at once backed away from the door while covering her face with both hands. It was with a desperate will that she tried to hide what she had seen.

"Oh god! Call your CV, do something!" she shouted, losing her voice at the same time.

The colleagues who were closest rushed up to Margaret. In a panicky fumbling with the keychain, they found the right key and then managed to open cell number two.

A dramatic sight met the correctional officers. Inside the cell, under a ceiling lamp, the beautiful fifteen-year-old Nassiva hung in a nose made of torn strips from bed sheets. Her body, which was dressed in a white nightgown, was still shaking in death throes as her blue-colored lips secreted frothy saliva. Blood and amniotic fluid ran along both legs, eventually dripping into a growing puddle on the floor around the placenta. The blue-purple umbilical cord was partially wrapped around the neck of the newborn baby lying on a wet chair cushion next to an overturned chair and moaned. The baby's bluish color indicated suffocation and required quick life action.

Suddenly, Ritva came rushing down the corridor, dressed in the usual dress. She nudged both correctional officers standing at the doorway, gaping in disarray as the organ tones from inside the cell faded out one last time.

"Damn! You cannot just stand there like fucking sheepheads," she exclaimed and went into the cell.

She quickly picked up the overturned chair from the floor and placed it directly above the baby who was moaning. Ritva climbed onto the chair without worrying about her dress, which she stumbled on for a moment. With a hidden kitchen knife, she cut off the noose while holding Nassiva's body with her left arm. She almost dropped her.

Four correctional officers from the Central Guard quickly came to the rescue along with two added correctional officers from the department. They hurried in and helped Ritva, who convulsively held Nassiva against her body with both arms. Eight arms received Nassiva and carried her out to the hallway, laid her on the floor and began CPR.

Ritva got down from her chair and turned around. In front of her stood an elderly guard commander with a heavily bushy moustache.

Nonchalantly, she lifted the chair away and placed the kitchen knife on it, then crouched down and lifted the little newborn baby into her arms. Quickly she removed the umbilical cord wrapped around her neck and soon found that she was holding a shapely little boy. She put a finger in the baby's throat and thus the airways became free of amniotic fluid and secretions.

The guard commander smiled as he extended his hand to Ritva.

"Good Ritva, then I can have that knife," he begged kindly but firmly as the baby began to scream so it could be heard outside of the hallway.

Ritva glanced at the kitchen knife, then smiled. Inside, she felt a tingling sense of an imaginary advantage, but her sanity knew better. She took the knife from her chair and handed it over with an innocent smile while responding with a cordial and humorous tone to her Finnish-Swedish accent.

"It's probably the hell in me the first time I'm so glad you guys are there. You should not be worried about the knife. You if anyone should know better, I am an old Romani person too," she added with a restrained smile that exposed two gold teeth.

Before leaving the cell, she was shown a framed photograph of the dresser standing in front of the bed. The photo showed a young, blonde boy with a charming smile, and the photo frame was decorated with a black mourning ribbon.

Ritva came out of the cell carrying the baby in her arms, just behind the CV manager walked in tow with the kitchen knife in his right hand. Ritva walked up to Margaret, resolutely handed the baby to her, and said, "Now this is your responsibility." Margaret looked alternately at Ritva and the baby with a terrified look. She tried to suppress the memories of what she had just experienced and did not want to connect that event to the baby wrapped in one of the prison service's towels. She stretched out her arms and accepted the baby with trembling hands. Margaret thanked her and at the same time corrected a flap on the towel.

"Now don't thank me," Ritva replied, smiling.

She turned and left. Margaret and the CV manager looked with a questioning look for the Roma woman as she walked past the other inmates standing some distance away and with Curiosity had followed the event. Staff continued life support at Nassiva until emergency doctors and paramedics came running on stretchers.

An hour later, inside cell number nine, Ritva took out a box from the top drawer. The motif on the box showed a black floating raven surrounded by stars, angels, and celestial bodies. She sat down on the bed and picked out a deck of cards from the box. The cards, which she systematically laid out, had different symbols.

A Syrian young woman named Yasmin stopped at the doorway.

"I heard what has happened. Where is the baby?" asked Yasmin with tearful eyes.

Ritva interrupted the laying of the cards and looked at Yasmin.

"The hospital I guess well, as does the girl. Why are you so committed to the girl and her baby?"

Yasmin looked at the cards laid out on the bed. She wiped away her tears, and then gave Ritva a glance. Yasmin turned around and left.

As she walked, she felt a deadly presence pass through her body with an unpleasant shiver. The question of Nassiva's state of health could well remain unanswered, as she hated the girl.

With intense eyes, Ritva continued to lay out the cards on the bed. There must be something seriously wrong with that woman, she thought with a shake of her head.

* * *

It was with some distance from the unpleasant event that Margaret walked through the corridor towards the office for a lightning-called crisis meeting. Nassiva's state of health was unclear, but she was alive. The baby had done well considering the circumstances when they left the prison by ambulance. There were reasonable chances that they would survive after all.

Margaret had experienced most things in prison service over the years, but this dramatic event was the worst she had ever faced. Severed wrists and drowning attempts were pure caress compared to what Nassiva had done in the morning. She wondered if there was any earlier hint or sign that the young girl wanted to kill herself. No, she said as she walked past cell number nine, where the steel door was open, and glimpsed Ritva sitting on the bed.

Margaret stopped. She turned around and looked hesitantly towards the doorway. She felt an allure and a challenge, at the same time as she felt an approaching discomfort within her. Although her defensive senses urged her not to go to the doorway, Margaret went there anyway. To contain her fear, she thought, and peered into the cell where Ritva laid out the last card incorrectly on the bed.

Ritva, concentrating on the cards, was fully aware that she was watching as the last card slowly turned over and the symbol of a Black angel appeared. A strongly unpleasant feeling crept up in Margaret as she grabbed the steel door. With a stomachache, she hurriedly walked away. The memory of the incident with Nassiva had etched itself in her consciousness, she did not need more drama than that. It was a sight that turned her reality into a bizarre nightmare.

Ritva sneered when she heard Margaret's rapid footsteps in the corridor, and she shouted with a Finnish-Swedish accent: " Run you! There is a curse on the girl. Even death despises her, that's how damn it is."

The sound of rapid footsteps in the corridor turned into running steps.

Ebola virus causes hemorrhagic fever or hemorrhagic fever with a high mortality rate. Ebola virus is a zoonotic virus that can infect humans and animals through blood and body fluids. There are five known species of Ebola virus: Zaire, Sudan, Côte d'Ivoir, Reston and Bundibugyoebola viruses.

Ebola virus is one of the most lethal pathogens for humans and non-human primates and must be managed in laboratories with the highest protection class, protection class 4. The virus attacks endothelial cells and spreads through the blood into the body and causes necrosis of the body's cells, which leads to a severe course of the disease characterized by bleeding from the body orifices.

Mortality is 50–90%.

Chapter 2

21 MAY 2014

IN THE CAPITAL Freetown in Sierra Leone, President Ernest Bai Koroma sat in his office waiting for the Minister of Interior and the Minister of Health to come for a lightning-called emergency meeting. The telephone conversation with the Minister of the Interior half an hour ago sounded serious, too serious to postpone the meeting until tomorrow. Even though it was late at night, the dinner table and the waiting wife had to have some patience. It was a frustrated president's wife he would come home to, a problem that had to be addressed then. Ernest Bai waited patiently. As he sat immersed in thought, he noted that during his second term as president-elected, he managed to keep the stability and peace that had once been created during his first term in office, after many years of corruption and bloody civil wars that were then ravaging the country.

Being greedy and thirsty for power, such as Zimbabwe's President Robert Mugabe, was not something Ernest Bai aspired to. He chose instead to build the country's infrastructure and distribute important government posts within parliament.

To achieve political order and affinity, governorships were also assigned to the local chiefs who represented the different tribes in the country. It brought increased popularity not only to the president, but also to the party, All People's Congress, which then resulted in his re-election as president in 2007.

Ernest Bai rose from his leather-covered English chair, took a shortcut over the zebra skin on the floor, and then stood at the window facing the front of the government building. Normally, the president would walk around the zebra skin. To show dignity and respect to the late zebra, whose life ended with a 470NE, an English double bouncer signed by William Evans.

Ernest placed his hands behind his back and thought again about the telephone conversation with Interior Minister Musa Tarawallie. Undeniably, there was a serious tone in Musa's voice when he was very anxious for an emergency meeting already tonight. Musa would also arrive together with Health Minister Miatta Kargbo. Musa had time to mention that there was a serious threat and a devastating crisis before the call was interrupted due to poor telephone connection or copper thieves.

If Miatta comes with Musa at this time of day, it really was not a courtesy visit, Ernest thought. A feeling of unease eluded when the clock in the office showed 23:45 and the light from a staff car passed by and stopped outside at the main entrance.

* * *

In the Eastern province, one of the four provinces of Sierra Leone, lies the country's third largest city Kenema. The province of the same name, moreover, borders neighboring Liberia, where the dreaded Ebola epidemic had broken out with full force. The town of Kenema was a regional economic center for other diamond trade, and now faced an epidemic.

Man had found the majority infected just outside the city, where the number of cases also increased alarmingly.

When the first military vehicles rolled into Kenema at dawn, it was after a joint decision by President Koroma, Interior Minister Tarawallie and Health Minister Kargbo. Quarantining the city was a demand from the WHO, after a nightly talk's deliberation.

Surveillance at all border crossings, especially the border zone with Liberia, was tightened in the belief that the spread of the dreaded virus could be prevented. It turned out after a few weeks that the measure came too late and infected people had been found in both Kenema and Kailahun district. In addition, there was a suspected case in the capital Freetown, which has not yet been confirmed.

Outside the hospital in Kenema, Kaiss tribe chieftain Kai Londo sat on an old camping chair and waited with weighted shoulders for a message. He was a man who had aged both in time and eternity and was as skinny and thin as the clothes he wore. The border of malnutrition was nearby. Kai had lost his appetite and had not eaten regularly for the past few weeks. He straightened the headdress that crowned his head. His previously prosperous round face had taken on a fresh look, with sunken cheeks and high cheekbones, which admittedly held his dark sunglasses in place.

Between his thumb and forefinger in his right hand, he held a rosary. With an accustomed movement, he let one bullet at a time slide away along the string while praying to higher powers for mercy. There was heavy grief on Kai's shoulders after losing first his wife and the following week also daughter, Neneh, in Ebola fever. Now he was waiting for word from the hospital about his only grandchild, who had also become seriously ill.

Kai's ordeal was again put to the test when he was deprived of the right to give his wife and daughter a dignified burial. This involved oiling the body, dressing it in formal clothing and then ending the whole ceremony by giving the deceased a kiss and a hug before putting the body into the soil. Due to the elevated risk of infection, the bodies were instead cremated according to certain directives from the WHO.

Kai's leadership as chief also began to be questioned by some members of the Cissi tribe. It was for superstitious reasons, since the chief had not shown the strength to follow the rituals of the tribe, even when it came to his own relatives. It could be seen as a weakness and that the gods had abandoned their chieftain. For Kai, the question was not truly relevant now, his only thought was whether his grandson Jusu Sawie would survive or not. On a tree trunk on the other side of the road sat four men from the Cissi tribe. They wanted to share the chief's heavy grief through their participation.

* * *

Nurse Audrey Limpton, a volunteer for MSF, came out of the hospital entrance and stopped. With a lump in her throat, she wiped away the tears from her cheeks. She straightened the bangs on her sweaty forehead, trying to look as unfazed as possible. Audrey was relieved to put her hospital uniform back on after wearing the warm safety suit for just over an hour. It had been a demanding hour trying to keep Ebola patient alive by extremely small margins. After the hour, she and Dr. Sheik Umar Khan were replaced at the security gate.

Just over a month ago at Heathrow Airport outside London, Audrey's self-created picture of the situation in Kenema was a little more... human than what she now faced in the harsh reality. That people would die was included in her calculations, but it was a bit naïve to think that it was only the old and sick who were at risk. She had not counted on young people and certainly not children, at least not to the extent that was now going on.

This is not right! Audrey thought as a warm wind caressed her cheek, bringing her auburn hair to life. The Sierra Leonean women regarded her appearance with both admiration and envy, while the men looked after her with wistful eyes.

Colleagues from the organisation Médecins Sans Frontières considered Audery to be a sweet and charming young woman. Her intelligence and level of knowledge in healthcare was a resource for the team after her nursing training in Cardiff, UK.

Audrey watched the skinny chief crouched on an old roadside camping chair. On the way, buses, cars, and motorcycles passed in both directions.

"Londo!" someone shouted through an open car window as a young Black man stuck his head out and waved eagerly from a well-used passerby Peugot 404 from 1973.

Kai made no effort to wave back. Instead, he became aware of the people on the other side of the road, who suddenly stood up and looked in his direction with anticipation in their eyes.

Anxiety rose when he realized that it was not him they were looking at, but at someone or something behind his back. He turned around while his right hand hugged the rosary tightly. At the hospital entrance, he saw the maroon-haired woman in a nurse's uniform standing and looking at him.

"I have to do this," Audrey said to herself with a doubtful conviction.

With a heavy sigh and determination, she reluctantly walked with slow steps towards the chief. The squalor-heavy air spread a foul stench from organic garbage lying everywhere, and from sewage ditches. At times, the air filled with smoke as the makeshift cremation site just outside Kenema was used and spread across the city with the help of the damp trade wind.

Audrey stopped in front of the chief and saw a motorcyclist pass by with a body bag hanging over the gas tank. It was a young, Black man who, in addition to sun-bleached shorts and a T-shirt, also had a white mouth guard hanging under his chin and his hands tucked into yellow rubber gloves. An absurd sight where he disappeared among all the crowds and vehicles on his way with his deadly cargo to the cremation outside the city.

An hour earlier, Jusu Sazie, a seriously ill eight-year-old boy, was lying in his camp bed in an isolation room. His critical state of health meant that he was sometimes completely unaware of his situation. He also did not understand that his mother and grandmother had died, or that he was one of the contributing factors to their deaths.

A few days before Jusu was taken to the hospital, he was seriously ill at home and had terrible nightmares. In the dream, a group of costumed people, consisting of four white people in blue full-face robes with glass hoods, took him away to a waiting car. The villagers stood in a semicircle and watched with questioning looks.

The state of health was at a critical stage. He was emaciated due to malnutrition and dehydration and had a remarkably high fever; he had also not been able to retain fluid or solid food for the past few days. The fluid that was successfully given to him was in the form of a drip intravenously. His dazed state of mind often led to hallucinations of creatures in blue safety suits stabbing him with needles. One of them was merciful and tried to quell the fever with a wet, cool cloth.

In the primitive world of Jusu, his mother, grandmother, and grandfather were always around him. There was no real existence of a father, but his male role model was and stayed a grandfather. For some inexplicable reason, none of them were by his side. He had shouted but never got an answer. A cry that was in fact perceived as a faint rustling sound from infected lungs.

He woke up for a moment and perceived the faint outline of a young woman with auburn curly hair. She was dressed in the same blue security dress he had seen earlier and gently wiped blood from his eyes, nose, and mouth. The bleeding was a sign that the boy's life was in its final stages. Jusu could not stay awake and fell asleep again. The last thing he felt was someone dabbing his forehead with a cool cloth, just like Mom had once done.

Dr. Sheik Umar Khan walked up to Jusu and took his pulse while Audrey put the cloth back in the stainless-steel barrel of cloudy water. She reached for the drip stand to change the drip but got an unpleasant feeling. Audrey turned around and together with Sheik she saw little Jusu lying on his back with his head resting on his side against the pillow. The boy's eyes gave a lifeless, blank gaze, and Sheik could only conclude that He had passed away and hopefully reunited with his mother and grandmother. He looked at Audrey with a resigned look and motioned to stop the treatment, covering her body with a white sheet of paper.

Inside the security gate, Sheik and Audrey were helped to remove their safety equipment, which always happened under strict safety regulations. In the next room, two people were seen in security suits and wrapped the boy's lifeless body in a black body bag.

A dark-skinned man dressed in a white security suit carried the body bag having Jusu's stays to the back of the hospital where a motorcyclist was waiting. The dark-skinned motorcyclist was dressed in sun-bleached shorts and a T-shirt. On his feet, he wore flip-flops. The protective equipment he wore did not even protect against the road dust. There was a dirty mouth guard hanging under my chin, and my hands were tucked into yellow rubber gloves. The body bag was placed over the gas tank of the motorcycle and lashed during a brief exchange with the man in the safety suit. The motorcycle kicked off and the youth drove off to once again be regarded as the angel of death by those around him.

Audrey tried to meet Kai Londo's gaze through the dark sunglasses. They annoyed her. You can fucking take off your glasses! she thought to say in anger and frustration instead of showing the despair and sadness that she really carried. After paraphrasing what she was going to say, she said, "I'm sorry to announce that we couldn't save your grandson." After a short breath, she added; "I can only regret, sir."

Kai's reaction was not as Audrey had expected. His mouth stayed in a half-open position whereupon his lower lip became drooping and exposed gums at the lower tooth row. He took a deep breath, wheezing because of asthma symptoms. Audrey bit her lower lip and wanted to say something more. But... What more could she say? Did she really have anything more to say at all? Would she be so emotionally involved in her job as a volunteer?

Audrey turned around and slowly started walking back towards the hospital building. The messenger of death had fulfilled his task. That is how she felt inside when the headache started to make itself felt. It was time to take a tablet before the headache got worse. Must drink more water, she thought.

The WHO (World Health Organization) was founded on April 7, 1948, in New York. Margaret Chan, born 1947 in Hong Kong, has been Director-General of the WHO since November 2006.

Margaret Chan holds a PhD from the University of Western Ontario. She was Director of the Hong Kong Department of Health from 1994 to 2003 and in this capacity had to deal with both avian influenza and SARS, both of which claimed lives in Hong Kong. From 2003 to 2006, she also served at the World Health Organization.

Chapter 3

21 SEPTEMBER 2014

UP ON THE third floor of the WHO headquarters in Geneva, the 66-year-old Director-General, Dr. Margaret Chan, the door of Dr. Chris Sjogren-Lester. Chris thanked her with a smile as he walked in and she politely held open the door to her office with a humble look.

"Come in dear. Take a chair, and we will exchange a few words before you leave," she said as she closed the door behind her.

He sat down on one of the chairs at the conference table, which was placed with a relaxing view of Lake Geneva. Chris, whose appearance was very reminiscent of American actor Alan Alda from the television series M.A.S.H., was originally from Chicago and had had a religious upbringing. In addition to medical school from Harvard University and the University of Minnesota, he specialized in virology and epidemiology. Then, like his older brother Owen Lester, he enlisted in the U.S. Army at Fort Detrick in Frederick, Maryland. At the turn of the millennium, Chris quit Fort Detrick and moved to Sweden in connection with an offer of employment at the security laboratory P4 at Karolinska Institute. There he was part of a research group in pandemic diseases.

Dr. Chan sat down opposite his forty-two-year-old colleague and placed a folder, labeled Sierra Leone (Kenema), on the table. She shuddered as she met Chris's friendly gaze with a serious look.

"We currently have a primary Ebola problem that seems to be escalating completely in the affected states of West Africa, Sierra Leone, Liberia and Guinea. I want to emphasize that it is quite serious."

"This is not good. Of course, I feel the same concern as you about the situation that has arisen," Chris said. "Especially after Dr. Sheik Umar Khan became infected and passed away after only a week or so."

"We really lost an important resource and colleague, with his sudden passing. What upset me most during the meeting was that the Minister of the Interior, Musa Tarawallie, did not want to understand the meaning of what this virus can do. The ritual burial customs of the tribes cannot be considered when the risk of infection is so imminent. My thoughts also go to the young Norwegian girl who became infected," added Dr. Chan and showed an even more concerned expression on his face than before.

"She's alive anyway. Speaking of staff, this English nurse Audrey who worked with Dr Sheik Umar Khan, have we received any response about her test results?"

"No, not yet. The girl should be flown back to London and to the Royal Free Hospital as soon as there is a technical opportunity, and when the girl's health allows it," the Dr replied. Chan and shook his head worriedly.

"I can't really understand how the staff could have become infected to this extent, given the safety regulations that prevail in

Kenema. There must have been some carelessness in the actual handling of the security gate, or even a lack of judgment. This needs to be addressed urgently, otherwise we face a terrible catastrophe."

"How many people have died up to this date?" asked Chris.

"Confirmed infections are three hundred and the number of dead right now is 99," Dr. Chan said with a sigh. "Can we count on you to take on the role of head of this new epidemiology team? We really need your experience and knowledge. Plus, you are good at organizing and delegating," she concluded, referring to Chris' training and experience at Fort Detrick, one of America's premier military bases developing sophisticated biological and biological defense weapons.

"I can take on the assignment if you want. When should I start?" asked Chris, glancing at the wristwatch. He had a flight to fit.

"When to start! Now on the spot. When you get home, contact Erica Saphire at Ollman Saphire Laboratory in San Diego. You already know her." Chris nodded, and Dr. Chan continued.

"The contact with the Centers for Disease Control and Prevention I transfer to you. I assume that there will be some form of cooperation with Fort Detrick. I'll email you a list."

Chris looked at his wristwatch, concluded it was time to leave, and got up from the table.

"Good, I'll get in touch with all concerned. Now I have to go so I don't miss my flight."

Dr. Chan stood up and shook Chris's hand with a worried smile.

"I can also promise that the financial issues will work out. The World Bank has pledged a greater financial contribution, which will further benefit our work and research, so that we may get a vaccine in time."

"That sounds good. We must try to stop the spread of the virus and ensure that staff do not become infected. The situation is urgent and the risk of a wide-ranging..."

"Pandemic. Yes, it was going to be a devastating disaster," interrupted Dr. Chan with a determined grin.

"I'll get in touch," Chris said, opening the door.

"I'm counting on it," Dr. Chan replied with a smile.

Chris smiled, then walked out and closed the door.

Dr. Chan sat down at his desk. She pondered as she weighed the pen between two fingers. She dropped her pen, then picked up the phone to make a call, while opening Outlook to draft an email.

Chapter 4

21 SEPTEMBER 2014

DR. SJÖGREN-LESTER WALKED with his suitcase rolling behind him inside Terminal 1, the international hall at Cointrin International Airport. An airport that was a bit unique because it had a French and a Swiss part.

Chris stopped at the headlines outside a newsstand and parked his suitcase on edge. From one of the headlines, Neu Zürcher Zeitung, he could read: *The Ebola virus is spreading in Europe. Is it the beginning of a pandemic? A French aid worker is suspected of having contracted the Ebola virus on his return.*

Chris shook his head and was bitterly aware that the biggest threat after all was not the Ebola virus, but thoughtless and inquisitive journalists who made headlines to reach the public with the latest news material. It often resulted in twisted theories and speculations with a single purpose; to create headlines. The world did not need misleading information that could lead to chaos and unrest.

"That's enough misery, we don't need any more," he said, his thoughts turning to his lovely wife, Linda. He had met her at the turn of the millennium in connection with her employment at Karolinska

Institute, where Linda managed finance. A year later they married and moved to Knutby and later to Upplands Väsby.

Chris took out his cell phone. It might be a clever idea to call Linda and let him know that he was on his way home so he might not have to take a taxi home from Arlanda Airport. Hopefully, he could have a few words with his ten-year-old son Jacob. If he is around, that is, Chris thought hopefully as he put his cell phone to his ear and heard the first signal.

Linda responded in her silky voice and told her that she and Jacob were on their way home from the Pentecostal church. Jacob had attended Bible class, something he did regularly twice a week. Chris then had a father-and-son conversation and concluded that everything was fine with both Jacob and his schooling. The conversation turned back to Linda. Chris was promised that she and Jacob would be at the international terminal to meet him.

Chris grabbed his suitcase and started walking towards gate eight. The thoughts around the problem of RNA viruses grew in his head. There was no doubt that the safety regulations and the measures decided by the WHO did not help. Nevertheless, Ebola fever spread at an alarming rate, not only in West Africa but also in some countries in Europe. Dr. Chang's concern about a coming pandemic was not unrealistic, which Chris reluctantly agreed to when the medical staff were infected and dying one by one, despite all countermeasures.

Arriving at gate eight, Chris sat down on one of the chairs at the boarding desk. Only ten minutes remained before boarding the SAS plane that was to fly to Stockholm-Arlanda. Chris thought of Jacob and Linda putting the thought process on something completely different than viral diseases and pandemics. These were thoughts that gave him something more loving, and something to long for. A safe, carefree life where God had a close place, of course.

Chris took the opportunity to say a silent prayer with clasped hands, which began by thanking the lord and his blessing before boarding. That Chris and Linda had received God's gift, namely their son Jacob. That his life story led to the first meeting with Linda, who later became his wonderful wife. Chris ended the prayer with an addendum, while he was at it, that the flight would be pleasant and carefree, Amen. Surely that could not be too much to ask.

There was a crackle in the public address system when a boarding announcement was heard. Chris got up and grabbed his suitcase, then walked over and stood in line at check-in with the plane ticket in hand. In three hours, he would meet his family after spending two days at a world conference in Geneva. He looked forward to it and longed for home. By God's will, the week passed normally without any unexpected surprises. A new outbreak of avian influenza or the Ebola virus is gaining a foothold in Europe and spreading uncontrollably, for example.

God had other plans.

God who loves children, look to me as a little one. Wherever I turn in the world, my happiness is in God's hands. Happiness comes, happiness goes, you stay, Our Father.

Chapter 5

22 SEPTEMBER 2014

At ten pasts three in the afternoon, the school day was over at Runby middle school in Upplands Väsby. Jacob and his friend of the same age, Robert, walked across the schoolyard with their backpacks propped up behind their backs and were on their way to the bikes. Jacob happened to stumble upon a curb as he was about to cross the lawn. With a few quick stacking steps, he managed to regain his balance with his slender body. Robert was quick to react and grabbed Jacob's jacket. He had an almost identical physique but had short-cropped dark hair that was hidden under a sports cap.

"Look where you're going," Robert urged as he dropped his jacket.

"Now you sound like my mother," Jacob replied, embarrassed, feeling overprotected as he straightened his bangs.

"It seems to be my life's mission. Are you coming to floorball?"

Jacob did not have time to respond until he felt a powerful blow that hit the backpack from behind. A ten-year-old boy named Jimmy ran mockingly past and waved his floorball stick. On the opposite side, David ran by with his floorball stick and a smile on his face.

"Is God going to punish me now? Haha. Idiot," Jimmy shouted sarcastically as he stopped at his bike. He ran his fingers through his short-cropped hairstyle.

Jacob did not answer. He knew what awaited him, so he slowed down in his steps with Robert. Jacob preferred to avoid a conflict with Jimmy. With a bit of luck then maybe...

Jimmy leaned over the bike to unlock, when he saw that the rear wheel was completely flat and even the air vent was removed.

"What the hell!"

"What is it?" asked David as he stopped at his bike parked next to him.

"Then look! Someone has messed up my bike."

David looked at the rear wheel, then shrugged.

"I don't have a pump with me," he enlightened.

Jimmy turned his gaze to Jacob and Robert, who had stopped and waited. He could quickly set up that it was undoubtedly Jacob who was the saboteur, otherwise he would have come here and picked up his bike. Robert was complicit in this sabotage too, Jimmy thought.

"Why don't you come here! Don't you dare?" cried Jimmy to Jacob.

Jacob looked at Robert, who looked at both Jimmy and David. He slowly started walking towards his bike.

"Are you the one who let the air out on Jimmy's bike?" asked David. Jacob shook his head.

Robert started walking after Jacob who was a few steps ahead. He was fully aware of Jimmy's sadistic, and not least provocative, manner towards Jacob. Not a day went by without Jacob becoming Jimmy's little chicken at school. It could be enough that he happened to look at Jimmy just for a moment to become a trigger and motive for Jimmy and his overly harsh actions against Jacob. It usually ended with violence such as punches and kicks that Jacob received. Jimmy lacked human restraint and the ability to expect the consequences of his uncontrolled actions. Robert had, at least during school hours, always been Jacob's protector and this afternoon was not going to be any more different than before.

When Jacob arrived at his bike, he was greeted by Jimmy who stood in front of him face to face.

"Why don't you answer?" he asked with a mocking smile, waiting for a reason to shut Jacob up.

Jacob looked at Jimmy, then lowered his gaze to the ground. Jimmy grew impatient and nudged Jacob when he did not get an answer. Jacob looked at Jimmy with innocent eyes.

"God does not exist! Do you hear that? You are just lying," Jimmy said provocatively.

"Stop!" said Robert, stopping next to Jacob.

"Don't get involved in this!" urged Jimmy in a threatening tone.

"God sure exists, Jimmy. You cannot just see it," Jacob said in a convincing manner, hoping it would toy his own fears, at least a little.

Jimmy stared at Jacob with a hateful look and kicked Jacob's bike in sheer provocation.

"You've said that so damn many times, prove it!" Jacob pointed to the rear wheel of Jimmy's bike and said succinctly, "There."

Jimmy stared at the rear wheel, and then at Jacob with a surprised expression on his face. Then he looked at the rear wheel again and once again stared at Jacob with an unchanged expression on his face.

"Huh! Has God let the air out on my bike, why? You are lying," Jimmy said with a provocative smile. "Do you know one thing, you lie all the time," he repeated as the smile disappeared and changed into a menacing face with pressed lips.

"You hit me with the bandy club and God responded to it by letting the air out on your bike. It is called karma, in case you did not know it," Jacob replied with conviction, then ran his hand over the saddle of his bicycle.

Now it was the last straw for Jimmy. He grabbed Jacob's jacket and pulled him close to him.

"Do you think you're funny now? Are you going to have a bang?"

Jimmy acted with his right arm to hit Jacob when a Chevrolet van stopped at the side of the road and honked as the side window was hoisted down. A less attractive man with a shaved head stuck his head out.

"Jimmy! Give a fuck about that."

It was Henke, Jimmy's father, who got out of the van. He was dressed in Ragnsell's work clothes and walked with determined steps towards the boys. Jimmy let go of Jacob and began gesturing with his arms, pointing at his bike at the same time.

"What! He is let the air out on my bike," Jimmy shouted, hoping that Dad Henke would see the situation as justification for giving Jacob a go.

"It wasn't me," Jacob excused himself, reluctantly looking at Jimmy's dad and his big, tattooed hands.

On the finger knuckles of the left hand, it was tattooed with a letter on each finger H.E.N.K.E. On the right hand between the thumb and forefinger, a swastika was tattooed. Jimmy's dad looked no less eye-catching when a tattoo appeared at one throat section. All the earrings that sat in both earlobes undeniably reinforced the impression of his appearance.

"Fuck it, Jimmy," Henke replied irritably, looking at the bike.

"He said it was God who let the air out to punish me," Jimmy said.

"It was God who..." Jacob said when his father Henke interrupted him in a sizzling tone.

"You put that off, there's no God. I'm fucking living proof of that, idiot."

Jacob swallowed the lump in his throat and then backed off two steps when he reluctantly met Henke's hateful gaze.

"There you hear your little shit!" hissed Jimmy.

Jimmy's dad rolled the bike towards the van. He looked back and saw that Jimmy was still standing by Jacob and kicking his bike.

"Are you coming today?" shouted Henke.

"See you at the game tonight."

Jimmy caught up with his father and Henke handed the bike to Jimmy as they walked.

"Here, take your fucking bike," Henke said irritably.

Jacob and Robert stood and watched as Jimmy tried to get his bike into the van. Henke ended up grabbing the bike and heaving it into the car with a bang, and then the rear doors slammed shut.

David got on his bike and called out to Jimmy as he was about to get in the car.

"See you at the game!"

Jimmy gave a thumbs up and then gave the finger to Jacob and Robert before getting in the car and closing the car door. Henke started the engine and kick-started. David looked after the car as he rode away.

Robert looked at Jacob and looked relieved.

"Nobody likes Jimmy. You should not be afraid of him," he said as he got on his bike and straightened his back.

"I'm not afraid of him. I just find him unpleasant. Then I know that God is with him and trying to get him to think better, a hopeless job you might think. But Jimmy does not know about it and is not receptive to it yet. He will have to keep pumping air into his rear wheel and get detained with calls to the principal," Jacob noted, who reinforced the feeling of hopelessness by rolling his eyes.

Surprised, Robert looked at Jacob. He could not understand his forgiving attitude towards Jimmy, who was often his tormentor.

Robert shrugged. "Okay."

Jacob got on his bike, and they rode off home. That will be fine, he thought to himself.

Chapter 6

22 SEPTEMBER 2014

AT THE HOME of the Sjögren-Lester family, Jacob sat with his mother Linda and ate dinner. Jacob's thoughts had stuck to what Jimmy's father had told him earlier that afternoon.

Linda sat across from and studied with her son, who was poking at the food while he pondered. She smiled as Jacob's forehead began to crease and he sat for a moment completely absent with chewed food in a half-open mouth and homemade ground meat sauce around his lips.

"But honey, what are you thinking about?" asked Linda with a restrained smile.

Jacob, who suddenly jumped, gave her a confused look, and swallowed the food.

"Is Dad going to work long tonight?"

"I don't know, friend. But I am going with you to floorball today if that is what you were thinking about?"

"I didn't think about it... Mom, I met Jimmy's dad when..." Jacob let the words die down when he realized that one should avoid discussions that would inexorably lead to conversations with the teacher about Jimmy. He wanted to avoid it because it would punish itself on an unguarded occasion.

"Honey, has Jimmy been stupid to you again?" asked Linda, her charming smile changing into a serious expression on her face.

"He's always stupid, Mom. Jimmy's dad told me that God does not exist and that he had proof of that. How can he be?"

"Did he say what the evidence consisted of?" asked Linda. *She would certainly break down Jimmy's father's unfounded hypotheses about God and all religion in* general *for his kind-hearted little son.*

"Yes, he said he was living proof that God doesn't exist," Jacob replied hesitantly.

"He has not accepted God's blessing, but that is proven. Eat now, baby."

"I said that too, but then I meant that Jimmy..."

"Honey. Eat now," Linda repeated, then took a bite from the plate.

* * *

The floorball match was at times both heated and rowdy, and there were two main characters who stood out during the match. Among the players, it was of course Jimmy who deliberately gave Jacob slaps and unfair club hooks. Was not it, Jimmy blocked him in another improper way, especially when the referee was not looking or nearby. The other main character was, of course, Henke, who disrupted the match with his loud protests from the stands.

Jacob, who was not even close to the ball, had Jimmy's stick hooked around his shin when the referee was busy elsewhere. This is despite Jacob trying to stay away from Jimmy. At a blowout, Jacob took the opportunity to protest, and the referee gave Jimmy a reprimand.

Henke smiled and gave him a thumbs up.

Linda, who was sitting a short distance away, looked at him angrily. She bit down so as not to start any conflict on the grandstand. Linda hated this Nazi-tattooed fellow to such an extent that she made the hell pale. At the same time, it triggered gross deeds of thought, which led to her having to ask God for forgiveness. Especially when God Almighty was worshipped to commit murder on her behalf.

In the heat of the battle on the field, Jacob tried to take the ball from Jimmy while they ran side by side. What Jimmy did not notice was that his right shoe was no longer tied. The shoelaces were dragged along the floor while Jimmy ran and Jacob accidentally stepped on the shoelaces, causing Jimmy to come to a complete stop, who went headlong to the floor. The referee noticed it and blew the match off when Jimmy resorted to hand over Jacob.

Henke hurriedly stood up and roared with black eyes.

"That's fucking deportation!"

The judge turned to Henke and gestured clearly with his hand for him to sit down and calm down. Jimmy stood up with slightly burned knees and limped up to the referee.

"He hooked me on purpose," he protested, grimacing a little more to show how much pain he was suffering now.

"There is no question of a curvature, but he happened to step on your shoelaces."

"Men ..."

"No buts, I saw it," the referee replied firmly, wanting to get the match going again to avoid getting into unnecessary arguments.

Jimmy at once began gesturing with his arms and club.

"Are you stupid all over your head?!"

A ball suddenly rolled between Jimmy's legs, and he caught sight of his shoelaces. The truth was closer than he first thought. The judge held Jimmy with a determined look, could see how the boy's face changed color. The referee pointed to the stands.

"Two minutes, my good lord. So are the rules."

Jimmy felt stupid in front of the referee and the team. There was only one person guilty of this and it would cost him dearly. He glared angrily at Jacob who was standing next to Robban. Jimmy turned around and threw the club onto the pitch in pure frustration and anger at the referee's sharp urge. He ended up having to pick up the club before going to the stands, where Henke stood with his arms waving up in the air and screaming.

"Now you get to take me fuck give you, judge bastard!"

Henke looked around to see if he was getting support from the audience, but none of the parents or the other bystanders said anything. Henke turned to Linda who was standing a short distance away and just shook his head, something he could not take. With determined steps, he walked towards her to read the louse of her.

As Jimmy sat down on the substitutes' bench, he looked a little worriedly at his father, who stopped by Jacob's mother. Linda stood up with a short prayer of self-discovery and strength. Now she was faced with Mr. Lucifer herself, and she certainly did not intend to do so in a sitting position.

"So, your godforsaken kid is going to have to rough and play ugly games against my kid, apparently that's okay?" exclaimed Henke with his distorted sense of reality.

Linda made eye contact with Henke and did not flinch her gaze or do anything else that could be interpreted as weakness or fear. She at once gave an answer to the speech.

"Maybe it's about time, considering all the evil your son has inflicted on Jacob. Do you have no human values at all? Do you have no shame in your body?"

"Shame! And it should come from you. Move the hell back to Knutby and that fucking cult you once came from. You, you hypocritical bastards, may well sacrifice yourselves for your fucking faith by committing collective suicide, so we get rid of you."

"Then you may want to attend and join us in killing yourself. It would be considered an incredibly good deed in that case," Linda replied, unable to help but sneer.

Henke came off completely when the referee blew the match off, and Jacob's team won 12–9. He turned muttering around and walked to Jimmy who had taken the loss hard. He slammed the club against a chair several times while swearing uncontrollably, like the child of letters he was. It was not only the loss of the match that was exposed in Jimmy's wounded soul, but also the personal struggle between him and Jacob, which became a disaster with the sending off.

* * *

On the way home, Robban got a ride from Linda and Jacob. Amid the joy of victory, he realized that they had a study day the next day, something that both Jacob and Robban had completely forgotten about. It was a message that also surprised Linda before she stopped outside Robert's gate.

"But hey! Why didn't you say anything about this earlier?" she asked worriedly.

"I didn't think about it. I forgot."

"But my friend, me and dad have to work tomorrow. What should we do with you then? You cannot be home alone all day," she noted with a deep, resigned sigh.

"Jacob can be with me tomorrow," Robban suggested, smiling.

"Yes, Mom. I can be with Robban tomorrow," repeated Jacob, who thought it was an excellent idea.

Linda pondered quietly. As far as she was concerned, that was okay and that would be a quick solution to the problem. She also could not believe that her husband Chris would have a different view. Robert, who lived with his father and grandmother, had a good family, a common opinion for both Linda and husband Chris. The aunt could be perceived as a little confused from time to time, which was normal considering her age. She was at home all the time and Jacob had been with them before without any problems, Linda noted.

"Do you think it's okay for your grandmother?" asked Linda as Robert got out of the car with his floorball club and training bag.

"I can ask her."

"Yes, do it. Tell her that I am calling tonight to check that everything is okay. Your dad is working tomorrow, right?"

Robert nodded and thanked him for the ride. He closed the car door and walked to the gate while waving to Jacob and Linda as they drove away.

Jacob looked out the back window and saw Robert drop his bag on the stairs and key in the door code. He did not have time to see more than that until the car turned left around the corner.

* * *

During the evening, Linda talked to Robert's grandmother on the phone. From another room, Jacobs could be heard discussing with Chris about the floorball match. Robert's grandmother had absolutely no problem having Jacob at their house.

"He's an adorable child, little Jacob," she expressed proudly, as if Jacob were her own.

Linda was a little embarrassed by all the flattery about her son. She thanked her for her help and the conversation ended. Now the babysitting is solved for tomorrow, thankfully. Now she did not have to bother her parents about it. They have put up so much anyway, she thought in front of the hall mirror as she looked at herself.

Linda opened Jacob's bedroom door and looked inside. He lay in his bed with Chris sitting next to him and together they said an evening prayer with clasped hands. Prayer was a routine and security for the Sjögren-Lester family. After evening prayer, Jacob crawled under the covers and was stopped by Dad. Chris hugged him and gave him a kiss on the cheek.

"I love you, son," he said proudly as he stood up to let Linda out and gave her a kiss on the cheek. She gave Jacob a huge hug and a kiss on the forehead.

"I love you above anything else on earth," she said, bringing a charming smile in return.

Jacob turned off the light while Linda and Chris walked out, leaving the bedroom door slightly ajar. Jacob was a little afraid of the dark, and the small streak of light that came from the hall gave him security. With God's presence in the room, Jacob put peace and quiet to sleep. He was now protected from all the forces of darkness, namely Jimmy and his father.

Linda was lying in bed admiring Chris as he entered the bedroom dressed in his customary pajamas. She felt a desire and ideally, she wanted to rip off her nightgown and just throw herself at her beloved man. Chris managed to lay under the covers before Linda crept closer with her charming smile. He gave her a smile back and kissed her tenderly on the mouth.

"I want you. Can you cope?" asked Linda as she laid her head on his chest and relentlessly began fingering his pajamas.

Chris felt a little tired after the day's work but could not say no to his lovely wife. He sat up and took off the top of his pajamas, exposing his hairy chest. Linda was not late in taking off her nightgown. She lay down and her beautiful hair settled over the pillow.

A real cougar," Chris said as he lay over Linda and felt her warm body against his. Linda pressed her nails against

Chris's back, gently pulled his fingers and said, "Kurr, meow."

Chris kissed her while his hands intuitively searched Linda's breasts. It started her erection center like an annealed bed of coal that was blown on. Chris caressed her breasts slowly and teasingly. She closed her eyes and felt his stubby beard growth as he closed his lips around her areola. They loved with intensity and without a clue what tomorrow would bring.

INSHA'ALLAH — GOD WILLING.

Prayer in the hour of danger

The Lord keeps you; the Lord is your protection at your right hand. The sun shall not harm you by day, and not the moon by night. The Lord will keep you from all evil, He will preserve your soul. The Lord will preserve your exit and your entrance from now until eternity.

Chapter 7

23 SEPTEMBER 2014

It was approaching eight o'clock in the morning when Chris and Linda stood by the car outside the house on Lillvägen 3. They waited patiently for Jacob who tried to pull his bike out of the garage. It was a sable lawnmower that insisted on hooking onto the bike all the time, which angered Jacob to the breaking point. Hearing Dad's call behind him did not improve the situation significantly.

"Jacob. Now you need to think methodically. See where the problem is and then find a solution," Chris urged in all good faith.

At the same time, he could not help but smile at Jacob's growing frustration. Linda gave Chris a light nudge with her elbow.

Jacob opened the garage door wide open. Rolled the bike back into the garage and then rolled the lawn mower a little to the side. On the next attempt, the bike came out of the garage without any problems and with a deep sigh he closed the garage door and locked. He then walked with the bike to his parents and said goodbye. He would cycle home to Robban on his own.

"Honey, now you ride straight to Robert. You do not stop anywhere along the way, promise me that," Linda urged.

"Mom. You do not have to worry about me, I have God by my side," Jacob said with a reminder that he was a big guy before getting on the bike.

"Do you have your phone with you?" asked Chris, unlocking the car with the remote.

Jacob thumped the backpack hanging behind his back with his elbow.

"You have to promise to call if something happens, no matter what," Linda urged. "You must not forget it, promise me that."

"Yes," Jacob replied in an irritated tone.

Linda hugged him and then a hug came from Chris. Jacob rode away while they looked after him. Of course, it will be fine, Chris thought.

Jacob rode on the sidewalk parallel to Hagvägen and as Chris and Linda drove by, they waved to him. Jacob waved back as the car continued and disappeared out of sight at Runby square.

Linda took a deep breath. Should she really let Jacob ride his bike by herself? She gave Chris a questioning look as he sat driving with completely different thoughts, work thoughts. Jacob could take care of himself and was careful. But he was only ten years old and that was Jimmy, she thought. The inner feeling of being an irresponsible mother penetrated her consciousness.

* * *

Jacob cycled down Billsbacke in the direction of the train station. Arriving at the station, he led the bike down the stairs and continued through the underpass and then made his way up the stairs on the other side of the train station, where the buses left. He continued cycling along the Central Road and turned right into an archway that had its passage through the rental property, opposite Medborgarhuset and a nearby patisserie. He then cycled past the playground to the residential area on Finnspångsvägen.

He stopped at the center gate and placed his bike against the wall of the house. After locking it, he keyed in the door code and heard a buzzing sound. He opened the door and disappeared into the stairwell, then went up the stairs as the gate door slowly closed again.

On the first floor, he stopped at a door. It said Magnusson in the mailbox. Jacob pressed the bell twice and listened intently for Robert's quick footsteps from inside the apartment. Nothing was heard. He waited a bit before ringing again. Then there were footsteps slowly walking up to the front door. The door opened and an elderly lady with glasses and set hair appeared in the doorway.

"Hello! Now I am here. Is Robban home?" said Jacob with a smile. Strange that Robban was not standing there at the front door, where is he?

"Hello. Robert is with his dad at work today," the aunt replied, and then looked a little anxiously towards the hall and kitchen.

"Well," Jacob said a little sniffly.

"I'm doing the food. You can come back this afternoon instead," the aunt said before abruptly closing the front door in front of Jacob's nose.

He walked slowly down the stairs, feeling a little... abandoned. When he came out of the gate, he stopped for a moment, put his hand in his trouser pocket and picked up a hundred-crown note. *Candy,*

I am going to buy candy. Jacob unlocked the bike and rode the same road he came from.

His plan now was to buy some pick & mix inside the tobacco shop and then cycle home and watch movies or do his math homework.

Said and done, Jacob came out of the tobacconist carrying a white paper bag of candy for the cost of twenty crowns and looked pleased. He got on his bike and started cycling along the footpath in the direction of the civic center. He stopped at a crosswalk. Jacob had changed his mind, instead of cycling home, he was going to the playground. There was a chance that Robert could have come home earlier.

* * *

Jimmy's father, Henke, drove the garbage truck along the Central Road and was in a bad mood. He had just been to a pizza restaurant and picked up garbage. He was able to set up, despite several verbal requests and written messages from the sanitation company Ragns Sells, that they were still mixing food scraps with the remaining garbage in the barrels, something they would not do. This resulted in Henke simply having enough of these damn parasites.

"Imagine that you are fucking Blackfeet don't learn at some point. You are fucking not home now!" Henke shouted to the pizza maker who lit a cigarette at the entrance to the store. Henke turned red with anger when the pizza maker showed such nonchalance by just shrugging his shoulders and continuing to puff on his fucking cigarette. As a result, Henke the bull threw the bin away in pure frustration, got into the garbage truck and drove off with a flying start. Then he screamed with his fradga running from his mouth.

"Fucking camel driver! Have you ever heard of waste sorting?"

Henke approached a crosswalk where he spotted a fair-haired little guy with a blue mountain bike. As the boy stood still with his bike and looked in his direction, Henke became convinced that the boy had seen him in the green garbage truck. With that belief, he did not break, but kept the same speed.

Suddenly, the boy stepped out onto the road with his bike right in front of the garbage truck. Henke panicked and began to crank the steering wheel to the left, while panicking brakes. A thump was heard from the passenger side of the cab. Henke closed his eyes to the strong conviction that he had hit the boy. The garbage truck stopped with a sharp rock.

Jacob stood with the bike only five centimeters from the green bumper of the garbage truck and was completely paralyzed with his mouth wide open. He stared at the turn signal flashing at head height as the ticking sound of the relay could be heard from inside the truck cab. A car honked. Jacob winced and found that he was still alive and unharmed. He looked around and saw two scratches on the passenger door of the garbage truck. He then looked at the handlebars of the bike and found that the right handbrake lever as well as the handlebars were the cause of the scratches on the car door.

Jacob heard someone get out of the truck cab with a loud bang of the door. He started walking with the bike and just as he passed the front of the garbage truck, a bald, tattooed man appeared out of nowhere.

"What the hell are you doing?!" shouted Henke when he caught sight of the boy.

Jacob thus received a new shock and only stammered when he caught sight of the devil's offspring. He felt it splash in his underpants and thought that now was the last moment and that He would be beaten to death here and now. Suddenly, Jacob rushed off with his bike across the road and in front of a taxi that suddenly had to brake. On the move, Jacob threw himself on his bike and pedaled as fast as he could towards Medborgarhuset, which was on the opposite side of Central Road.

"Is that you?" shouted Henke with surprise when he recognized Jacob who disappeared to the right through an archway, fifty yards away.

Henke got into the garbage truck and pulled the car door shut in pure anger.

Jacob stopped inside the arch and turned to make sure he was not being followed. He tried to calm down by breathing more calmly and getting his heart rate down. Jacob rolled back on his bike towards the vault mouth, staying as close to the tunnel wall as possible. He peered cautiously out at the mouth of the tunnel to see how the green garbage truck drove in the direction of the train station and puffed out while his heart with wild efforts wanted to leave his body.

The boy remained straddling his bike and felt immense relief. Completely unexpectedly and out of nowhere, he felt a knock on his back. In a flash he turned around and suddenly came face to face with Jimmy. Next to him stood David with a grin. Just behind Jimmy stood Anna dressed in a T-shirt and denim skirt.

Jacob, who had just escaped Jimmy's father by a hair's breadth from death, now came face to face with the devil's own offspring.

"Why are you standing here pushing?" asked Jimmy, teasingly pushing Jacob's bike.

"Rest a little," Jacob replied just to say something, glancing a little at the bag of candy he was trying to hide behind his back.

"What do you have in the bag? Is it candy?" asked Jimmy, patting Jacob on the cheek with a mocking smile.

Suddenly, without any warning, Jimmy grabbed Jacob, ripped him off his bike, and then pushed him onto the asphalt. During the fall, Jacob dropped the candy bag on the asphalt and Jimmy was not late to take it. He tried to get up but was suddenly stopped by Jimmy's foot on his chest. He handed the bag of candy to David.

"Hold it," he said before straddling Jacob with a wicked sneering grin.

"You're not so cocky now," Jimmy said, laughing.

Jacob was completely silent. Then there was a small chance not to be beaten ... More than that, he did not have time to think until he got a slap. Then came the return that hit the other cheek while Jimmy taunted him with schadenfreude. Jacob lay completely still with tearful eyes, hoping that some adult would come by. He silently prayed to God for help as tears began to flow down his cheeks.

Now the position of power was restored, according to Jimmy, who felt victorious. He looked alternately at Anna and Jacob with a growing smile. His eyes twinkled in a way that showed he had an idea.

"Anna, come here," Jimmy ordered, and she took three steps forward.

"No, stand next to me, close to me," Jimmy said, waving impatiently.

"What are you going to do?" asked David.

"You'll see. Stand over there so no one comes," Jimmy ordered, pointing to the vault mouth.

Anna stood next to Jimmy and sensed that something exciting was going on. Jimmy slipped his hands under her skirt and tore her panties down to her ankles. Anna was both embarrassed and horrified by his actions.

"What are you doing, Jimmy!" she shouted in horror, and at once crouched down to pull up her panties.

"Nope. Wait! Anna... Do you need to pee?"

"No!" replied Anna but stopped and instead looked very questioning.

"Well, you're probably a little pink," Jimmy said, then put a palm on Jacob's cheek.

"What do you want me to do... No! Do you want me to?"

Anna began to giggle as she began to sense Jimmy's intentions and pointed embarrassedly at Jacob. Jimmy nodded with twinkling eyes.

David looked worriedly at Jimmy and Anna and then at Jacob who was lying on his back against the asphalt with red-swollen cheeks.

"Jimmy lay off."

"Shut up David. Grab some candy."

Jacob lay petrified and shocked when he realized what was going on. Anna giggled and removed her panties and then stood straddling Jacob.

"Good Anna. Now back off a little," Jimmy said, grabbing her calves. He then steered her as she took a few steps backwards and stood just above Jacob's face.

"Now you can crouch down," he urged with a mocking smile as he eased his skirt a little to see.

Anna crouched down gently while Jacob's head disappeared inside her skirt. Jacob closed his eyes and was horrified because he saw Anna's inner thighs and glimpsed her vagina. He must Be doing something bad quick, he thought. Jacob panicked, managed to wriggle his arms off Jimmy's knees, then placed his firsthand Anna's buttocks and gave her a push. Anna screamed as she lost her balance and fell over Jimmy. She fell backwards, which ended with Jimmy's head disappearing inside her skirt and she started straddling him.

Now Jacob got the chance and quickly got up. He grabbed his bike before David could intervene and then ran as he threw himself over the bike and pedaled away. As he passed the three bikes that were inside the tunnel, he took the opportunity to kick the first bike so that it toppled over the other bikes lined up next to it. This could give Jacob a slight head start.

Anna sat straddling Jimmy's face and laughed hysterically. At the same moment, she accidentally splashed some urine which resulted in Jimmy getting a small jet right in his face and thus panicked and screamed. David ran over to help Jimmy by lifting Anna away, who could not stop laughing. She managed to get up as Jimmy quickly rose from the asphalt, spitting and sizzling.

He glared angrily at Anna as he tried to wipe her urine off with his jacket sleeve. Jimmy was not angry, not angry, but holy cursed as he fixed his black gaze in the direction Jacob disappeared.

Psalm 121

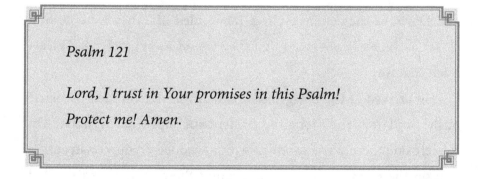

Lord, I trust in Your promises in this Psalm!

Protect me! Amen.

Chapter 8

23 SEPTEMBER 2014

JACOB WAS TERRIFIED, yes, so scared that he feared for his life while cycling fast towards the playground in the courtyard at Finnsspångsvägen. Behind him, he heard the excited voices of Jimmy and David as they came cycling, it sounded like they were getting closer. Jacob was convinced that they would soon catch up. At least it felt that way.

He arrived at the playground, which was surrounded by dense bushes and trees and a longitudinal fence of impregnated timber. On the left side there was a sandbox with a wooden frame construction and on the right side of the playground there was a black-painted swing set built in a steel tube frame. He saw the bushes as a possible hiding place and instinctively he turned left towards the sandbox and jumped off the bike at speed, then plunged down and crawled under the fence and into the bushes. At the same moment, the bike hit the wooden fence and was left lying over the sandbox with the front wheel spinning in the air.

Jacob crawled among the bushes and heard Jimmy and David getting closer. He found a good, sheltered spot under two densely grown bushes overlooking the walkway. He heard Anna shouting from a distance, it sounded like she was not keeping up with Jimmy and David's pace and was falling behind. Jacob spotted a rough stick and had an idea. Whether it was good remains to be seen, there was not enough time for any further reflections.

Lying on his stomach, he reached for the stick, but it was a little too far away. Jacob crawled a little closer, managed to grab hold of it, and crawled back as Jimmy and David got closer and closer.

Jimmy held the bag of candy around the handlebars while he pedaled on his bike. He smelled of urine and, to put it mildly, felt violated and laughed at. The thought of tearing Jacob to pieces like a crazy pit bull terrier was at least nearby if given the opportunity. In addition, he was angry with David, who with his passivity reacted far too late when Anna took the liberty of pinking him.

He had intended to humiliate the godforsaken boy and make up for what happened at the floorball match. The idea came from a movie that Jimmy had found at home and seen on a few occasions. It was a DVD that his dad had hidden carelessly in mom's drawer in the bedroom.

He was riding his bicycle feverishly with ominous thoughts of revenge when it suddenly came to a complete stop. He felt the rear wheel lock and without a second thought he looked down to the left towards the rear wheel. He was horrified to see that a stick was stuck between the spokes, then it slammed.

Unfortunately, Jimmy unconsciously steered to the right and the bike collided with the adjacent fence. He had no chance, flew over the handlebars, and landed with his head against a rock on the lawn and then lay down.

Jacob, who saw the whole event, watched in horror as Jimmy lay there motionless on the lawn next to the stone, with Blood flowed from his head, nose, and mouth. Not a sign of life appeared.

David came at high speed and swerved to avoid colliding with Jimmy's bike that was across the walkway. He threw himself off his bike and ran up to Jimmy while his bike fell over Jimmy's. He shook Jimmy as he shouted, but the boy showed no signs of life. He pushed Jimmy and screamed in panic. David feared the worst as he watched the pool of blood at Jimmy's head grow larger.

Jacob wanted to crawl away but then saw the bag of candy lying on the walkway. He was going to reach for it, but just then Anna came cycling and stopped half a meter away. She screamed and started crying when she saw what had happened. She rushed over to David who held Jimmy convulsively and just cried.

Carefully, Jacob crawled off in the direction of the playground while Anna and David were busy with the lifeless Jimmy. He crawled under the fence and then continued up to the bike that was overturned in the sandbox. Raised it, hitched up on it and quickly rode away. Suddenly, he heard Anna screaming right out with anguished panic in her voice.

"He's dead, he's dead! Mom, Mommy!"

Jacob cycled as fast as he could out onto Finnsspångsvägen and then turned right onto Optimusvägen. Jacob understood what he had done and the guilt inside him was impossible for a ten-year-old boy to oversee. He had done something terrible and unforgivable, an act that God detested.

He quickly approached the intersection of Optimusvägen and Central Road but was so preoccupied with his thoughts that he did not notice two masked youths armed with a sawn-off shotgun and axe coming running from the tobacco shop. At the same second, Jacob cycled right out into the intersection where two cars and a bus had to brake.

Both robbers threw themselves into a dark-colored BMW, which drove off with screeching tires in the direction of Väsby station and then disappeared to the right.

Jacob, who carried a sinner's confession within him, trampled for his life. He had to flee from this hell and at the same time asked God for help. A prayer that fizzled out, believing that God had turned his back on him.

More than that, he did not have time to think before the next problem appeared out of nowhere. From the T-junction in front came a police car in full emergency with blue lights and siren on. Jacob once again got a big lump in his throat that was suffocating him as he met the police car at high speed. He quickly turned right onto Björkvtovägen while the police car drove past in the direction of Central Road. At the same moment, a dark BMW passed at high speed in the direction of Apotekskogen.

* * *

On Finnsspångsvägen, an ambulance reversed and stopped at the entrance to the playground. The paramedics quickly pulled out a stretcher and hurriedly rolled off towards the playground. At the scene of the accident stood a group of parents. One of them was Jimmy's mother, who was terribly upset and sad. Jimmy's mother, Gun-Britt, had just finished a harrowing phone call with her husband

Henke while she was crying on her knees on the lawn hugging her cell phone. David's mother sat crouching next to her, trying to comfort her as far as it went, while feeling immense relief that her son was unharmed.

Paramedics quickly took care of Jimmy. An emergency doctor was able to decide that Jimmy was alive, but given the boy's injuries and his deteriorating condition, he rushed to the hospital.

As Jimmy was being wheeled away on a stretcher, somewhere nearby a cell phone rang. It had been heard twice before without anyone reacting, everyone was busy taking care of Jimmy and comforting the other distraught children who had seen the accident.

Anna's mother had given up all her work as a social worker when she received the news of what had happened. She went straight to the scene of the accident and took care of Anna by holding her tightly. Questions were raised as she felt deep despair over what had happened to Jimmy. Deep down, she was not particularly surprised. Rather, it was expected that something serious would happen when it came to Jimmy and his constant ill-fated antics. Not even Astrid Lindgren's little Emil could compete with Jimmy when it came to mischief of this caliber.

But why did her daughter ride her bike around with David and Jimmy without wearing her underwear? Why is a stick inserted into the rear wheel of one of the bikes? Now the ringtone from a cell phone somewhere nearby was heard again, but no one reacted. Anna's mother assumed that she would get answers to the questions once Anna had calmed down. She was also eternally grateful that Anna did not lie injured next to Jimmy.

She picked up her distraught daughter and then carried her to the car. When Anna was put in the back seat and fastened with her seatbelt, her mother saw through the rear window how a green garbage truck at high speed was riveting behind her car. Henke threw himself out of the cab, leaving the driver's door open as he ran towards the playground with heavy steps.

Karolinska Institute was founded in 1810 in Stockholm on the initiative of King Karl XIII, partly as part of training more field surgeons (see also Master of Surgery) to increase Swedish war preparedness. Among those who took part in the establishment of KI was Jacob Berzelius, whose research in chemistry laid the foundation for the newly formed university's scientific profile.

In 2010, Karolinska Institute celebrated its 200th anniversary.

Chapter 9

23 SEPTEMBER 2014

On the second floor at Karolinska Institute in Solna, Linda sat at her desk with her cell phone next to her ear, waiting anxiously for an answer with a flickering gaze. She bit her lower lip when she interrupted the call and put her cell phone on the table. She had tried to call Jacob five times at regular intervals during the morning, but no answer. Even worse, Jacob had not called back, or for that matter sent a text message, which he always did for missed calls. A routine that both Linda and Chris had told their son with God's will. Staying connected with family was important.

Why doesn't he call? He must have seen that I called... Or has he not? she thought as she searched feverishly for logical answers to avoid fears.

There was a knock, then the door opened, and Chris came in. Linda's worried gaze met him.

* * *

In a bicycle storage room, Jacob sat and froze while wiping away his tears. He had been crying persistently as his mind tried to find a solution to his atrocity. He was not only sad and heartbroken, but also terrified of what was to come. He had prayed to God for help and asked several times for forgiveness for his wrongdoing. He had prayed that Mom and pappa inte would be angry with him because Jimmy's death, it was an accident. He also said a prayer that God would take diligent care of Jimmy.

The question remained, what would he do now? He wanted to call his mother but had lost his cell phone somewhere along the way. After a while, he abandoned the idea of trying to connect with his parents. They would not want to hear from him because he had become a murderer, a Black winged angel, something that the bride of Christ had talked about during the Bible hours in Knutby's parish. Going to the police and confessing to your crime was also not an excellent choice. Then he would be locked up for the rest of his life as a murderer and have his black evil soul examined together with that pastor Ragnar Åbjörnsson from Knutby. Jacob shuddered at the mere thought when it occurred to him that Robert would not want to hear from him either. He was abandoned, lonely, and hunted like game. Hated by all. But...

"Uncle Owen!" exclaimed Jacob, and suddenly there was a small glimmer of hope in that total, eternal darkness in which he found himself.

Whatever happens, I will be here for you, my boy. So had Uncle Owen said on a few occasions, and he always stood by his word. He was a military man, Jacob thought with a small hope for the future. But then he suddenly realized that he did not have a cell phone.

Jacob thought about how to connect with Owen.

"I have to hide so the police don't find me or worse, Jimmy's dad does. But where and how?"

Suddenly he remembered what Owen had said about approaching dangers in the dark in the woods and other unknown places. *It is almost impossible* for a person *to find a specific tree in the forest* when *all the trees are identical. Should you hide,* then *the best place where there are a lot of people, for example in big cities. You blend in with the crowd and then you are not seen.*

* * *

Linda had called Robert's grandmother without much success. After that, Linda and Chris had discussed who should go home to find out what had happened to Jacob. Chris was convinced that there was a logical explanation for why his son did not answer the phone, and therefore perhaps we should wait a little longer. At least until Robert's grandmother was found. In addition, Chris had a tough time getting out, as he had to be down in the security bunker P4 with the research group. He oversaw an ongoing test project that had the highest safety class. They tried to create a synthetic RNA virus with the hope that it might create antibodies against Ebola virus that could then lead to a sustainable vaccine.

Linda was fully aware that she was leaving and put on her jacket. She gave Chris a kiss on the mouth.

"Honey. Do not forget that God is watching over our son," Chris said to calm her worries as he took out the car key from his pants pocket and handed it to his wife.

Linda nodded, trying to force a smile. Then she took the purse that was on the desk. "I'll call when I know more."

"Drive carefully," Chris said, opening the door for his wife and giving her a kiss.

* * *

Inside the emergency room at Danderyd, Henke settled down in the waiting room after having been out smoking and letting the worst of the frustration settle down a little.

How are you made as a human being when you try to kill a poor kid? He leaned his elbows on his knees, then let his chin rest against his palms.

Sure, Jimmy was not God's best child, but who was that? he thought, trying to find a forgiving attitude towards his son's past doings. One thing he was determined about, he would find that freak of a kid from Knutby and use the boy bastard as a baseball bat to pound some common sense into that dad. And would it end so badly that... Then even God cannot help them, Henke thought, swallowed a lump in his throat and stood up.

Jimmy was still unconscious and lying in the hospital bed. Mom Gun-Britt was sitting next to her, having recovered from the early shock. She held Jimmy's hand in hers and had a tough time deciding which of them most needed the human touch and touch.

Gun-Britt had previously heard various distraught versions of how the accident had happened, and who caused it. Everything pointed to the fact that the boy Jacob was involved, which was not impossible, rather highly likely. And if that was the case, then Jimmy was not innocent, she knew that. If Jacob engaged in this accident, then he would have the opportunity to tell his version and take responsibility. She gave her unconscious son a pleading look and shook her head.

There was a knock on the door and a male doctor came in. He looked at Jimmy's values and could see that the boy's injuries were serious, but not life-threatening.

"We will bring Jimmy up for X-rays again, to make sure there has been no further bleeding in the head," the doctor informed as Henke entered the room.

"Has he woken up?" asked Henke. Gun-Britt shook her head.

"No, not yet. I just told your wife when you came in that we will x-ray Jimmy one more time to make sure there is no more internal bleeding in the head, but I will get back to you later.

Henke pulled out a chair and sat down on the other side of the bed. He caressed Jimmy's cheek with his tattooed hand as the doctor left the room.

"They're going to get the hell out of this, I promise you Jimmy," Henke grumbled.

"You are fucking shouldn't mess anything up. It is bad enough as it is, and I do not want any more nonsense or retribution. Make sure it sticks in there," Gun Britt said firmly, pointing demonstratively at her head.

Psalms 25:15-21

My eyes always look up to the Lord, for He pulls my feet out of the net.

Turn to me and have mercy on me, for I am alone and oppressed.

The anguish of my heart is great, bringing me out of my distress! Look to my suffering and toil, forgive me all my sins.

Behold, how many my enemies have become, how they hate me with violent hatred.

Keep my soul and save me, let me not be put to shame, for I flee to you.

Let innocence and honesty preserve me, for I hope in you.

Chapter 10

23 SEPTEMBER 2014

"IMAGINE THAT IT would be so difficult to get the management of that NCC building on Magnusladulås street to understand. Can't they take on board what the cake had to say instead?"

Fredrik Nilsson muttered irritably as he drove out onto the motorway from Rotebro with his Volvo CX70 in the direction of Stockholm. He was both stressed and irritable. He had planned a round of golf this afternoon with a colleague from Ture Berg's haulage company, something he did not want to miss. The traffic towards Stockholm was still quite intense even though it was late morning.

He drove out into the left lane and overtook some cars. When he reached the height of the slip road at Sollentuna, he suddenly saw a small fair-haired boy riding a blue bicycle along the shoulder of the road on the right side of the highway. Fredrik reacted to two things, partly that the boy was on a life-threatening highway and partly that none of the other road users who were closest to the hard shoulder in the right lane made any attempt to stop and help the boy.

Frederick cast a quick glance in the rearview mirror. He had a lorry from Poland behind him. Damn, this fucking right lane is full of cars and will certainly not let me in, Fredrik thought and felt frustrated by the traffic situation. Braking and at the same time trying to cross the hard shoulder was not even to think about, he reasoned and reached towards Cell phones to call. Then he saw a police car coming in the opposite direction. Frederick flashed his horn as he pointed frantically to get the officers' attention. The police car turned on the blue lights when it stopped at the shoulder of the road and two police officers hurriedly got out of the car.

"Good! They saw the boy, then they took care of him," Fredrik said relieved to himself, and was able to relieve his conscience as a fellow human being and father of three to children who were the same age as the boy on the bike. Hopefully, they were not riding their bikes on some heavily trafficked road like this lad.

Fredrik overtook a white van from Grönsaksgrossisten while he tapped his cell phone to call his wife home. At the same moment, he saw in the rearview mirror how the white van flashed right and drove onto the hard shoulder and then stopped with its hazard lights on.

* * *

Linn Segerström in police car 1167 drove north on the highway together with her colleague Dan Stormare. They passed the Chest exit and were on their way to the police station in Sollentuna after conducting passenger transport to Kronobergshäktet, which was their first work assignment during the morning shift.

She noted that the traffic was quite dense in the direction of Stockholm and was relieved not to have to sit in the queues. Suddenly, they met a Volvo XC70 that started flashing its high beams and a male driver in the car waving frantically at the hard shoulder.

"Here's one who's in a hurry," she noted.

Dan looked a little startled at the blue Volvo and at the waving driver.

"Is it to us he? Look kid!" exclaimed Dan, pointing to the southbound traffic. "Damn it!"

Linn spotted the boy riding his bicycle along the hard shoulder.

"Oops! Where did he come from?" she exclaimed, and at once drove onto the hard shoulder while?

Dan turned on the blue lights. Linn stopped abruptly as she and her colleague unfastened their seat belts and hurried out of the car. Dan was quick. He managed to get over to the center railing and then started waving at the boy who stared at him in horror as he rode his blue bike.

"You kid. Stay there!" shouted Dan.

It had the opposite effect and the boy rode away at a hell of a speed. Dan folded his arms up in the air and at the same time looked at Linn a little incredulously, who now turned around and shook his head. She called the AFCOS from her hand radio. Dan managed to get back across the road and stopped at Linn. She gave him a look of disbelief.

"That was talented. You should go on a new charm course at preschool. Pedagogy is clearly not your strong point when it comes to children," she said with a small sneering smile and started walking towards the police car.

* * *

Initially, Jacob was determined to follow Uncle Owen's advice. He was going to Stockholm, becoming invisible and trying to contact his uncle. The U.S. Embassy could help, he thought.

The route was fairly mapped out and clear. He would cycle the old road to Stockholm and hopefully he would not meet any police or Jimmy's father in a green garbage truck.

The bike ride from Upplands Väsby past Rotebro went painless as he stuck to footpaths as far as possible. When Jacob passed Häggvik's interchange, he could see the highway on his right. After passing by Knistavägen and Volvo trucks, it turned out that there had been a traffic accident at a roundabout a little further on. He did not dare to cycle past because the police were on site, but instead turned and cycled onto Knistavägen past Volvo's truck workshop and then through the tunnel under the highway.

Once out on Norra Kolonnvägen, he approached an industrial area that he did not recognize. A little further on, he saw the large newspaper printer. The only reference Jacob had to walk on to orient himself was the highway, which he could now only hear because of a cloudy section of forest. The question was, does he have to get there and try to follow the highway?

Jacob cycled into the forest and was then able to make visual contact with the highway, which felt a little safer. He followed a narrow path until he reached Upplands motor, just before Sollentuna interchange. Now a new problem arose because the forest ran out right there.

He did not want to let go of contact with the highway. It could not be that far to Stockholm either, he thought as he looked at the hard shoulder along the highway. There he can cycle instead of crossing the impassable stump fence with stone boulders.

"If I cycle a little on the edge as fast as I can, I'll get to Stockholm," Jacob said to himself, despite knowing that cycling on the hard shoulder was a significant risk.

He led the bike down over the ditch and then onto the hard shoulder. There he got on his bike and pedaled on as fast as he could, terrified of being discovered by the police.

When Jacob passed the exit to Sollentuna, he was lucky. There were no cars coming now, so with determination he stepped on for king and fatherland. As he passed the viaduct and the slip road from the Sollentuna interchange, he saw a huge T-shaped glass building further away.

There's Stockholm, finally! he thought with relief as a car began to honk. Jacob saw a blue Volvo XC70 driving in the far-left lane where a man waved and said something from inside the car.

Jacob was terrified thinking it was a civilian police officer and looked feverishly around to find a way away from the highway. Suddenly, a police car came from the opposite direction and turned on the blue lights. Jacob watched as it drove onto the shoulder of the road and came to a complete stop, while his heart was leaving his body. He saw two police officers where one of them ran over to the center railing and shouted, "You kid. Stay there!"

Jacob was not going to stop, instead he quickly shifted gears and increased his speed while looking back at the two police officers who disappeared among the cars. After about two hundred meters, he saw a white van standing on the shoulder of the road with its hazard lights on. Behind it stood a small man of foreign descent. As Jacob got closer, he slowed down and became uncertain about the new situation but saw an opportunity to pass. He approached the van and den short stature man with mustache. He wanted to pass it but became hesitant.

"Hey buddy!" the short man said, stretching out his arms with a big, gleaming smile.

Jacob stopped and looked in surprise at the man who looked incredibly happy to see him.

"Hi," Jacob replied, a little hesitantly.

"Are you going home, buddy?" the short man asked as he walked over to Jacob.

Jacob nodded and, just in case, placed one foot on the pedal to be prepared to stab if something should happen. The man saw Jacob's reaction. He smiled again and waved his hands.

"No, no. You do not be afraid of Shamun. I mate and I drive you."

Shamun stretched out his hand and greeted Jacob, who was a little reserved and hesitant.

"You live in Stockholm?" he asked, and Jacob nodded. "Good mate, then you ride with me. The police over there, not good."

Jacob got off the bike with a smile and with a short sentence of thought he thanked God for his help. Shamun took Jacob's bike and put it in the van, then took two apples from a blue Arla basket and handed one apple to Jacob. They got into the van and their hazard lights were turned off. The white van started rolling in the direction of Stockholm.

* * *

Linda came driving on the E4 with the family's white Mercedes combi heading north. She had passed the Kista interchange and saw the large, T-shaped hotel on her left as she drove by. For a moment she thought she saw Jacob sitting in an oncoming white van, but the thought disappeared as quickly as it came when she suddenly saw a police car drive off the hard shoulder in front of her. Linda slowed down because she was driving too fast and then kept a comfortable distance from the police car. She thanked her creator that she did not have time to pass before the police car drove out. There could have been costly fines, in the worst case the driver's license.

The police car drove off the highway at the Sollentuna exit, whereupon Linda continued north and increased her speed. The thought of what she thought she had seen came back. What was the likelihood that she had seen correctly? Why would he be in a van towards Stockholm? Linda tried to tell herself that she had seen the wrong thing.

* * *

When the white van passed Do Norra, Shamun and Jacob saw two police cars with blue lights on the slip road. Jacob reacted at once at the sight of the police cars but could feel relieved as they drove by. Shamun, who was on his way to Årstahtorna, was a talkative man who wanted to know a little more about Jacob. Especially after finding him on the highway for some strange reason.

"What's your name, buddy?" he asked, taking a bite of his apple.

"Jacob," he replied, fixing his gaze on his half-eaten apple.

"Aha! Jacob, nice name, genuinely nice. You show me where you live, ha?"

Jacob nodded and pointed straight ahead towards Norrtull as they passed the cemetery and the exit to Karolinska and Solna. "Your mom and dad, them at home, ha?" asked Shamun with a restrained smile.

"Mom is home and Dad will be home soon."

Jacob avoided eye contact and looked out the side window. Shamun drove out onto Norra station street and soon had to stop for a red light at the intersection with Sankt Eriksgatan.

"I follow you home. I tell your mom that I found you and will drive you home. Good, ha?" suggested Shamun.

The light signal switched to green, and he started driving. The proposal was not appreciated at all by Jacob, although he understood that Shamun wanted well. When he saw Sankt Eriksparken, he saw his chance and pointed to Västmannagatan.

"Over there I live," he said as Shamun turned onto the sidewalk and stopped.

"Okay, will you I follow you home?"

"No, you can't, Dad can be home," Jacob replied quickly, almost stammering.

Shamun spread his arms with a surprised expression on his face.

"But mate, I'd love to talk to your dad. I am sure I like him," he exclaimed, not seeing any obvious obstacles in meeting Jacob's father.

"You can't. Dad drives a garbage truck, and he does not like foreigners. But I like you!" added Jacob, who feared the mere thought of a nasty encounter with Jimmy's father.

Shamun's smile disappeared, and his mustache drooped a little. He looked firmly at Jacob, who did not dare meet his gaze, but instead directed it down to the floor.

"Your dad doesn't like blackhead, ha?" asked Shamun with a disappointed expression on his face.

He took a business card from the dashboard on which he wrote a phone number and handed it to Jacob.

"Here, you see my number. You are in trouble, you call me, and I will help you then, okay?"

Shamun, feeling some unease, wanted to become Jacob's future support. As a father of five, he felt he had the right conditions and experience to help Jacob.

"Thank you," Jacob replied with a forced smile, tucking the business card into his jacket pocket.

"Come, I'll help you with the bike," Shamun said, opening the driver's door at the same time.

The tail lift went down as he climbed onto the lift and with a firm grip lifted the bike down to Jacob, who thanked him for his help. He jumped down from the tail lift and closed it again. It was not a good feeling, to let the boy go to a father who had racist views and prejudices. Jacob said goodbye and began walking with his bike across the street while Shamun patiently stood still, keeping a watchful eye on traffic.

Jacob got on his bike and pedaled off on Västmannagatan while for a moment he turned around and waved to Shamun. As he rounded the corner at a property, he got off his bike and leaned it against the wall of the house. He then crept up to the corner and looked cautiously towards Sankt Eriksgatan. There he saw the white van drive off in the direction of the Vanadis roundabout. Jacob got on his bike and pedaled off along Västmannagatan in the direction of Karlbergsvägen and Odenplan.

Jacob did not know where in Stockholm he was. He also did not know where he was going. He knew only one thing, that he must somehow contact Uncle Owen for help. Jacob was scared, the thought that he would never, ever get to meet Mom and Dad again did not want to let him go. To never be forgiven for the terrible thing he had done, that no one would understand, was an unbearable feeling for a ten-year-old boy.

Jacob could never have imagined what fate awaited. A life story that soon would change his life so completely and where the parents' Search over time would enter two different worlds.

Prayer for a child.

Jesus, you are the friend of the children. You have said in the Bible that the angels of children see the face of God and that the kingdom of heaven belongs to the children. I pray for this child. Preserve and protect it. Let it grow up in security and love. Bless parents to nurture and raise their children with all love and wisdom. Give them firmness and calm. Let this child have a happy and meaningful life through faith in you. Amen

Chapter 11

23 SEPTEMBER 2014

ON THE DRIVEWAY at Lillvägen 3, a white Mercedes combi was carelessly parked. On Runbyvägen below, a few cars passed as well as an elderly gentleman who was out walking their dog. At the Sjögren-Lester family's villa, the front door opened, and Linda came out with a worried look. She had set up that Jacob was not home. Everything looked the same as when she and Chris left the house this morning.

If Jacob had come home alone or with Robert, traces of them would have been seen. Linda closed the front door and locked, then ran to the garage. She opened the door and looked inside. Jacob's bike was not standing there. She made a resigned gesture with her arms, then closed the garage door.

She got in the car and backed out of the driveway.

On the way home, Linda had tried several times to contact both Robert's grandmother and Jacob but received no response from either of them. Linda got the feeling that Jacob, Robert, and his grandmother were simply engulfed in the earth, just as if they had never existed.

Arriving at Finnspångsvägen, she drove into the yard and stopped outside the middle gate. She got out of the car and hurried through the gate, which fortunately was open. When she stopped at the front door on the first floor, she checked the nameplate, then rang the bell. She pressed the bell twice more but not a sound was heard from Inside the apartment. Instead, she saw someone come through the gate and groan, then she heard someone with heavy steps walking up the stairs.

An elderly woman with glasses and set hair came walking slowly up the stairs carrying a grocery bag from Coop, it was Robert's grandmother. When the older woman spotted Linda, who was standing at her front door, she stopped at the step and said hello. Then she took the last steps up to the landing with some effort.

"Oh God, thank you! I finally got a hold of you," Linda said, thinking it was all over and Jacob was safe.

"Well, you say that. I went to the doctor and then done some shopping at Coop. You must take advantage when Robert is not home," said the aunt, dropping the grocery bag on the landing to get the keys out of her jacket pocket.

"But where are Robert and Jacob?" asked Linda, looking down at the stairs in the stairwell.

"Robert is with his dad at work," the aunt replied as she inserted the key into the door lock with some precision and turned it over.

"Is Jacob there too?"

"Jacob? No, I do not think so," she replied, looking a little puzzled as she opened the front door.

Linda took to her forehead.

"Think? Please, man, you must know if Jacob is with Robert's father," Linda said desperately, feeling it all turn into an ominous illusion in her reality.

"I really don't know. Jacob came this morning and wanted to play with Robert. Then I told him that Robert was with his father and then he left," the aunt informed, grabbing the grocery bag, and carrying it into the hall.

"Why didn't you call and tell me?" asked Linda with a growing lump of worry in her throat.

"Would I call, why?"

"Last night we talked on the phone about Jacob being with you and Robert. They have a study day today."

"It was boring. If I see Jacob, I will let him know that you have sought him, I will do that, goodbye," the aunt said, closing the front door.

Linda stood speechless, staring at the front door. She came out of the gate while wiping away tears from her cheeks. Robert's grandmother was her guarantee that Jacob would be in a safe place. An awareness and faith that was suddenly snatched away from her.

What should I do now? she thought as she looked around and caught a glimpse of the playground a little further away. She walked with quick steps in the direction of it, which was currently empty of people. On her left side was the swing set and on her right side was a sandbox.

She continued walking in the direction of the underpass. Linda met a woman with a stroller in the same place where Jimmy had crashed. She cheered the woman on and asked if she had seen her son with a blue bike and gave a more detailed description of the person and age.

The woman shook her head and replied that she had not seen a boy with that description. Linda was about to leave when the woman started telling her about a bicycle accident with two boys that had happened just over two hours ago. The woman pointed to a rock in the lawn beyond the fence about five meters away. Linda noticed that there was dried blood on the stone and saw that the adjoining wooden fence was broken. The woman wished Linda good luck in finding Jacob and then walked away with the stroller.

Linda took out her cell phone and tried again, with growing panic, to call Jacob. When the first signal sounded on the phone, a familiar ringtone sounded nearby. When the next signal on the cell phone came, it sounded again. It cannot be a coincidence, she thought as she looked around for the sound. The ringtone came from the bushes, and she crouched down to look.

About an arm's length away was a cell phone. Linda got up, stepped over the fence, and forced her way through the shrubbery. She found the cell phone and there was no doubt that it was Jacobs. On the back cover was a picture of a red heart with the text *Jesus Loves Me*. Linda was convinced that Jacob must be one of the boys involved in the accident. It must be so because his cell phone was in the bushes at the same place where the accident had happened.

* * *

Inside the office at Karolinska Institute, Chris Sjögren-Lester had just finished a telephone meeting with Dr. Erica Saphire at Ollman Saphire Laboratory in San Diego, USA. For Erica, it was an early working morning considering the nine hours of time difference. Chris and Erica had jointly drawn up an action plan for how their collaboration for a vaccine against Ebola virus and RNA would work in practical terms.

They agreed that the RNA virus must be attacked with some type of antibody. Earlier, Chris had had an interesting conversation with a German scientist who shared a theory about that there could be positive qualities in The Influenza medicine Favipiravir. Chris decided that it might be worth doing some clinical tests with mice and gave permission to start the tests. The German research team and Chris' research team would perform independent tests and then review the results in parallel.

He got up and went to the coffee maker to pour a mug of coffee while he pondered the conversation with Erica. He sat down at his desk and then glanced at his cell phone. When does she call? he thought and looked at the clock a little worriedly and concluded that Linda should have made it home and maybe gone to Robert's grandmother. In and of itself, that could be the reason she had not heard from her yet...

What if something has happened? But then Linda would have called, he thought, feeling both uncertain and worried. Oh, got to knock off the thoughts. Sitting here and being worried for no valid reason did not help anyone, it would rather become a distraction with the focus on the work. Linda will call, he finally noted.

Instead, he began to think about the ways by which the Ebola virus spread through his body. The virus first attacked white blood cells via the lymphatic system, then continued via the liver and spleen to spread the genome. It was a question of being able to isolate it.

Chris picked up the phone, but hesitated, then put it back. No, I will send an email to Travis Warren instead, he reasoned, considering the time difference. He felt an inevitable nervousness about making contact.

Travis was a former work associate at the Fort Detrick Research Institute. A highly skilled molecular biologist who stood for a strong loyalty to his country. How would Chris be treated after resigning at Fort Detrick and moving to Sweden?

He opened Outlook on his computer and then authored an email to Travis. He hoped for a collaboration and that the email would not end up in the trash on Travis' computer. Chris pressed Return and the email was sent away when the cell phone suddenly rang. He looked at the display. It was Linda and he answered instantly.

The conversation did not turn out quite as Chris had hoped. Linda did not start the conversation by telling her in a calm voice that she had found Jacob unharmed. No, her voice was in despair, and Chris could almost hear tears streaming down her cheeks. She was so upset that it was sometimes difficult to understand what she was saying. After a few repetitions and an unsuccessful attempt at mastery, it became clear that Jacob was missing. He was seriously injured after a bicycle accident with Jimmy. Moreover, no one knew where the son was. Linda was at the playground near Robert's home and was completely perplexed. He ended the conversation by asking Linda to go to the patisserie at the civic center on Central Road and wait there. He himself was going to take a taxi and had already left the office with his jacket under his arm on the way to the elevators.

* * *

Just before the phone call with Chris, Linda had met some mothers in the playground. The need to talk about the accident was great among the mothers, even though none of them had been present at the place where it had happened. There were several different theoretical courses on events presented, all based on what they themselves had heard. Ominous rumors spread avalanche among parents in the neighborhood.

Linda hurried back to the car and then drove around the block to the pastry shop where she parked. Inside the patisserie, she ordered a cup of coffee and sat down at a vacant table. She had to recover and try to collect herself before her husband arrived. From her purse, she took out a small make-up mirror and began to examine her appearance with critical eyes. The mascara had stained around the eyes and on both cheekbones and looked almost terrible. With her left elbow on the table, she leaned her head slightly to the side against the palm of her hand, trying to hide the war painting. She took a sip of her coffee and looked embarrassed at the other guests who were busy having coffee and talking. No one had paid much attention to her.

Outside the patisserie, a yellow 020 taxi stopped. Chris reached for an American Express to the Yugoslav elderly taxi driver, Rica Novac.

Chris came carrying a tray with a coffee mug and sat down at the table in front of Linda. She stood up and hugged him tightly as her body shook. They sat down and she started from the beginning by telling them everything. She also told mothers about the accident ravens who told her theories about what might have happened about the accident. Jimmy's mother had arrived, but why hadn't she heard from her if Jacob engaged in the accident? A question she had asked herself without finding a reasonable answer.

"Shall we start by going home to Jimmy's parents before we do anything else?" suggested Chris while holding Linda's hand.

"Gunn-Britt should reasonably know what has happened to Jacob and Jimmy. Hope by God that not that Henke is home," Linda said. "I can't manage meeting him now, he's a disgusting person."

Chris drank his coffee and stood up. Linda looked at her coffee mug, which was half-drunk, and then pushed it away. She got up from the table and took her purse. Together they left the patisserie and got in the car. Chris started it while looking at Linda with a determined look.

"I'll confront Henke if it turns out he's home."

Linda nodded as her thoughts grinded. Why doesn't he get in touch? Why doesn't anyone contact us? Could this be God's trial? If Jacob is injured, someone must contact him if he is in hospital. Why is it so quiet? Just as if Linda and Chris did not exist at all?

Prayer for forgiveness

God, be gracious to me according to your goodness, blot out my transgressions according to your great mercy. Two me clean from my iniquity, cleanse me from my sin.

For I know my transgressions, and my sin is always before me. It is against you that I have sinned and done that is evil in your eyes.

Turn away your face from my sins, wipe out all iniquities. Create in me, God, a pure heart and give me again a bold spirit.

Do not reject me from your face, nor take your Holy Spirit away from me. Let me rejoice again in your salvation and hold me up with a willing spirit.

Chapter 12

23 SEPTEMBER 2014

ALONG KARLBERGSVÄGEN AND around Odenplan, Jacob had cycled around to different shops and asked politely if he could borrow the phone. It would certainly have gone well, if Jacob had not been so honest and told him to call Uncle Owen in the United States. If nothing else, it supplied a valid reason for staff to start asking questions: Where did he come from? Where were the parents? And why would he call Uncle Owen in the United States? Jacob apologized for disturbing and with a U-turn he left the store urgently. The staff saw the little blonde boy get on a bike and disappear.

At Odenplan's subway entrance, he met a teenage girl, dressed in a leather jacket and torn jeans. She was kind enough to lend her cell phone. She unplugged her headphones after listening to Justin Bieber, then handed Jacob the cell phone with a small smile. But problems arose when Jacob asked for the country code for the United States, then she at once took back the cell phone with the fear of being ruined.

The girl walked away while Jacob remained completely uncomprehending at her reaction. Suddenly, he saw two police officers walking towards him from Upplands street. He took his bike and started walking along Oden Street in the direction of Sveavägen.

At the same time, a woman with a stroller came out of the subway entrance. With quick steps, Jacob caught up with the Woman. Quite unexpectedly, the woman was suddenly accompanied by a little boy who was leading a blue mountain bike. She also noticed that he looked back at two police officers who disappeared through the subway entrance.

The woman became very pensive about the strange boy and was about to ask when he gave her a sweet smile. She got off and smiled back at the adorable boy. It turned green and together they crossed the street. Jacob politely thanked him for the company and got on his bike. The woman was left with the stroller and looked with surprised eyes after the boy as he cycled towards Sveavägen.

Arriving at the intersection of Oden Street and Sveavägen, it was just past four o'clock in the afternoon. Sveavägen was heavily trafficked and on the sidewalks most people walked in both directions. A little further to the right, Jacob saw a McDonald's restaurant. Apart from the apple given to him by Shamun, he had not eaten since this morning and was extremely hungry. A hamburger menu would not sit amiss in his rumbling stomach. But he was hesitant. Would he dare to go in and eat? He could at least cycle past and see how many people there were in the restaurant. If there were a lot of people, he could walk in and blend in with them, just as Uncle Owen had told him. Jacob slowly began to cycle there.

Inside the McDonald's restaurant, there were many guests, but no police officers as far as Jacob could see when he stepped in. Arriving at one of the checkouts, Jacob was able to order a Big Mac menu and paid with his last money. With a few crowns left, he took his tray of food. He stopped and looked around, wanting to sit down at a window table where he could keep an eye on his bike. A short distance away, he saw a family with children begin to get up from one of the window tables and put on the outerwear. Once at the table, he sat down with his food tray and got a good overview of the bike and the entrance.

He ate his food with a good appetite. Meanwhile, he looked curiously at the children who either talked to each other while they ate or ran around playing while their parents tried to calm them down. Jacob felt a little abandoned when his thoughts went back to mom and dad. He missed them tremendously. It made him sad and made him feel a strong despair. He wiped away his tears with his hand as he ate the last of the burger with fries.

While drinking Coca Cola from the cup, he suddenly saw two uniformed police officers enter and join the queue right at the entrance. Jacob stared at them in horror and saw that one of the police officers was looking in his direction. With his eyes on the table, he began to finger nervously with the hamburger box. He looked up cautiously, the police officers were still standing, and Jacob did not want to challenge fate by trying to pass them. He saw a girl come out through a revolving door just beyond the cash registers. What if he could get out of there?

Jacob got up and took the tray from the table and then walked towards the revolving door. When he reached the door, he looked around. Everyone seemed busy with completely different things. He walked in through the revolving door and just as he entered, he met a girl who was on her way out.

"Hello there! Where are you going?" she asked with a warm smile.

"Was going to leave this one," Jacob replied a little shyly, swallowing a lump in his throat at the same time.

"Oh thanks, I can take it. There are tray carts out there, just so you know for the next time you eat with us," the girl explained as she accepted the tray with outstretched arms.

"Can I come out here?" asked Jacob, smiling gently.

"But little friend, there is an exit out there. It's the same one you came in through."

"I can't."

"Why not?"

"There are some people who are stupid to me," Jacob lied, then directed his gaze to the floor.

The girl opened the revolving door slightly ajar and saw three teenage boys standing at the entrance teasing each other. She let go of the revolving door, and then turned to Jacob.

"Okay it's the boys mischief, then you can come with me, and I'll let you out through the staff entrance."

She extended a hand that Jacob happily grasped and together they walked through the staff room. The girl opened a door, and Jacob walked out. He politely thanked him for his help and then disappeared around the corner.

Jacob carefully walked over to his bicycle that was standing at the entrance. He looked around, then unlocked the bike and led it to the sidewalk. It was now half past six in the evening and he started cycling along Sveavägen in the direction of Sergel Square. He knew roughly where he was, but he had no idea what would happen next. It had begun to get dark and soon it would get dark. Where would he go? How would he connect with Owen, his only hope?

Chapter 13

23 SEPTEMBER 2014

On a ward at Danderyd Hospital, Jimmy was bedded. He was in a private room with his mom and dad on either side of the bed. Jimmy had woken up from his unconsciousness a few hours ago. Gun-Britt had shown her gratitude by wiping away her tears with a smile. Henke had walked over to the bed, grabbed the headboard, and then gave Jimmy a small smile but said nothing. Jimmy was too dazed and tried to talk, so he was allowed to sleep and rest. Talking had to be done later because a severe concussion had been confirmed.

Gunn-Britt sat and read Swedish Women's Magazine after Jimmy had gone back to sleep. Henke had ad nauseam browsed through all the newspapers available in the department. The only thing he had not touched in reading was a Bible that was in the dayroom. He got up and said he was going out to smoke. Gunn-Britt nodded disinterested and continued reading the latest gossip about Laila Bagge. She heard the door open and close as Henke left the room, looked up for a moment and gave Jimmy a watchful look, then returned to Laila Bagge's celebrity world.

Henke opened the door leading out to the stairwell and collided with a woman who was in a hurry. Henke was about to apologize but quickly changed his mind when he saw who he had collided with. In front of him stood Anna's mother Charlotte Metzer, a person he held in high esteem and absolutely did not want to meet.

"You'll fucking see you for when you go!" he hissed, glaring at Charlotte as if she were some shit the cat had dragged in.

"What room is Jimmy in?" she asked firmly, ignoring Henke's verbal attacks.

"Yes, how so?"

"Either you say so, or I go and ask the staff. Which will you choose?"

Henke looked at her and there was no doubt that she was serious.

"He's in room 7 and Gunn-Britt is there."

"Thank you. That was not that hard, was it?" asked Charlotte as she started walking.

Henke shrugged and then walked towards the elevators with a sense of defeat. That bitch is going to interfere in everything, take me fuck, he thought bitterly.

Gunn-Britt was in the middle of Laila's love story when she heard the door open. She did not even look up, but said a little succinctly:

"Did you swallow smoked?"

Charlotte stepped into the room and stood on the opposite side of the bed.

"I don't smoke," she said.

Gunn-Britt jumped when she saw social worker Charlotte Metzer standing next to the bed where Jimmy was still sleeping.

"What are you doing here?" asked Gunn-Britt in surprise.

It was not the first time they had met. They had supported it.

on each other several times inside the social welfare office when Gunn Britt and Henke had been to meetings about Jimmy's possible continued schooling and future. There was no doubt that Jimmy's future was highly uncertain, something that Charlotte had not doubted deep down without any misconduct.

"I want to talk to Jimmy and to you," Charlotte replied, placing her purse demonstratively at the headboard.

"About what? Jimmy is asleep as you might see and he needs to rest after everything he has been through," Gunn-Britt said as she stood up and threw the rolled-up newspaper on the window table.

"Well, then the police will have to question him when the time comes. I can instead talk to you as a responsible parent, does that work?"

"But please, now you can actually say what it is about."

"I've had a scary conversation with my daughter, Anna."

"Hey you frog jaw! I know what your daughter's name is. What has she said that has made you so fucking upset and made you come here," Gunn-Britt hissed. "Can't this wait a bit until Jimmy is back on his feet?"

"No, it can't wait! Jimmy has ripped off Anna's panties and forced her to urinate on poor Jacob. Then he touched her genitals! My daughter is heartbroken and thinks the police will take her," said Charlotte, who at the same time tried to contain her emotions as hard as she could. It was not only her daughter who had been violated and insulted, it had also been as a mother and a woman.

Gunn-Britt stared at the distraught woman in front of her in surprise. How can a ten-year-old get such abstract ideas? Jimmy was not even sexually mature for the horror.

"Stop and prove! Do you know what you are accusing my son of? He has done a lot of stupidity, but that he would produce something so stupid..." Gunn-Britt interrupted the sentence as Jimmy moved in bed.

He woke up and, in his sleep, -drunk state he saw Charlotte standing at the edge of one of the beds.

* * *

The Sjögren-Lester family's white Mercedes kept quite a high speed on the motorway in the direction of Danderyd Hospital. They had been at Jimmy's parents' house but apparently no one was home. At least no one opened the door. Chris was a little frustrated with the situation. Instead of sitting in the car and wasting precious time waiting until Jimmy's parents would show up, they decided to go to Danderyd Hospital in the meantime.

Linda closed her eyes and in silence prayed to God for help in finding Jacob while Chris concentrated on traffic and driving.

At the emergency room at Danderyd Hospital, they walked through the entrance with an inner hope. Injured, yes maybe, but alive and found. The nagging worry and despair dug deeper into their Christian souls and hopefully that torment would end soon.

They introduced themselves to the nurse sitting inside the door of the clinic. Linda took over the conversation and told them in short terms that they were looking for their son. When the nurse got Jacob's social security number, she keyed it into the computer. It turned out that no Jacob Sjögren-Lester was registered as being entered in the patient register. The nurse offered to check inside the reception just in case, which she did.

Chris and Linda went and sat down in the waiting room. There sat a pensioner couple, a younger mother with a child in a sulky, and a Roma woman who showed signs of pain in the stomach area. The Roma woman, named Ritva, winced when she saw Chris and Linda sitting a short distance away. Linda perceived the woman's reaction as unpleasant.

Ritva got up from the couch. Wearing high-heeled, black shoes and traditional Roma attire, she walked past them while giving them a serious look. She stopped in front of Linda and continued to stare at her, then smiled and walked on to the reception. Linda felt a cold shiver that made her skin knot. There was something about the woman's gaze that was unpleasant.

The woman knocked on the door and a nurse opened the door with a professional smile.

"How long will I have to wait?" asked Ritva with a noticeable irritation and a clear Finnish accent.

"I'm terribly sorry, but we're working as best we can. You will see a doctor soon," the nurse replied kindly.

"I think you have put this into practice to let me as a gypsy girl just sit and wait and wait. The Social Insurance Agency does the same thing and its hell in me racism. You have no interest in healing me. No, we are to be eradicated from this hell that you call democracy."

From inside the waiting room, the conversation between Ritva and the nurse could be heard. Linda was frightened and reacted by grabbing Chris's arm. He put his hand over hers to calm her down and became a little puzzled by the Roma woman's harsh statement.

"I can only regret that you take it that way. As soon as a doctor becomes available, we will call you in," the nurse promised with professional composure.

"I'm not going to fucking go. I will have help, now!" Ritva persisted, staring angrily at the poor nurse who needed to leave. The nurse picked up the phone.

"That doesn't help!" exclaimed Ritva, resolutely banging her fist on the reception desk.

At the same moment, two stout guards came out of the emergency room and stood on either side of Ritva and received an angry look in response.

"If you only touch me then you..." Ritva marked, interrupting herself mid-sentence when one of the guards pointed decisively towards the waiting room with an equally determined look.

Ritva sneered, turned on her heel and walked to the waiting room. As she passed Chris and Linda, she saw how noticeably frightened Linda was. Ritva was given a special reason to stop with the guards just behind.

"It's too late. You will not find what you are looking for," said Ritva.

Linda and Chris were abruptly taken by her statement and stared at her in shock.

"What do you know about what we are looking for?" asked Chris instinctively as Ritva read his determined expression.

"I know a lot. You are looking for your boy, aren't you?"

Linda stood up and grabbed Ritva's arm. "Do you know where he is?"

Ritva rubbed her left upper hand against Linda's cheek with a smile. Linda, staring helplessly at her brown eyes, perceived for a fraction of a second how her brown pupils had turned black and the whites of her eyes bloodshot. She looked away and took a step back. To ensure that she had seen correctly, she looked again into Ritva's eyes, but they were normal again. It must have been imagination, she thought as she tried to capture reality.

The guards grabbed Ritva's arm and wanted her to go sit down, but Linda stopped them. "No, leave her alone."

Ritva had gained a psychological advantage over Linda. She snatched her arm from one of the guards as she said, "Well, you heard what she said. Go away," Ritva said in Finnish with an unpleasant look.

She turned to Linda and Chris stood up and stood between them.

"Do you know where our son is?" he asked with skepticism and some irritation.

"He's not here," Ritva replied without deviating, her gaze locked in Chris's eyes.

"You have already said that..." Linda managed to say before Chris interrupted her.

"The truth is, you overheard our conversation with the nurse when we came in. That is the situation. You do not know anything," Chris noted.

The nurse entered the waiting room and stopped. "No, unfortunately! He is not here. I have also called Karolinska, and he is not there either. I am terribly sorry," she said, wishing she had a more positive message to give.

Ritva raised her eyebrows while staring at Chris.

"Isn't it true that I happened to overhear your conversation with her," Ritva admitted, pointing to the nurse. "But I was right, because you Jacob is not here. She there has just attested to that."

"A wild gamble, I would say," Chris said when Linda grabbed his arm at the same moment. She felt a cold shiver creeping through her body.

"Gamble, you say, I want to call it facts," Ritva replied with conviction, adding: "What are you going to do now that you can't even call him?"

"What do you know about that?" asked Linda abruptly as she raised her eyebrows in surprise and reconciled herself to the idea of the Roma woman as a satanic magic pack.

"Your son doesn't have a mobile phone, he dropped it. And now it is in your purse," Ritva replied, smiling confidently.

Linda and Chris stood paralyzed with their mouths wide open. Chris felt an unpleasant shiver and a later dullness and had to sit down. Linda was still staring wide-eyed at Ritva, who in turn noted with a slight shrug that she was a magician. She opened her purse while holding Ritva with her gaze and picked up Jacob's cell phone with the display facing up and showed it with her arm outstretched while Ritva nodded. The nurse backed off two steps.

"On the back it says, God loves me in a heart," Ritva said, taking the liberty of turning the cell phone in Linda's hand.

Linda and Chris stared wide-eyed at Ritva. They felt guilt and a hopeless powerlessness over what Ritva knew when the truth appeared. They were now standing in front of a wildly strange woman who knew more about Jacob than they did. A sudden encounter with an unknown woman that turned into a nightmare. A nightmare that increasingly lived on and enveloped reality with a solid grip.

* * *

Henke was pissed off and so damn offended that it was unprecedented as he walked with quick steps down the corridor towards the emergency room. Fifteen minutes ago, he had set up that the fucking social worker, who was walking behind him with his wife Gunn-Britt, had not just one screw loose, but several. To top it all off the fucking misery, his son Jimmy had woken up.

During a high-pressure interrogation held by the social witch, it had crept up that Jimmy had found a Russian-made DVD with crude pornographic content. It had been well hidden under Gunn-Britt's underwear in a drawer inside the bedroom, causing Gunn-Britt to hit the ceiling like the left-wing woman she was. It was not just that Henke had the audacity to hide a DVD in her drawer. No, but also that her ten-year-old son had been there rooting and found that damn record. After watching the heinous movie, Jimmy had the bizarre idea that Anna would urinate on Jacob was born. Because it was done in the movie. A confession that Jimmy embarrassingly told his mother and the social worker. Jimmy's admission was anything but prompt when Henke entered the room after his smoke break and then got the shock of his life. It turned out that Jimmy's confession was only part of the truth. Charlotte also wanted to know if Jimmy had touched her daughter's vagina.

Jimmy reluctantly told how Jacob had pushed Anna so that she fell over him and was seated over his face. Then Anna, accidentally,

accidentally peed a small jet on his nose and mouth. In sheer panic, Jimmy tried to protect his face with his hands by pressing both palms against Anna's vagina and pushed her away.

Henke had to resolutely take the main responsibility when two aggressive women stood and scolded him for notes. The atmosphere between them thus became very rancorous and threatening. In addition to threatening divorce, Gunn-Britt had also promised a dissection of his intimate possessions with a dull knife in the heat of the moment. A measure that Charlotte was not at all slow to approve.

The doors to the emergency room were opened and Henke came out all red in the face. Suddenly, he spotted Linda and Chris talking to a Romani cart inside the waiting room. For some reason, two guards also stood behind the Traveler cart. Henke stopped and stared at them while a tantrum was imminent. Gunn Britt and Charlotte came right behind and saw the reason Henke stood and snorted like an angry bull.

At the same moment, both Linda and Chris saw Henke, Gunn-Britt and Charlotte standing at the reception and just staring at them with surprised expressions.

Finally, they show up, Chris thought and started walking towards Henke. More than that, he did not have time to think until he heard a roar and saw Henke come rushing towards him like a ridiculous bull terrier. When Henke had less than three steps left for Chris, he threw himself on top of him and both fell headlong to the floor between table and chairs.

"Henke! What are you doing?" shouted Gunn-Britt in panic as Charlotte stood and stepped on the same floor and was completely confused and surprised by Henke's move.

"You sanctimonious fucking idiots!" he shouted as he straddled Chris and kept a firm stranglehold on him.

Chris managed to hive his legs up and locked them in a scissor grip around Henke's head. Henke had to let go of his neck to try to get out of Chris's scissor grip. Guards came till rescued as Gunn-Britt rushed forward and grabbed Henke's ear and turned around.

With a deafening roar and both arms pushed up behind his back, Henke ended up on the floor and Chris was able to get up. At the same moment, paramedics came rolling in with a patient and behind them two sturdy uniformed police officers entered the emergency room.

The officers rushed into the waiting room and took over the guards' work by handcuffing Henke's wrists. It was not until then that Henke began to calm down and he was abducted under vigorous protests.

Chris was a little shaken by Henke's touches and gave Gunn-Britt another questioning look before walking up to her.

"Can I have an explanation as to why your husband jumped on me? We have searched for you and now I have completely lost my bearings. Oh God, what a mess!"

Gunn-Britt stared at Chris as her thoughts drifted through her head. Would she just give the bastard the jaw slap that her fellow failed at? Or would she patiently try to talk to him patiently about how inappropriate it is to endanger the lives of other people's children? She looked at Charlotte who was standing a short distance away, trying to mentally come back to reality. Given what Charlotte had told her about Jimmy's fucking ideas, it was safest to tread carefully anyway.

She would at least think about Henke and divorce properly because you could not have it like this.

"I guess I can start by telling you that Jimmy has messed Jacob up as usual," Gunn-Britt began as she tried to find the right words to describe what had happened.

"Is Jimmy here?" asked Linda as she took a few steps closer to Chris.

"He's in a ward. He hit his head against a rock after falling off his bike," Gunn-Britt replied, but avoided mentioning the actual culpability of the accident.

"But do you know where Jacob is?" asked Linda.

"Isn't he with you?"

"Nope. We have searched and have even been at your house and called," Chris replied with a hope that was now dashed.

Charlotte stepped forward to join the conversation. Now the truth will be told.

"Excuse me, I'm Anna's mother yes - as you probably know."

"What, is she also involved in this accident?" asked Linda.

"More than you could imagine," she replied, giving Gunn-Britt a determined look.

Gunn-Britt felt that she was losing face and then began to tell the whole story. It was better that she told her than that it would come out from a moderate social worker whose daughter happened to show her nipple to two of the same age. She would surely paint a scenario worse than reality and make herself and her daughter look like fucking victims of crime. No, it was just a matter of putting the cards on the table. Jimmy had suffered enough.

Chris and Linda stood like two nesting boxes when Gunn-Britt had detailed the whole event. Chris looked at Charlotte who was standing opposite, trying to hide her face with his left hand. He tried to take in what Gunn-Britt had just told him when Charlotte broke off the silence:

"What should I say? I can only regret what my daughter has done. I can only say sorry. My daughter is not a bad girl, you must understand that. You know how impressionable children can be, especially my daughter."

A police officer entered the waiting room and stopped by Chris. He wanted Chris and Linda to go with him to the police station in Sollentuna to sort out the whole incident. Henke had filed a police report against Chris for intentionally harming his son Jimmy.

Linda felt her legs wanting to give way, everything began to move in the waiting room. All geometry suddenly took on a life of its own or ceased to exist.

At the same time, someone turned up a white glow of light that increased in strength, as if the entire waiting room were bathed in light. Linda felt she had to sit down. With a little presence of mind, she tried to get to the chair that was closest, but she never made it. She fell to the floor handlessly.

A cry for help.

How long will you forget me, Lord?
How long should you hide your face? How long shall thoughts grind, my heart anxious day after day?
How long shall my enemy triumph?
Look at me, answer me, Lord, my God! Give new shine to my eyes, let me not fall asleep in death, let not my enemy say that he defeated me, my enemies rejoice at my fall. I trust in your goodness; my heart will rejoice in your help. I want to sing to the glory of the Lord, for He is good to me.

Chapter 14

23 SEPTEMBER 2014

It was nine o'clock in the evening and darkness had settled over Stockholm. Minor rain clouds passed and at times brought lighter precipitation. On the smaller streets, it was almost deserted. Only the street lighting and light from the surrounding apartments gave the impression that people were in safety and warmth. On the main streets, there were still a few people moving around who were going somewhere.

Sergel Square, or the plate as it was commonly called, was often a hangout and hub for those who were outside the framework of society, addicts, prostitutes, undocumented immigrants, and not least young people who were on the move. During the day, they were not seen because they blended in with all the people who commuted and had Sergel Square as a public thoroughfare or hub. There were often stressed people on their way home or to work via the subway network. People who could not or did not want to see the bottom scrap from the lower strata of society.

There, Jacob stood over his mountain bike and did not dare to get off the bike. He had previously cycled around the central parts of Stockholm looking for the American embassy. He was convinced that he would be helped to connect with Uncle Owen there.

Jacob stood with the stairs up to the culture house behind him and followed the passing people with his gaze. There were also some smaller youth groups that had gathered local gang circles. Every now and then a loud girl ran between two groups. Her behavior was like Jimmy's, except that she was loud, there was no way in the world to get her to stand still. Her enormous need for affirmation and always being the center of attention was at the top of her priority list.

Jacob's feeling of being alone and abandoned came back when he saw the youth standing there talking or laughing together. Some of them prank by chasing each other. Longing for Mom and Dad was still both a torment and an embedded fear, but he no longer cried.

He felt a few splashes of rain and looked up at the dark sky.

"No, please, no more rain," he pleaded as he pondered where to spend the night. He did not dare ask anyone he did not know, especially at this time of day. It was something that his parents had taught him, the risk of asking the wrong person for help was quite high even if God was by his side.

Jacob closed his eyes and began to begin a silent prayer. Again, with the hope that God would hear him. How long will you forget me, Lord? How long should you hide your face? How long will the thoughts grind, my heart anxious day after day? How long should ...

Suddenly, he felt a slight push behind his back and stiffened. He did not dare to look but stood motionless and squeezed his eyes shut even tighter. He heard someone harking and then spitting.

Then nothing happened, he only heard someone standing and breathing behind him. Suddenly, he felt a light tap on his left shoulder.

"Damn! Now you must react a little. Have you fallen asleep over the bike, huh?" said a hoarse and rosy voice.

"Now it's over. Thank God," Jacob muttered with a growing lump in his throat, a few drops of urine ending up in his underpants. He was convinced that it was the police who were behind him.

"What are you mumbling about? Did you have any bucks to spare?" asked the hoarse voice.

"What?" said Jacob, who opened his eyes and turned around.

He now came face to face with someone he had not expected to see. There stood a tall and slender guy with dirty, light blonde hair. He obviously had a challenging time standing still. To stand still at all for a few seconds, the guy had to adjust his standing position by moving one of his legs every few seconds so as not to fall over. The slender upper body twisted as he tried to regain his balance with the help of his flapping arms. The jeans that hid his slender stilt bones, had seen better days. Likewise, the denim jacket was as washed out as the trousers and there was no button.

"Huh! Yes, you could say that kid too," the guy noted. "Well, did you have a dime or?"

Jacob started digging into his pants pockets and found his last ten. He handed the money to the strange guy, who had to hold out both palms to make sure that the ten crowns would end up right in his hand. When it ended up in the palm of one hand, it did not lie still, it bounced. The guy put his other palm on top, so as not to drop the coin, before raising his hands folded in front of his face and saying, "But damn, lie still coin bastard I need you now."

"Do you need help?" asked Jacob kindly and was met by two gray-blue eyes staring at him unfocusedly.

"Does it look like that?" the guy asked with a small smile and then moved one leg to find the latest support and balance for his long slender body.

"It actually does. You may need some help. What is your name?"

"Pretzel, what's your name?" he asked as he managed to pinch the coin with one fist with some effort. He needed to free one arm so as not to lose his balance.

"My name is Jacob."

The fear slowly began to subside as Kringlan managed the feat of picking up the tian from the palm of his hand with his thumb and forefinger. Then he bit the coin with his mouth screaming with involuntary tooth loss while Jacob smiled. Kringlan could see that the ten-crowns was not a piece of chocolate in a gold-colored foil package, stretched out both arms and looked pleased. Jacob's smile changed into a surprised expression on his face when he saw a tattoo sticking out of one sleeve of his jacket, an image of Jesus crucified in a heart.

Could it be a sign?

The pretzel stared at the ten-crowns bouncing around in the palm of his hand and then alternately looked at both Jacob and the coin. He got decision anxiety, what if... Would he really take the ten crowns from that kid? It felt wrong.

"Is this all you had?" asked Kringlan as he stared at Jacob.

Jacob nodded, and at the same time became a little unsure at Kringlan's strange look.

"You can take it, you need it," Jacob said.

The pretzel took a wobbly step forward and grabbed his wrist. "Open your hand, kid."

Jacob was frightened, and at once stretched out his palm. The pretzel put the ten crowns back in his hand, then he closed it and patted it.

"I can't take from someone who has nothing," Kringlan remarked a little wistfully.

Jacob looked at him a little questioningly, then a smile came.

"May I ask something?"

"Sure, shoot!" replied Kringlan, shrugging his shoulders.

Jacob started laughing, his first laugh of the entire day.

"No, I'm not going to shoot you."

The pretzel frowned and looked at him questioningly before the token finally fell.

"Yes... No, not so. Stop fussing, ask instead," Kringlan grumbled.

"Is it God who sent you?" asked Jacob hopefully.

"What?" exclaimed Kringlan with a surprised expression on his face, becoming even more confused. "Where did you get that from?"

"I saw Jesus," Jacob replied with a twinkling smile.

Kringlan looked around with a surprised face and with his hand on his forehead he peered over the plate, on towards the entrance to the subway.

"Where?" he said, losing his balance and falling head over heels onto the hill.

The pretzel stood up with his hands supporting his knees, even though his legs were as unsteady as a newborn moose calf trying to get up for the first time. Jacob could not help but laugh, he was too funny.

"Nope! There," Jacob said, pointing to Kringlan's left arm. He pulled up his jacket sleeve and showed off the Jesus tattoo.

At least God had sent a funny guy, Jacob thought. "Do you believe in God?"

"Yes, and so do you," Jacob said, holding up one palm to do a high five. The pretzel smiled and answered the greeting with a clap of his hand.

"Once upon a time, I did it."

Jacob's smile died out and instead showed a disappointed expression on his face.

"But, why?"

"Do you know where Knutby is? A small hole outside Uppsala." Jacob nodded with a rediscovered smile.

"I went to Bible school there. My mom and dad lived in Knutby before I was born, that was a long time ago," said Jacob.

It began to creep into Kringlan's body and he once again found it difficult to stand still. In addition, he had to get himself a sieve to even get through the next night.

"You, Jacob. We'll have that talk by some campfire; I've got to move on."

Jacob's eager and curious gaze died out, even the smile disappeared and was replaced with an impression of disappointment and abandonment. He did not want to be alone and kindly asked me to go with him. The pretzel looked at him with a questioning look.

"Are you on the run, kid?"

Jacob lowered his gaze to the bike frame. He nodded reluctantly, and then looked at Kringlan with a pleading look. "Please!" he begged, a tear running down his cheek.

The pretzel did not want a kid behind him when he was fixing a strainer. Now if he could raise enough money. It would only lead to problems, something he had plenty of before. But, deep inside his crumbling soul was a feeling that did not want to leave Jacob in the lurch. It reminded him about his own heavy backpack that had tragic life secrets, which were hidden by sticking an injection needle in his arm daily to escape from reality. A backpack that was packed with both experiences and strong life stories and strongly spiced with social misery, betrayal, and abandonment. A survival process that had led to both addiction problems and prostitution.

"We do this, listen now. I will stick and fix a little, myself. When I am done, I will come back and if you are still here on the plate then you will come with me, okay?" promised the pretzel.

Jacob nodded most reluctantly.

"Good, then we have a deal. A stable tip, kid. If you have a home and a mom and dad, go there," Kringlan urged with a little hope.

"Do you promise you'll be back?" asked Jacob in an anxious tone.

The pretzel looked at Jacob with a serious look, then he started walking in the direction of the subway and stopped. He turned around a little unsteadily and reluctantly met Jacob's tearful eyes. A child's facial expression that seemed to say: do not abandon me, I am a child and need security, love. Her gaze opened Kringlan's hurt feelings embedded in a pus-filled boil in his heart, reminiscent of strong, dramatic memories.

"I will come as I have promised. Then I hope you have made the right decision, kid," he said before leaving.

It was with great bitterness and regret that Kringlan had even mentioned the godforsaken place of Knutby, a place he would rather forget and hide in his past. He got an unpleasant feeling that Jacob had managed to open his backpack that until today had kept secret for so many years. The memories he had once repressed had come back. The image of the coveted bride of Christ began to be recreated in memory. He tried to suppress it by thinking of something completely different, while at the same time turning the need for a sieve into a crying need.

Jacob remained standing over his bike and followed Kringlan with his gaze as he began to beg for money from passers-by. He walked across the plate towards the subway entrance and disappeared. Jacob was alone again.

* * *

From Kulturhuset, the audience from the evening's theater performances at Stockholm City Theatre came out through the main entrance. Among them, a middle-aged man went out. He was thin-haired and wore glasses. His long coat suited his posture but did not hide the incipient excess weight. The man in question was called Lars-Åke Rosén and his formal appearance allowed him to blend in with people unnoticed. He was chief physician and served on the Defense Staff in Östermalm, Stockholm.

He had just spent just over two hours at a lengthy theatrical performance. The play was about three one- 120

The same women and their life stories in the sixties, something that was not to his taste. He had sometimes sat and dozed Underneath the performance, but there were sometimes rude awakenings when one of the female characters on stage roared out her pain of powerlessness and disappointment.

Lars-Åke stood by the stairs leading down to Sergel Square and looked a little startled at the people passing over the square to or from the subway entrance. There were both uninteresting people and young people on aimless wanderings for lack of employment and money. It was young people who would do anything for little money, something that Lars-Åke had discreet experiences of. At Sergel Square you can buy everything in the form of goods or all kinds of services.

He spotted a fair-haired little guy straddling a blue bike below the stairs. He estimated that the boy could be ten or eleven years old. A young, attractive boy who had a Swedish background, given his appearance. The boy was alone, which looked promising, Lars-Åke reasoned. With a small discreet smile, he took the first steps down the stairs.

Philadelphia Congregation i Knutby (called Knutby Parish) is a free church parish in Knutby, Sweden.

Before 1992, there was no notable difference between the Knutby congregation and other small free churches. It was after the bride of Christ was dismissed from her seat in Uppsala Pentecostal Church and moved to Knutby, where she was a major source of inspiration for the congregation. It was received very positively but led to questions among some in the local community, in the Pentecostal movement and among some parishioners.

The congregation, with about ninety members, became nationally known after the Knutby drama in 2004, after which the congregation was forced to leave the Pentecostal movement.

Chapter 15

23 SEPTEMBER 2014

Linda sat in the waiting room of the police in Sollentuna and waited for Chris to arrive. He was currently being questioned by a male detective inspector about involvement in assault. Linda was stuck with her eyes on the windows facing the brick-clad archway. She too had been questioned about the altercation between Henke and Chris, an interrogation that went quickly. In a moment, she would be able to file a report about Jacob's disappearance and hoped that Chris would be ready before then. She wanted him to be present when the report was drawn up. The tiredness was excruciating and really, she just wanted to get some sleep.

The hope that Jacob would be found by contacting Jimmy's parents had been completely dashed in the hospital. Linda thought about the moment she met that white van on the highway. She was almost certain that it was Jacob who was in the passenger seat, but logic insisted on dismissing the idea. Why and for what reason Jacob would get into a vegetable truck with a wildly strange man and head for Stockholm.

He would never do that... if he did not have to...

No! Wait a minute now... In the unlikely event that he had been kidnapped, at least he would not be placed in full view inside the cab of a van. I must have seen wrong, she thought. A conclusion that made her lose another clue to her son.

A door opened and a female uniformed dog handler, Sandra Hediger, held the door open to let Gunn Britt out. She stopped to ask when Henke would be released but was only told that Sandra did not know. She then looked at Linda and gave her a sign to come.

Linda got up and walked over to Sandra while Gunn-Britt urged Sandra to find out when Henke would be released. She had an injured child to take care of.

"You'll have to wait a little while longer," Sandra said firmly.

"When is my husband coming?" asked Linda.

"It probably won't be much longer. Unfortunately, you will have to wait a bit before we can prepare your report", said Sandra. She turned on her heel and disappeared behind the door that was closed.

Linda and Gunn-Britt sat down on one of the sofas. On the table were various information sheets and brochures about the work and purpose of the police and how to apply for a passport in Arabic.

Gunn-Britt had a tough time making eye contact with Linda. There was no justification for what had happened. Not only was the personal guilt that felt like milestones, but shame had also taken a firm grip on her, thanks to her son. How could reconciliation be found with a mother whose son has disappeared without a trace? I am fucking cannot just sit here and not say anything, she thought frustratedly.

"Are you going to file a report on Jacob's disappearance?" she asked, trying to break the ice that had settled in the waiting room like a cold silence.

Linda, who had been staring down at the floor, looked up and gave her a determined look. She wiped away a few tears from her eyes, spilling tears before the devil's wife she was not going to do anyway.

"Surely it goes without saying that I should report my son's disappearance," Linda replied in an irritated tone, catching herself with her grumpiness.

"You don't have to touch it like that. I just want to help. I have apologized seven times this night and I can do it seven more times if that is what it takes," Gunn-Britt replied with a lump like a seal of guilt in his throat.

"Sorry. Everything is an indescribable nightmare that never ends. I cannot understand what is stopping Jacob from getting in touch. We are his security."

"Don't you think he's turned to someone he trusts?" asked Gunn-Britt at last.

Linda thought about what Gunn-Britt had just said. To whom would he turn? Grandma and Grandpa would have contacted him if he had gone there. With Robert, he was not. Could he be with someone from Bible school perhaps? She showed off a surprised look on her face as she thought. Has he cycled to...? Suddenly, the door opened, and Sandra looked at her.

"Then you can come with me."

Linda got up and walked over to her. They walked in and the door slowly closed again behind them. Left alone, Gunn-Britt began to think about her son Jimmy and the consequences ahead.

* * *

Chris walked with Detective Inspector Ulf Sandborg along the corridor on his way to the waiting room. The interrogation about Henke's handling went quickly and painlessly. Chris had explained that it was he who was attacked by Henke and not the other way around, which was then confirmed when Linda, Gunn-Britt and Charlotte had given their accounts of the incident.

When it came to the guilt in this accident with the boy Jimmy, Chris was incredibly surprised and wondered how Henke could have gotten Chris to be responsible for it. He was not even nearby, which half the staff at Karolinska Institute could vouch for.

Detective Sandborg adjusted the accusation and instead asked if Chris, as Henke claimed, was the instigator of the accident by hiring his son Jacob as the perpetrator and having induced him to arrange the accident in a deliberate manner. Chris had shaken his head while asking the detective if he was serious. Ulf had then shrugged and referred to the report that Henke had made and emphasized that he had to do his job as an interrogator. What Ulf thought personally was not part of the matter.

When Chris and Ulf turned left, they were met by Linda and Sandra who stopped. After a brief deliberation, Chris went with Linda and Sandra to file a joint police report about Jacob's disappearance. Ulf returned to his office; he would not spend any more precious time on what a personal fucking bickering between two dads was really.

Two men with diverse backgrounds, one with a clear fascist disposition, while the other slept with the Bible under his pillow and was more Christian than Jesus himself.

* * *

It was half past ten in the evening when Chris and Linda were on their way home. Despite all the earlier accounts with the police, Linda still had a need to talk about her thoughts. It was a way for her to hold back the panic attacks that were constantly trying to get a grip on her emotions. Chris, on the other hand, was tired and mentally worn out and just wanted to go home. It had been an exhausting day for both.

"We know Jacob participated in this bike accident, don't we?" asked Linda, taking his hand and holding it as a consolation. Chris nodded while concentrating on driving.

"He must have cycled to someone or he's hiding out somewhere in the dark," Linda added as she looked out the side window. But let us assume that he has contacted someone. We can exclude everyone in our closest circle of friends and my parents. Your parents and your brother we can also exclude. There is no way Jacob is heading to the United States by bike, right?

Chris smiled a little gently and for a moment a fantasy scenario appeared in which Jacob came cycling across the Atlantic. A tangible parable of Jesus crossing the Sea of Galilee. Linda looked at him questioningly.

"I'm with you baby, keep going," he urged with a sustained smile as he drove out onto the highway.

"For God's sake! What is so funny?" hissed Linda.

"No, nothing, honey. Absolutely nothing," Chris replied, and the smile disappeared in an instant.

"Okay, Jacob must have gone to a person or a place that he knows. Someone he feels safe with. The only place I can think of is Knutby," Linda said.

Chris braked while looking at his wife in surprise. Without warning, he accelerated at the same time as the car shifted down and accelerated away at high speed on the highway in the direction of Upplands Väsby.

"That we didn't think about it earlier!" he said as the speedometer showed that they passed 140 km/h.

The white Mercedes combi veered off at the exit to Upplands Väsby at high speed. The traffic light did show red, but Chris completely ignored it when he forced the car to the left so that it screamed about the tires. Linda held on convulsively.

while saying a silent prayer to survive this madness.

After passing the first T-junction at Vallentuna road, they arrived at a four-way intersection at the old pharmacy. Chris turned right and onto Almungevägen, it was the fastest way to Knutby. He reproached himself by passing through Torsåker avenue at high speed.

"That I didn't think about it before. He must be with Moa Waldarud," Chris said as he gave a direct thank you to his master, that he had given him a woman who could think clearly in tricky situations like this.

"Are we on our way to Moa?" asked Linda with a nervousness she could have done without. She held the doorknob, so her knuckles whitened, hoping fervently that she was wrong.

Chris nodded as they passed the entrance to the go-kart track ÖS-WE Ring.

"If Jacob is in Knutby then he is with her, there is no doubt about it. Hope to God he is there," Chris said. "If so, why doesn't she get in touch?" asked Linda.

"Please honey, I don't know. I don't have any answers at the moment."

The question was obvious to Linda, of course, but to expect Chris to contribute with a convenient answer was to set a little too high demands, she thought to herself. Instead, she was quick to see that an accident rarely comes alone, and that evil begets eviler when they came out on the long straight along Almungevägen. She glanced at the dashboard and saw the speedometer creeping nasty close to 180 km/h.

"Chris, our lives could end as fast as the speed we're at right now. If a moose were to cross the road in front of us, it is over," Linda said, hoping he would hear her.

Chris lowered the speed to 160 km/h as they passed by the T-junction with the signs that said the creation two and motorway.

They were approaching Knutby and had about three km left to the community when Chris braked sharply and turned left onto a smaller gravel road that turned out to be very poorly maintained. Linda felt anxious about meeting Moa again. Memories that she thought were erased came back. Chris turned right and passed some houses on the left, including Ragnar Åbjörnsson's villa, which was now repainted and had a new owner. It was a place where came on an errand and changed the lives of the entire congregation.

Chris felt a slight shiver as he stopped the car at a familiar brown two-story wooden house. In the light of the outdoor lighting, you could see the outline of the small timbered herb with grassy roof that stood on the plot, a place that Linda had strong memories of.

There were two vivid memories dating back to the year 2003, a year before the horrific murders became known. The first incident occurred when Chris was in the United States at a medical congress. Moa had, after they had rehearsed with the choir in the parish hall, invited Linda over for a cup of tea. They had sat down in this very shelter and had tea with some snacks. After that, they prayed together in the form of pastoral care, which caused Moa to let go of all inhibitions. She seduced Linda through a ritual lesbian sex act in the spirit of God. Linda had never told Chris about the incident for two essential reasons. The first reason was not to lure Chris into redemptive fantasies to start an intimate relationship with Moa. The second reason was not to give Chris a self-proclaimed valid reason for jumping into bed with Moa on the grounds that Linda had cheated on him.

A few days later, Linda received the news that she was pregnant, which she informed Chris during a nightly phone call.

She remembered the event very well because Moa had praised God for the gift that Linda was carrying. Moa wanted to believe that her love for Linda was one of the reasons Linda got pregnant. It was not an imaginative hope of Moa, but a strong conviction that this was the case. God had appointed her the bride of Christ and given her His blessing.

The second memory was that she caught Moa trying to seduce Chris during a pastoral care conversation. They would now once again meet the enormously beautiful Moa. Thank goodness I am in, Linda thought.

They got out of the car and looked around. On the turnpike, an A-tractor was parked. Despite being poorly lit, Linda got the impression that time had stopped. They had remained in the Pentecostal church for six years, five of whom Jacob attended Bible hour. After that, Chris and Linda chose for more practical and personal reasons, where travel time was one of the reasons, to go over to the Pentecostal church in Upplands Väsby. Since then, they had not set foot in Knutby until tonight.

Chris rang the bell while Linda was standing by, wanting to hold his hand to mark, but he gave her a glance and snatched his hand away when the front door suddenly opened. They stood Moa Waldarud dressed in a white, transparent negligee that did not hide much of her naked body. Chris came off completely and just stood there staring at her. Linda was equally surprised by Moa's challenging outfit and gave Chris an elbow nudge to stop staring like a male dog.

"Hello! But what a surprise!" exclaimed Moa with a warm smile and asked them to come in.

"Sorry to disturb us this late," Chris excused himself as he walked into the hall and looked around.

Linda reluctantly walked in, and Moa closed the front door behind her. She walked over to Linda and hugged her. Linda felt an adorable perfume scent that had been immortalized along with other body fragrances. A few creeping footsteps were heard from upstairs, and a door was carefully closed. "God, how I have missed you. I have thought so much about you," Moa said sincerely as she let go of Linda. She walked over to Chris and gave him a long, intense hug, something Linda would rather see undone.

"We have come here because we..."

Linda interrupted herself when she again heard a few quick footsteps from upstairs. Chris and Linda looked up without seeing anyone upstairs. Linda instead spotted a men's leather jacket hanging on a hook on a tambour major. She looked suspiciously at Moa, who let go of Chris and contributed a warm smile.

"Maybe we were interfering," Chris said, nodding discreetly towards the stairs leading to the upper floor.

"God no! We have just finished pastoral care exercise. Would you like a cup of tea?"

Linda took a marking step forward.

"No thanks. Jacob is missing and we are searching for him.

Is he here?"

Moa stood staring in surprise with wide eyes and her mouth wide open.

"Oh my God. Is he gone?"

Linda looked at Moa suspiciously.

"He's been missing since this morning," Chris replied.

"Poor child. Do you think he is here in Knutby?"

"We've been looking for him everywhere except here," Linda said as she wiped a tear from her cheek.

"Linda come, let's sit down in the kitchen and you can tell us what happened," Moa said and then walked towards the kitchen.

Linda and Chris followed while someone started showering upstairs. When Linda pulled out one of the kitchen chairs to sit down, she heard someone stop showering and there was silence Upstairs. When Chris sat down across from Linda, showering resumed. They gave each other a questioning look.

Pedophilia (from Greek parents, genitive paidos, "child" and philia, "love", "friendship") is a term for an adult's sexual attraction to prepubertal children and children in early puberty (usually 13 years or younger).

Since the attraction is aimed at young teenagers (people of puberty age), rather than younger children, the term hebephilia or efebophilia is used instead.

Pedophilia is a psychiatric diagnosis regardless of whether the person succumbs to the pull or not.

Different countries' laws criminalize sexual acts against children with different laws and depending on the nature of the crime. Crimes related to pedophilia include child pornography offenses, child rape, child sexual exploitation, and more.

Chapter 16

23-24 SEPTEMBER 2014

Jacob stood at the doors of the subway car with his blue bike together with Lars-Åke. They had boarded the subway at Hötorget and were on their way to Stadion's metro station in Östermalm. The meeting with Lars-Åke Rosén initially became a little tense when he appeared from behind and started talking to him, but soon Jacob realized that he was not a police officer. When Lars-Åke introduced himself as Lars and sounded both kind and accommodating, he politely introduced himself as Jacob and held out his hand to greet.

Lars-Åke showed him a humble and understanding side. His first questions about school and sports soon led to a more relaxed conversation. He asked some leading questions about Jacob's social status and when asked if he was all by himself, Jacob had replied that he was waiting for his brother who was called Kringlan. The longer the conversations went on, the more Lars-Åke understood that the boy was alone. The truth finally crept out when Jacob realized that Kringlan would not show up, which caused Lars-Åke to smile.

When asked if Jacob was hungry, he received a nodding answer along with a small smile. Lars-Åke then offered two enticing options to choose from. The first was to be invited to McDonalds, the second to go to Lar's home and get hot chocolate and good sandwiches. Should Jacob have nowhere to go tonight, he would have to sleep in a guest bed.

At last, Jacob had been heard after several prayers to God for help. He thus chose hot chocolate with sandwiches and a bed to sleep in. The day had been long and dramatic, and crawling under a blanket to sleep was something Jacob longed for.

Arriving at Stadion's metro station, Jacob led the bike out to Valhto Road. It had started to rain, and it was blowing cold as he waited for Lars, who was walking just behind. Lars explained that it would be a short walk in this severe weather.

"You can stand some water, can't you?" he asked, smiling.

Jacob nodded smiling and longed to get into the warmth and security. Together they walked along the walkway through Lindallén in the direction of Gärdet. They passed the pedestrian crossing on Valhto Road, then continued in the same direction. They stopped at gate number 129. Jacob placed the bike against a telephone cabinet and locked it, while Lars keyed in the door code and then opened the gate and held it up for Jacob. The rain turned into a heavy shower as they hurriedly entered the stairwell while the gate door closed again.

When Jacob entered, he was greeted by a beautifully furnished hall. He took off his shoes and hung up his jacket on a vacant hanger while Lars hung off his long coat and then straightened his jacket.

"Yes, my friend, here I live. Shall we go to the kitchen and prepare hot chocolate and sandwiches?"

Jacob nodded, feeling his hunger make itself felt.

They went into the kitchen where Jacob sat down at the kitchen table. LarsÅke brought out butter, milk, cheese, squash, and smoked ham from Pålsson. Then he put up six loaf boards from Skogaholm.

Within minutes, a platter of six sandwiches with ham and cheese, garnished with some tomato slices and sliced squash, was standing on the kitchen table. After a few moments, a mug of hot chocolate was also on the table in front of Jacob. It was just a matter of chopping in, and Jacob started eating with a good appetite while Lars-Åke sat opposite and studied him in a little more detail while he took a sandwich.

Meanwhile, Jacob told us about all the dramatic events that had taken place during the day, and it was with great empathy and sometimes with tears in his throat. Lars-Åke saw a tear running down Jacob's cheek and reached out his hand to comfort. Jacob got up from the table and walked over to him, hugging him as he cried. Lars-Åke took the opportunity to strengthen trust by comforting the boy while he saw potential opportunities with the blonde active child creature who for the moment sought comfort and security.

This *cannot be true! The boy was risk-free and if he had the opportunity to go to the police he would not do it, he was terrified.*

When Jacob had been allowed to cry and find peace, he let go of Lars-Åke to wipe the last tears from his cheeks. He sat down with reddish eyes and drank some lukewarm chocolate. He had gained confidence in Lars and felt a sense of relief to let out his feelings and burdens in front of him.

Lars-Åke got up and started clearing the kitchen table before Jacob was guided around the apartment. It was a three-room apartment with furniture that was in the same English style throughout the apartment. English oxblood-colored leather group with side tables on each side and a large glass table, a sturdy oak bookcase, yes - all in the typical English bourgeoisie class.

Jacob sat down on the sofa while Lars-Åke went to his wheeled, antique globe that stood on the parquet floor and opened it. He poured some whiskey into a glass and then closed it again. He took a seat in an armchair and began sipping the whiskey with a smile.

"Mmm, sometimes the world is unfair and puzzling," said Lars-Åke. "What do you think will happen if the police find you?"

"I'm going to go to jail, and I'll have to sit there all my life," Jacob replied with a bubbling feeling in his throat.

Lars-Åke saw a strong concern in Jacob's tearful eyes.

"Do children end up in jail?" asked Lars-Åke, taking another sip of his whiskey.

Jacob gave a nodded answer with strong conviction.

"You don't have any money either, I guess?"

"No, no money," Jacob replied, fixing his gaze on the floor.

"This is too good to be true, Lars-Åke thought, bringing the whisky glass to his mouth with a slightly shaky hand and taking a sip.

"I can help you with some money if you want. Do you want to make some money?" asked Lars-Åke after swallowing the whisky and setting the glass down on a base layer on the glass table.

Jacob lit up on the couch, now God had finally helped him by sending Lars to him. He nodded eagerly. "I'll do anything. I need to connect with my uncle in the United States."

Lars-Åke smiled and nodded. He got up and then disappeared out of the hall. When he returned, he stood in front of Jacob at the beautiful living room table, held out a five-hundred-crown bill between his fingers, and held it up. Jacob stared at the banknote with a strong feeling of want, while Lars-Åke with raised eyebrows showed a small smile. This was childishly simple, Lars-Åke thought and swallowed some saliva.

"What should I do?" asked Jacob eagerly.

"I want you to undress while I film you with my camcorder. Do you want to do it?" Jacob looked at Lars in surprise.

"Just that?" asked Jacob, standing up. "We can start with that."

"Okay, but why should I undress?"

"You'll see. I am going to get my camera," said Lars-Åke as he placed the five-hundred-krona note on the table.

He disappeared out to the hall while Jacob looked tempted at the note on the table. Should I just undress and get five hundred crowns for it, Jacob thought uncomprehendingly. From inside the kitchen, Lars-Åke asked if he wanted something to drink and suggested orange juice, Jacob accepted.

Inside the kitchen, Lars-Åke took out two glasses and a pitcher of orange juice from the fridge. From his trouser pocket, he took out a foil package and squeezed a tablet onto the sink. From one of the kitchens drawers, he retrieved a tablespoon and crushed the tablet into powder form, which he then poured into the orange juice.

When he entered the living room, he handed one of the glasses to Jacob, who gratefully accepted it.

"Are we going to compete to see who drinks from their glass the fastest?" suggested Lars-Åke with a smile.

"Okay, I'll win!" exclaimed Jacob victoriously.

Lars-Åke started counting down from three, and at one Jacob started drinking. He poured himself the orange juice so that it began to ooze from the corners of his mouth, which made Lars-Åke's perverse fantasies grow.

"I won!" exclaimed Jacob triumphantly as he set the sticky glass down on the table. Lars-Åke smiled, then hurried to lift the glass and could see that there was an imprint on the table glass on the mahogany table.

"You were a witty one to me," he said, carrying both drinking glasses out to the kitchen and then disappearing into another room. He came back with a video camera and a black tote bag. Jacob stood at the table and glanced at the five-hundred-crowns note.

"You can take the money now if you want. But then you must promise me that you will do what I ask of you."

"I promise," Jacob said with wild delight, taking the note from the table. He looked at it and folded it neatly before pushing it into one of his trouser pockets.

Lars-Åke began to instruct Jacob on where to stand and undress. He also wanted Jacob to dance sensually by performing rocking movements with his lower body. Jacob, who believed that this was a game, slowly began to dance across the parquet floor, doing pirouettes while with a little hesitation he began to undress. Lars-Åke filmed and excitedly focused on the blonde boy's tender body.

"Good Jacob! How clever you are. You dance beautifully, my friend."

Lars-Åke then asked him to sit on the floor and take off his trousers. Jacob did as he was told without question, it was just a game. When he was about to take off his socks, Lars-Åke spoke up, he instead wanted Jacob to take off his underpants and then get up and play with his dick. Jacob hesitated and looked embarrassedly at Lars-Åke, who was getting all red in the face.

"Why?" asked Jacob, beginning to feel dizzy.

Lars-Åke walked with determined steps up to Jacob, who was still sitting on the floor. He held out his hand and asked for his money back. Jacob felt his head start spinning and absolutely did not want to give the money back. Instead, he took off his underpants and stood up completely naked. Lars-Åke smiled with a disgusting sexual arousal and authoritarianism. There in front of him stood a young, beautiful boy right in front of the camera masturbating.

Lars-Åke took a quick breath and ordered Jacob to unbutton his pants. Jacob was in a completely different, drugged, world when he unbuttoned Lars-Åke's pants, after which he pulled out his erect limb.

Jacob heard the commanding voice as if through a giant tin can in a dark voice. It commanded him to open his mouth, and he obeyed. He felt something warm and stiff put into his mouth as reality slipped away from him. Suddenly, something went down his throat and his gag reflexes reacted. At the same moment, he received a severe blow to the right cheek.

* * *

Jacob woke up in a double bed, dazed with singing headaches and oppressive nausea. He did not really understand where he was but felt that someone was behind him when he changed position. Suddenly, two hands took hold brusquely tag around life on him from behind, someone parted his aching buttocks. It hurt so much when something slid into his ass, and Jacob closed his eyes. The pain wanted to make him scream right out, but he did not dare. The last time he screamed in pain, he had a pillow pressed against his face and nearly choked.

Lars-Åke breathed quickly when he once again enjoyed sex with an underage child. This time it was more enjoyable, as he chose not to film this rape. He already had many exciting film clips of the wonderful, young boy and finally he could enjoy a little extra without thinking about camera angles and poses. This untouched boy belonged only to him. God, how nice, he thought as his body shook in an orgasm.

Jacob did not resist; he was completely powerless and in an apathetic state. All he could do was pray to God for help and reconciliation before consciousness drifted away from him again.

* * *

It struck seven in the morning when Jacob woke up. He looked around and could see that he was alone in bed. When he stood up, he felt pain in his tail, and he grinned badly. He heard someone showering inside the bathroom as he snuck out of the bedroom.

In the living room, he found his clothes. Suddenly, the shower was turned off and Jacob panicked. Quickly he got dressed while braving the pain, this was his only chance to get out of here. When he heard the shower turn on, he could breathe out slightly.

He snuck out to the hall and hurried to put on his jacket and shoes as quietly as he could, then walked to the front door and felt it locked. Carefully, he turned the lock and a click was heard from the locking plunger. Silently, he tried to open the door, but it was still locked. He looked up at the door mirror and saw that there was another lock, a seven-lever lock.

Suddenly, the doorbell rang with a late knock. Jacob was horrified and panic increased when a male voice called from the stairwell.

"Open! It's the police."

Jacob heard the shower turn off inside the bathroom and the sound of two wet feet sliding in the bathtub with a squeaking sound, then it became quiet. It felt as if time had stopped. Suddenly, the doorbell rang again. Jacob ran to the living room and in a panic, he looked around. Balcony! He ran over and opened the balcony door facing the backyard. Quickly out onto the balcony, leaned over the railing and looked down at the ground. It was two floors down to freedom, he noted, and became even more despairing. Would he just jump? He had to, because now a door was opened from inside the apartment. But... The gutter!

"My only chance! I must do it. Oh, how much it hurts," Jacob whispered, grimacing.

Jacob grabbed the rod with his feet and with his arms climb-

They climbed onto the narrow balcony railing and took a quick grip around the black downspout.

"Don't look down," Jacob hissed to himself, locking his gaze horizontally on the black downspout.

Balancing he took another step to get next to the downspout. He took another grip around the downspout and wall bracket and fumbled a little with his legs until the soles of his shoes took hold against the façade. Slowly he began to climb down. Then he felt someone grab his jacket and look up in horror. On the balcony, a man wearing a black leather jacket was grabbing Jacob's jacket. At the same time, he heard agitated voices from inside the apartment. One of the voices belonged to Lars, and he sounded both resigned and scared. Jacob stared with tearful and terrified eyes at the man standing on the balcony.

"Kid! No need to be afraid. I will help you," said Detective Inspector George Lindmark of the Stockholm police.

George felt how the fabric of the jacket began to slip out of his hand and then lost his grip on the jacket. He tried to take another grip, but Jacob slid to the ground and was out of reach.

"Are you okay? Can you stay there, and I'll come down... Stay, you don't have to be afraid."

When Jacob finally contacted the ground, he ran for his life towards Artillery Street. Behind, the man shouted on the balcony.

"I'm a cop for fuck!"

Jacob stopped at Artillery Street for a moment to orient himself. He saw Valhto Road and the Seven Eleven store that rounded the corner of the property and ran there. Arriving at the corner of the property, he peeked cautiously out. He saw the bike leaning against the façade and about seven meters further on, two uniformed police officers stood by a police car. Behind them stood a civilian car with the passenger door wide open. Would he be so cheeky? Would he even dare to go up and take the bike when the police were so close? What would Owen have done? he thought. He had killed Lars and cycled away like a hero, he guessed.

With that conviction, just as if nothing had happened, he walked towards the bike. Both officers looked at him a little startled but showed little interest in contacting him. No, why should they? A kid who was on his way to school, just like all the other kids passing by. They had completely different tasks to address.

When Jacob reached the bike, he nervously swallowed a lump in his throat and glanced at the police officers at the same time. He unlocked it and sat on it. At the same moment, a plainclothes policeman came running out of the gate and was about to say something to his colleagues when he saw Jacob cycling away in the direction of Gärdet. He recognized the boy; it was the same kid he almost got hold of out on the balcony.

"You kid!" shouted George and began to run after, while the two uniformed police officer looked in surprise for the colleague whose open leather jacket swayed like a black coat as he ran.

Jacob pedaled for king and fatherland while avoiding sitting on the saddle. A little further on, it turned green at a pedestrian crossing, and he took the opportunity to cross the street just behind some cars passing by. He cycled across the tree-lined avenue, the parking lot, and the walkway that divided Valhto Road in two directions. Jacob turned around for a moment and found that the officer was left on the sidewalk across the street due to the intense morning traffic.

George gestured irritably with his arms as he watched as the boy cycled across the other part of Valhto Road and continued onto

Artillery Street in the direction of Karlavägen. He walked back to his colleagues who were still standing by the police car with questioning looks.

"You should have picked the kid," exclaimed George irritably, and at the same time felt a frustration that would not let go.

"How the hell could we know?" replied the older police colleague.

"It's fucking a peddo we've seized in the apartment as you're supposed to... Fuck the same... he's gone now," George stated dejectedly.

"What kind of guy was that?" the younger colleague asked.

"He left the apartment by climbing down the gutter out on the balcony. Damn, I was this close to getting hold of him," said George and held up his clenched fist.

George started walking towards the gate but stopped and turned to his colleagues.

"We have the suspect anyway. He will just get dressed, then we will come down with him. He is going with a damn speed to Kronoberg," George stated firmly. Then he disappeared through the gate, which closed with a click.

Chapter 17

24 SEPTEMBER 2014

THE VISIT TO Moa's home brought nothing but Moa's dismay and despair at the disappearance. She then calmly began preaching to convince Linda and Chris that Jacob would be found unharmed, with God's help. It turned out that she had some contacts in the police force that she could use.

According to Moa, she had not seen Jacob or heard rumors that he was staying in Knutby. She was convinced that in that case she would have heard about it. Despite the tragedy that happened ten years ago, she stayed in her leadership position within the congregation, although not officially.

Neither Chris nor Linda had reason to doubt what she had told them, to think that she would hide Jacob from her own needs was to run away without any credible grounds whatsoever. Moa's love for children and that they loved her back was no secret, but to suspect her of kidnapping was unreasonable.

At 09:15 Linda came out of the police station in Sollentuna. She had been inside and handed over a photo of Jacob that showed a young blonde boy with a charming smile, as well as blue intense eyes with a confidence in the future. Two hours earlier, she had agreed with Chris that she would stay home if Jacob were found or came home of her own accord.

After Linda drove Chris to work, she went to the police station with the photo.

Chris was in a more awkward position. He could not be away from his vital work and research, even though he wanted to be at home and support Linda. At P4, some important development talks with the research team awaited as well as a telephone meeting after lunch with former colleague Travis Warren at Fort Detrick. Moreover, he told himself, Linda was just a phone call away and would keep him informed throughout the day if something were to happen. It gave him some peace of mind.

Back in the hall, Linda had kicked off her shoes and carelessly tossed her jacket on top of the dresser next to the coat hanger. With her mobile phone in hand, she went straight to the bedroom. As she walked past the bedroom door of Jacob's bedroom, she stopped. Her heartbeat faster as she considered looking into the bedroom. She felt a faint hope that she would find him asleep in her bed, and that everything that had happened was just a diabolical nightmare that would not let go. She opened the door and found that Jacob's bed was still empty and made. She walked over to the head end of the bed and took the pillow that was under the covers. With the pillow in her arms, she left the room and closed the door. She went to her bedroom where the double bed was waiting, put her cell phone on the nightstand and threw herself on the bed with Jacob's pillow pressed against her chest. She closed her eyes as she felt tears streaming down her cheeks.

Shortly after eleven o'clock, Linda woke up to the phone ringing. She rushed to answer and heard a male police officer announce that a blue children's bike had been found near the boat club at Cairo Boat Club next to the swimming area. Two patrol cars had been sent to the scene, one of which was a dog patrol. The officer took the opportunity to ask for the frame number of Jacobs bicycle to be able to find the bike that had been found. After the conversation, Linda sat wide awake on the edge of the bed while the thoughts once again went around in her head.

Would Jacob have cycled to Cairo all by himself? Doubtful. What if... What if Jacob and Robert had built a hut while they had been there with the school? Or does someone else have his bike?

Ten minutes later, Linda was sitting in the white Mercedes and backed out of the driveway with a flying start. Once out at the roundabout at Mälarvägen, she turned right and drove at high speed towards Ed's church, and then took off on the slightly more winding road towards Cairo beach.

Arriving at Upplands Väsby Båtsällskap, she saw two police cars parked at the steel gates of the boat club. She parked the car and got out. The dog handler Sandra walked up to her along with her Malinous. She informed them of what they had found and that her colleagues were currently checking the frame number of the found bike. Sure enough, two police officer came rolling with a blue mountain bike that had a puncture on the front wheel. Linda recognized the bike.

It turned out that the frame number that Linda had said was almost correct on the found bike except for two digits that were damaged and thus could not be read.

* * *

At half past two the search ended. They had searched the entire marina area as well as the immediate area around the boat club and the bathing area. Linda informed Chris once again about the found bike and any question marks that remained, as the frame number could not be found at this time. She also could not tell with one hundred percent certainty whether it was Jacob's bike or not.

The search for Jacob itself was fruitless, showing that Jacob had not been in the harbor itself, unless he had climbed over the fence. There was only one concrete trail that Sandra's dog marked, and led from where the bike was found down to the water.

After a conversation between Ulf and Sandra, it was decided to search the waters around the boat club with the help of divers from the fire brigade. In any case, the boy had been missing for over a day and all you had to go on was a blue mountain bike, which may have belonged to Jacob.

Upplands Väsby fire brigade was called in with reinforcements from Sollentuna fire department. Volunteers from the boat club also took part by dragging along the lake bottom outside the moorings.

Linda did not believe at all in the police's theory that her son could be lying on the lake bottom. According to her, it was too far-fetched to believe that Jacob would end up in the water, he had respect for water and was also able to swim. Her thoughts were then confirmed by the dragging and diving efforts once the search had been completed at dusk.

* * *

During the evening, Chris and Linda sat at home each with a mobile phone and a telephone list to once again call everyone in the circle of acquaintances, including Pentecostal church members in Upplands Väsby, class students and teachers who were worried about Jacob. They also called around the Pentecostal church in Knutby and inquired. None of them had seen or heard anything about Jacob.

Finally, Linda called Gunn-Britt with some despair and hesitation. Partly to hear what it was like with Jimmy and partly if they had heard anything about Jacob, which was not likely. True, they had heard nothing. Jimmy remained in the hospital and there were hopes that he would be able to come home tomorrow after the doctor's round. In the case of Gunn-Britt's miserable bloke, Henke, he had been released as Chris had withdrawn his complaint after Henke's police report against Chris was dismissed by the prosecutor.

Chris and Linda looked at each other with eternal wonder, how could this happen to them? What is next? Tomorrow would be forty-eight hours since Jacob disappeared, and not a sign of life since. Only one bike that you could not even ascertain was his bike. Amid all the worry and despair, skeptical spiritual and existential questions were slowly born.

Why did God allow this to happen? Why were they never heard despite countless prayers for help? Could reality be so cruel that God had reclaimed the gift of their lives? That Jacob might not exist anymore but had become an angel? Had God really abandoned them and turned his back on them?

الإ هلإ ال نأ دهشأ هللا لوسر دمحم نأ دهشأ و هللا (*ʾ ašhadu ʾ an lā ilāha illā-llāh, wa ʾ ašhadu ʾanna mu ḥ ammadan rasūlu-llāh*), *or* دمحم هللا الإ هلإ ال هللا لوسر (*Lā ʿilāha ʿillā llāha wa Muhammadun rasūlu llāhi*), *that is, "there is no god but God and Muhammad is the Messenger of God".*

Chapter 18

24 SEPTEMBER 2014

At 9:30 p.m., A dark blue Toyota Prius taxi was parked a little tucked between two trucks in a parking lot. The glow of the streetlights was reflected on the Taxi Courier logo and the taxi sign on the roof. Behind the wheel, a 25-year-old man was waiting impatiently. The man's name was Ali Naharaim and he was originally from Syria. He had lived in Sweden for five years and was a faithful Muslim.

He drummed his fingers on the steering wheel and became increasingly impatient to sit and wait. He was logged into Taxikurir's traffic system for free, which meant that he could not wait forever. The car also had GPS and was visible to traffic control. Turning down multiple runs would not help him, quite the opposite.

Ali was, in addition to a taxi driver, also a courier in the name of God. His undertaking was the first phase in a recruitment process for young refugees. With the help of a well-established network of contacts, who worked at various refugee facilities in Stockholm, Muslim refugees were recruited.

Now he was waiting for a contact person who could not keep up the times. Suddenly, he caught a glimpse of a woman wearing a burqa disappearing behind a white van parked on the opposite side. The woman looked forward again and waved discreetly to Ali. Her name was Hadishe and she was originally from Iraq. She started walking towards the taxi with two young Muslim girls, dressed as her, in tow.

Ali got halfway out of the car and waved impatiently to her to hurry up. She increased her steps as she pushed both girls, who were between 12 and 15 years old, in front of her. When she stopped at Ali, she received a stern lecture.

"Damn woman! I said nine o'clock. Not half past ten! Do you get it – What!" he shouted, spitting, and upset at having to sit here and wait. No respect whatsoever. It is unbelievable how a Muslim woman can become so Swedishized in such a fleeting time.

"Ali! I got in trouble, you must understand," Hadishe defended himself pleadingly, pointing to one of the girls as the scapegoat for the delay.

Ali gestured with his arms that he did not want to hear her excuses and instead opened the rear passenger door of the taxi. With an angry look, he motioned for the girls to get in the car, which they did. Hadishe sat down in the passenger seat next to Ali. He keyed on the taxi computer and saw that he was still number one in Skärholmen.

"Fort, call the taxi courier and order a taxi to Heron city."

Hadishe took out her iPhone to do as she was told. A minute later, the computer pepped up and Ali received a drive from Heron City which he accepted at the press of a button. He started the car and drove away.

"Now fucking woman, not one more time! Next time I'll take you to Iraq and let everyone fuck you like a little whore."

Hadishe at once showed his submission by curling up in his seat like a beaten dog and was terrified. She was scared to be forced to return to their homeland and be subjected to dishonor, shame, war.

"Nope! You do not do that. I help you get God's warriors. I arrange all the wives of warriors. Sorry! Next time I pass the time, next time will be good, great," she promised dearly and holy to emphasize how important she was both to Ali and to the Islamic Empire.

"I'm going to fuck you!" hissed Ali with black eyes as he stopped at the entrance at Heron City and glared at her angrily.

"Now? Here?" exclaimed Hadishe, horrified.

Ali covered his face with both hands and prayed to higher powers for mercy and strength. He turned on the taximeter, shifted into the right gear and then continued towards Södertälje.

The journey on the E4 southbound took place in silence that was occasionally interrupted with a slight cough from the back seat. What needed to be said had been said, at least for Ali. The anger had subsided, and he felt that he had gained control of the situation.

Hadishe, on the other hand, was still worried about whether Ali would make his earlier threat a reality. There was a solution to the problem. If she had to have sex with him as a disciplinary measure, she would be willing to let go and give him that little extra. She kept thinking as the dark blue Taxikurir hybrid crossed the bridge over the Södertälje Canal and continued south towards the Buying.

At the Järna exit, Ali turned off the highway and then right onto Route 57. Hadishe recognized herself when she saw the road sign, Katrineholm, Gnesta, Järna. As they passed past the county border and Järna, Ali felt he had to lighten the printed mood.

In Arabic, he began to tell the girls in the back seat that their lives in the future would be both bright and successful, through the care of Toh and Ali. A future where their future men would become real heroes and be honored with both wealth and respect. The struggle for Muslim supremacy had begun according to Toh's will.

"INSHA'ALLAH!" exclaimed Ali triumphantly.

The girls in the back seat nodded and repeated what Ali had exclaimed as they pondered where they were going. Hedishe had faithfully agreed with one: INSHA'ALLAH and ended with a chattering battle call.

The journey continued past Gnesta while Ali promised far-reaching promises of a better life in Iraq under the presence and protection of God. The difficult hardship and sometimes dangerous journey that the girls had recently lived through was a test of adulthood from Toh. Hedishe nodded in agreement.

After passing Björnlunda, they approached Sparreholm. Ali braked and then turned right into a plot where an older wooden villa stood a little secluded from the road. There was a glow in the latticed windows and someone with a boyish appearance was looking out of one of the windows. Ali got out of the car and opened the back door for the girls, they got out of the car and looked around at the pitch-black surroundings. Ali pushed the girls in front of her towards the entrance of the house while Hedishe walked behind to show her respect for Ali, hoping for the best for herself. She knew what was going to happen when she stepped through the door of this house, something she prepared for.

Ali unlocked three locks on the steel-encrusted front door and opened. With an inviting gesture, he let the girls go in before he went in and closed the door. He locked two locks with two different keys and Hedishe took the girls with him to guide them around the house and show them where to spend the night when they met two young dark-skinned boys from Somalia.

Half an hour later, the two Somali boys sat with the newly arrived young girls, dressed in burqas on a worn fabric sofa in the living room. While the TV was turned on at high volume and a freight train passed by nearby, the children could hear from an adjoining room how Hedishe was verbally chastised in Arabic by Ali, while the headboard hit the wall in time with her moans.

From time to time there was a wailing voice from Hedishe when Ali had shown his adulthood. A few minutes later, the television was the only thing that could be heard. It was as if time had stopped. The door opened and Ali stepped out with a grinning smile as he nearly unbuttoned his pants. Behind his back, the bottom of his white shirt hung down his lower back as he walked to the kitchen. It was time for a few glasses of invigorating orange juice and a moment of presence with Toh. Still in the room, Hadishe lay naked and leaning forward on the bed with his butt in the weather. She begged for mercy as the pain pounded persistently in her vagina and anus.

The congregation of Hedvig Eleonora was formed on 17 April 1672 by a breakaway from the parish of Holmkyrkan. Until 1737, the parish was also called.
Ladugårdsland parish and has also been called.
Östermalm Parish. From the congregation was erupted 1724 Burgher widows' house parish and 1749
Hedvig Eleonora poorhouse parish. In 1819, Djurgården's country parish was split off, which reverted in 1868. In 1879, the General Institute of Manila for the Deaf-Mute and Blind Parish was incorporated, which in 1864 was split off from Djurgården's country parish. On 1 May 1906, Engelbrekt parish and Oskar parish were split off.

Chapter 19

24 SEPTEMBER 2014

THE MORNING HAD been as terrible as the past night at Lars. Jacob turned onto Storgatan and stopped for a moment at Hedvig Eleonora church in Östermalm. He admired the beautiful church building as his pulse slowly went down. There was a peacefulness about the Church that lulled him into an inner sense of security.

A feeling of dirtiness, disgusting, punished, hunted, and completely abandoned smoldered in his despairing consciousness. The feeling was unprecedented. In addition, he had pain in his tail, which led to painful problems with sitting on the saddle when cycling. To top it all off, he also had to pinch again extra hard with his sore opening because he felt that some kind of fluid was flowing out, which was uncomfortable. He needed to go to the toilet as soon as possible.

Jacob saw an elderly lady coming out of the large wooden gate at the church entrance, showing that it was open. Would he dare to go in and ask for a toilet? Outside the entrance stood a mountain bike leaning against the stone wall. Jacob had stepped into the church hall itself with extensive ornate decoration in the form of beautiful architecture all over the hall. He walked past the pulpit and up to the main altar, which was beautifully decorated with a crucified Jesus in the middle of the eye-catcher.

He looked around him with wide eyes and spoke.

that the church hall was empty of people. When he turned to go back, he saw a huge church organ adorned with beautiful façade pipes perched on a ledge directly above the entrance to the hall. Jacob opened the door to the armory and collided with a female priest. He stood motionless, his eyes fixed on the floor, and the unpleasant smell of lube and feces that he had felt this morning made itself felt again. Reluctantly and with flushed cheeks, he slowly looked up at the chief theologian Christina Grenholm, who looked at him in surprise with a warm smile.

"Oops! Did it go well, my little friend?" asked Christina.

"Sorry. In fact, it was not my intention," Jacob excused himself, believing that he was to blame for the collision.

Christina melted like a dollop of butter in a hot frying pan. The boy was adorable with his doll-like appearance. He was so cute that it was almost punishable and had a huge charisma.

"Oh, but please friend. You should not apologize for this."

"Nope. But... Is there a toilet I can borrow? I need one now," Jacob whispered as he marked by pulling on the back of his pants.

"Of course, come and I'll show you where the toilet is."

Christina reached out to Jacob, who grabbed it, and they walked out of the church. When they arrived at the gate at Storgatan, Hedvig Eleonora's congregation was opposite.

Inside the toilet, Jacob sat and tried to squeeze out the remaining liquid and it was with painful attempts. When he was finally about to dry himself, he felt a stinging pain around the anus and there was blood on the paper. Tears flowed, not only for the pain he felt but also for the despair and violation he was experiencing at the same time. When he finished, he folded together a stack of soft toilet paper and put it in his underpants as a soft cover for his butt. Then he dressed and washed his hands repeatedly before going out.

Before leaving the congregation, he went to the office where Christina was sitting with her planning calendar. Jacob politely thanked him for borrowing the toilet and Christina began to smile with twinkling eyes.

"May God be with you, my young man," Christina said with a sustained smile.

Jacob walked over and gave her a hug.

"Where are you going now?" she asked as Jacob let go of her.

"I'm going to go to church and pray a little. There has been some atmospheric disturbance on the line," replied Jacob, who turned and left.

Christina laughed so that tears ran down her cheeks and she felt the draught of air from the hall as the front door opened and then closed. She got up and looked out the window, where Jacob entered through the gates and continued the gravel path up to Hedvig Eleonora church.

* * *

It was almost one o'clock in the afternoon when Jacob stopped with his bike outside the main entrance to Stockholm Central Station. He locked the bike while looking for police officers. Then he walked towards the entrance closed together with other people to blend in and become invisible. Jacob was hungry and was aware that there were several cafes and restaurants inside the central station where you could eat your fill. He had done this with his mother several times.

In the entrance hall, Jacob came up to the famous ring and kept a watchful eye around him. On the opposite side, he saw a café.

He put his hand in his trouser pocket to pick up the five-hundred-crown note... as... did not exist! In despair, he began to search through all his pockets and all he found was ten crowns and the home keys. Jacob became angry when he realized that he had been duped.

He must have taken the money while I slept, Jacob thought, clenching his fists in pure frustration. For the first time in his Christian life, he felt a desire for revenge. It was the first time he wanted to beat Lars to pieces. It was an emotional explosion of hatred flowing out of his mind.

Jacob was so hungry that his stomach protested with a palpable stomachache. He looked with tempted eyes at the people sitting and having coffee. Either they ate buns, pastries, or good sandwiches. Jacob noticed a middle-aged man, dressed in a long coat, standing at the counter buying coffee and a large sandwich consisting of liver pâté on rye cake. He sat down at a table and ushered in with a sip of coffee while flipping through a magazine. He took the sandwich and was about to take a bite when he hurriedly stood up and stared in horror at the clock outside in the waiting hall. He put the sandwich back on the plate, grabbed his bag and hurried off with quick steps towards one of the platforms.

Like a hungry bird of prey, Jacob was in battle mode. There was now basically only one obstacle left, finding the courage to walk up and snatch that sandwich without anyone noticing. How it would practically work with all the people in the vicinity remained to be seen.

Jacob looked around and could see that all the people in his eyes seemed to be busy with other things. The sandwich was available on the table just inside the black ropes that separated the café. He looked towards the cafeteria again as a younger, dark-haired girl began to pick and dry off the tables one by one. Now it was urgent. Jacob walked towards the cafeteria and focused his gaze on the sandwich lying there on the table. He only had to reach out his left hand and grab the sandwich as he passed by quietly. Suddenly it would be gone, and no one would notice. He had a few steps left and quickly looked at the girl standing a few feet away with her back to him.

When Jacob passed the table, he grabbed the sandwich, but the plastic wrap was stuck on the saucer which happened to slide along and broke on the floor. With hurried steps, Jacob closed his eyes and waited for someone to start calling him. But no shout was heard. He walked around the waiting room for a while and then started walking back towards the entrance with the sandwich hidden inside his jacket.

The National Criminal Investigation Unit's mission consisted of four parts: combating serious organized crime, international cooperation, crisis preparedness and unique events, and combating mass and serial crime.

The main task was to combat serious organized crime at national and international level and to impair the criminal organizations' ability to run in Sweden. Since this assignment required cooperation with police authorities in other countries, the Swedish police's international cooperation was within the remit of the National Criminal Police. This included the Swedish police's peacekeeping activities, where Swedish police officers take part in peacekeeping missions abroad.

The National Criminal Police's assignment also included coordinating the police's efforts if events of national concern. In crisis situations, the National Criminal Investigation Police, as the central operational police, was able to quickly change its operations and coordinate the police's efforts at a national level.

Chapter 20

24 SEPTEMBER 2014

During the morning, Detective Reneé had dropped off his nine-year-old adopted daughter Haphy at Bagarmossen's school. The girl was originally from Uganda, which was one of the reasons Reneé had started driving her to school and it then became a routine measure after the divorce three years ago. Her long professional career in the police force was no guarantee of her daughter's safety, she was aware of that. Haphy could sometimes face harassment and racist abuse from other school students, not only because of the color of her skin, but also because her forty-two-year-old mother was a police officer and a woman with skin on her nose.

Reneé turned onto the small stretch of road, which was a final extension of Drottningholmsvägen from Fridhemsplan, and stopped at the barrier guard. She showed her worn police ID through the side window and the boom went up. Reneé drove into the large police garage that was well protected under Kronobergsparken.

Inside his office, Reneé hung off his leather jacket on the office chair by the desk. Then went out and was soon back with a white coffee mug with the police's weapon symbol. She ran her palm under the mug to wipe away spilled coffee before setting it on the desk.

Reneé had just had time to sit down and take a sip when George Lindmark came in with a coffee mug and sat down on a chair in front of the desk. He took a sip of his coffee and smacked contentedly.

“Good morning, dear colleague!” he said after swallowing the coffee, adding: “Mmm, that’s good. There was a significant difference in this type of coffee.”

“Good morning. It went well this morning,” I heard.

“Oh! The actual raid and arrest went well but it was a bit too uneventful for my taste. Okay, except for a little guy who just managed to escape by bike,” he relentingly told me in a disappointed tone.

“Do you have any indication of the boy?” asked Reneé, taking another sip of his coffee.

“Description? He looked well like all the other kids. Normal physique and light blond hair. Guess between nine and eleven years old. He climbed down the chute from the second floor, and I got the impression he was more terrified than scared as he ran away from the back.”

“We need to find him, I guess the boy is probably a victim who is also an important witness in the investigation.

Did you bring any forensic evidence?” George smiled contentedly.

“We have two laptops, as well as a desktop computer that is technically checking through right now. In addition, we found a video camera and a lot of memory cards. Let us hope that we can restore what has been cut. Like I said, we’re working on it.”

“Good. Have you had time to start questioning this LarsÅke Rosén?’ asked Reneé as she turned on her computer.

"I had a brief interrogation this morning. He has admitted to having ugly films and many photos stored, but the boy who disappeared did not want to know.

He had been alone all night," George replied, shaking his head slightly before drinking his coffee.

"But the camcorder?"

"It was used yesterday evening. However, I haven't seen the content yet, Lelle is looking at the material."

"Good, then he'll review it. Then we will have a little chat with Mr. Rosén. Is he sitting here at Kronoberg?"

"Second chamber with restrictions from the prosecutor," George said with a smile.

Reneé got up from his desk when there was a knock on the door at the same time.

"Come in," Reneé shouted, as the door opened, and a blonde colleague of the same age named Lelle came in with a laptop under her arm.

"Good morning. You, George, look at this," he said, placing the computer on some stacks of paper on his desk and starting a movie clip. "Is this the guy you saw running away this morning?"

George and Reneé watched the video that showed how a fair-haired boy performed oral sex on a man. The boy's innocent blue eyes with enlarged pupils strongly showed that what was going on was not voluntary. During the act, the man pushed his penis into the boy's throat causing him to retch. They did not see the face of the perpetrator and therefore could not find him. Reneé shook her head, then walked around the desk to get her jacket.

"That's enough, Lelle. Try to see if you can find the boy in our records," she said as she pointed to George who was still sitting and closed his eyes, to get up. It was still just as damning and grotesque to review these photos and videos despite all the years of service in the police force.

"We go to the detention center and begin an interrogation of this man. We are going to take some photos that we can then compare with the movie clips. Now, we have no face that can find the perpetrator, only the blonde boy. We will see if we can get recognition, with a bit of luck. Were there more clips?" asked Reneé.

"I've produced eight so far. Have not looked at all of them yet, but it is a case of complete rapes of this boy and other victims. Several rapes have taken place in the apartment, so we have at least one crime scene that has been clarified," Lelle noted.

George got up and walked with quick steps past Reneé and Lelle, stopped and opened the door.

"Good, then we have a work plan to follow. Come, and we will have a chat with that cuckoo," said George before disappearing out.

* * *

In an interrogation room inside the detention ward, George and Reneé sat on separate chairs at the table. On the table was a tape recorder with an external mic. The door opened and a correctional officer let Lars-Åke in. George got up and stepped aside a little. "You can sit there," he said, pointing to a chair. LarsÅke sat down with a regretful look and moistened forehead.

"Hi, my name is Reneé Grahn and I'm a detective inspector at the National Criminal Investigation Department," Reneé said, avoiding taking the hand that Lars-Åke had intuitively held out.

George pressed the record button on the tape recorder and said at the same time: "We have already been introduced to each other since this morning. It's on now."

"Then we start with the interrogation of Lars-Åke Rosén. The presents are Reneé Grahn and George Lindmark. I would first like to inform you why you have been arrested and what you are suspected of," said Reneé, moving the microphone forward slightly towards Lars-Åke.

Lars-Åke nodded and flickered his eyes to the edge of the table.

"Yes," he replied.

"Good, you are suspected of child pornography offences, rape, or aggravated sexual exploitation of a minor. I would add the distribution of child pornography," Reneé said.

Lars-Åke nodded with blinking eyes.

"We've looked at some footage that we found in your camcorder. Do you know the content of these videos?" asked Reneé.

"Maybe."

"Maybe! fun trek. Was it you film or was it someone else?" asked George.

"Maybe I was the one holding the camera."

"Maybe the word is not something we use here in the department," George said irritably as he leaned against the wall and folded his arms.

"No one else participated in this rape?" asked Reneé, locking his gaze.

Lars-Åke shook his head.

"Yes or no. We cannot tape your shakes with your head," Reneé enlightened.

"I was alone," Lars-Åke replied.

* * *

Inside her office, Lelle sat at the computer with two monitors standing on the table. On one screen was a photo of the fair-haired boy, which had been taken from one of the videos. On the second screen scrolled photos of missing wanted children and young people that Lelle methodically compared to. A picture of a fair-haired little guy with blue eyes and a charming smile appeared on the screen.

"Bingo! There we have him. Jacob Sjögren-Lester."

Lelle stood up and pressed the print button on her keyboard at the same time. He took the papers and left the office.

* * *

"At the first initial interrogation, you said you were alone for the whole past night, but that's not quite true, is it?" asked Reneé.

Lars-Åke did not answer but kept his eyes on the table.

"Personally, I think you are answering my colleague's question. I saw the kid at your house, and was this close to taking him," said George as he placed his elbow tightly on the table and measured between his thumb and forefinger in front of his face. "Got it?"

"Yes, yes... I had company," Lars-Åke replied reluctantly. "Did that party consist of an underage boy?" asked Reneé as she pushed George's arm away from the table.

"I met him at Sergel Square. I wanted to help him."

"Were you there ragging?" asked George and sat down next to Reneé.

"No, I was at the cultural centre and saw a theatre performance. I met him on my way home."

There was a knock on the door. George gave Reneé a questioning look and asked with a gesture to the door if he should open it. It knocked again. Reneé turned off the tape recorder and with a deep sigh she gave George an annoyed look that smiled a little teasingly.

"Come in!" shouted Reneé, giving George a determined look again. "You'll have to wait a minute," Reneé added to Lars-Åke

The door opened and Lelle poked her head through the doorway.

"Sorry to bother. Can we exchange a few words?" he asked, looking at Reneé.

Reneé saw in Lelle's intense gaze that he had found something important to the investigation and went out with him. The door closed after them.

Chapter 21

24 SEPTEMBER 2014

At 13.00 Linda's phone rang on the kitchen table at home on Lillvägen in Upplands Väsby. There were five signals, then the signals stopped. Ten minutes later, it rang again from an unknown number. Linda came running around dressed in an open dressing gown and a towel wrapped around her hair. She had just showered and did not have time to dry herself until she heard the cell phone ring.

She answered and heard a female voice introducing herself as Detective Inspector Reneé Grahn from the National Criminal Investigation Department. Linda, fearing the worst at first, sat down on a kitchen chair just in case. Would this conversation be the final message, that Jacob had been found...?

Reneé began the conversation by saying that they had made visual contact with Jacob at an address in Östermalm this morning. Linda puffed out and at the same time received tears of joy. She and Chris had been heard; Jacob was alive. My beloved boy!

Linda opened her eyes with her mouth half open when she realized that Jacob was in central Stockholm and that he had run from the police. Linda could not answer the question of why he stayed away from the police because she did not understand why Jacob should stay away at all. What happened?

She asked about the address where Jacob had last been seen, but Reneé referred to the confidentiality of the pre-trial investigation on an ongoing criminal investigation. Linda wanted to know more about it and why Jacob participated in a criminal investigation. Reneé could only go as far as to confirm that Jacob figured in the investigation, more than that she did not want to tell but suggested that Linda come to her for a conversation and name some photos. They agreed to meet today at Reneé's office at 3:00 p.m.

At 1:20 p.m., Chris received a phone call from Linda. It was with a certain tension in her voice that she told me that the police had seen Jacob in Stockholm. Linda could not tell in more detail but said that she was on her way to pick up Chris, then they would go on to the police station to meet Detective Reneé Grahn from Crimea.

After the conversation, he felt a sense of relief that Jacob was alive and not lying on any lake bottom in Lake Mälaren. But what would they meet a detective inspector from Crimea for? he wondered as he hurried back to his office.

When Linda drove into the staff parking lot at Karolinska Institute, Chris was waiting with his document portfolio. He threw his briefcase into the back seat before sitting down next to Linda and closing the car door. Chris was about to give her a kiss on the cheek but was suddenly pushed back into the backrest as she made a flying start. The white Mercedes swerved as it turned right onto Solnavägen in the direction of Kungsholmen when the clock showed 14:25.

* * *

Inside the office, Reneé sat with a new report in his hand. After skimming through it, she could see that it was newly arrived refugees, two young girls from Iraq who had disappeared from a refugee facility in Fagersjö. This was the seventh report of missing refugees on her desk.

She got the feeling that it could be some kind of organized disappearance. It was about children who had fled in mostly inhumane conditions across the Mediterranean and the whole of Europe to get to Sweden and safety, and then just disappeared completely without a trace. Was it some form of human trafficking or prostitution? Reneé wondered as she checked the time on her mobile phone. 14:50.

Chapter 22

25 SEPTEMBER 2014

This past night had been very exhausting for Jacob. He had spent it in a parking garage on Olof Palme's Street, freezing, crying, and sleeping alternately behind a parked car. In addition, a security guard had arrived, which meant that Jacob was wide awake and lay still. He saw how the security guard drove around with his car and then left. Jacob had then tried to find a new sleeping position on the hard and cold concrete floor while shivering and trying to go back to sleep.

At 17:30 Jacob came cycling on Klarabergsgatan at Åhléns department store. He had wandered around with his bike all day, trying to find the American embassy without success. Twice he had also visited the plate at Sergel Square with the hope of seeing Kringlan again, without success. Jacob had plucked up the courage to ask others who had stayed on the plate, including a prostitute who was leaning against a wall with a syringe stuck in one foot. No sensible answer ever came from her, only an indistinct murmur. The heroin had just taken over her consciousness.

Then he had come across an older man whose appearance and smell unabashedly spread around the synthetic Jacob keep a little distance from him. From a safe distance, Jacob had asked if he had seen the Kringlan. Man showed his toothless grin as he smiled and replied in Finnish dialect that Kringlan was dead and probably already cremated. There was a lot of dirty jacks on the plate, he said. Jacob got on his bike and rode away with a sense of inner turmoil creeping through his body. He was strongly reminded that Lars could be nearby and hurried away.

Jacob approached the second main entrance to Åhléns in the direction of Klara Norra kyrkogatan and saw a Romanian beggar sitting at the entrance with a coffee mug from Seven Eleven. He cycled slowly past and caught a glimpse of a banknote and small coins in the mug. Jacob was completely penniless; the last ten crowns went to buy a Rice fruit from an Ica store.

Jacob cycled up to the intersection at Klara Norra kyrkogatan. There he saw a coffee mug from McDonald's that stood on an electrical cabinet and rolled there. He poured out the contents of the mug and wiped it with a white napkin he found below the electrical cabinet.

The Romanian Roma, whose name was Gabor and looked to be about fifty plus, sat on a blanket at Åhlén's entrance. He had been sitting there since opening time trying to raise a few bucks throughout the day. In his coffee mug there was, last time he counted, about sixty crowns.

Alms that people were kind enough to give as they passed in and out of the entrance. A few times during the day he was hit by some careless mother with a stroller and a stressful existence. Gabor was careful to give thanks in Swedish and at the same time bless those who had time to stay to contribute to today's livelihood.

Something Gabor had not counted on this late afternoon was the little blonde guy with a blue bike who had stopped and put the bike against the façade wall. After that, the boy went and sat down at the entrance opposite him and simply put a coffee mug from McDonald's in front of him.

Now Åhlén's entrance became a source of income for two actors. Gabor did not appreciate the competition but kept quiet so as not to attract unnecessary attention.

Jacob tried to avoid Gabor's questioning gaze, focusing instead on the people passing by the entrance. It soon turned out that it was a winning concept, and after an hour Jacob had raised seventy kronor. A demanding situation for Gabor, who at the same time had not received a single penny since the boy had arrived. An elderly man stopped by Gabor and thought about putting a twenty-crown note in his mug, but when he suddenly saw Jacob on the other side, he changed his mind and instead put it with a smile in his mug.

The reaction was not long in coming, and Jacob saw Gabor have pitch black eyes. He tore off the blanket wrapped around his skinny body, flew up and shouted angrily in Romanian. Jacob was quickly on his feet and ran with his coffee mug up to his bike and pedaled off in the direction of Stockholm Central Station.

Gabor wisely chose not to run behind but returned to his seat and wrapped himself in his worn blanket. The competition was thus gone and now there was a small hope left to raise a few more crowns before Åhléns boomed again for the day.

Jacob stopped at the stairs that led down to Vasagatan and got off his bike. He counted the money and then put it in his jacket pocket.

He placed the mug from McDonalds down on the sidewalk next to the wall of the house, then he began to lead the bike down the stairs to Vasagatan. He had previously seen that there was a McDonald's restaurant on the left side when coming down the stairs.

When Jacob came down to the ground floor, a police car suddenly stopped next to the sidewalk. Jacob was terrified and thought for a moment that it was his last time in freedom. He looked around, there were no escape routes to take without being seen, his only chance of not being discovered was to stand and investigate the window of the Dressman store next to him. At the same moment, a crowd of people came down the stairs right behind him, giving him brief shelter as they passed.

He saw how the officers got out of the police car and hurried towards the entrance of the Dressman shop, something Jacob could see across the store from where he stood. There, at a pole stood the same toothless man that Jacob had previously met on Sergel Square. Now he stood and urinated against the post. The man, whose name was Kauno, suddenly had a different expression on his face at the sight of the officers approaching. During a chant of profanity and sharp protests in Finnish, he was headed towards the police car. Kauno was heavily intoxicated, but at least was able to have his temperamental temper when they arrived at the police car. At the urging of the officers, he reluctantly sat in the back seat with one of the officers.

Kauno looked out of the side window and saw the boy standing at the shop window, staring at him with wide eyes. Kauno recognized the boy, waved, and showed off his toothless smile. The boy hesitantly waved back.

Jacob started walking with his bike towards the McDonald's restaurant while looking a little anxiously at the police car that was blinking to drive away.

Kauno grabbed the front backrest of the passenger seat to lift his butt and straighten the sitting position. Then he saw a photo who was lying on the passenger seat and at once recognized the person in the picture. It was the boy with the bike!

"Wait, wait a minute!" shouted Kauno eagerly, who turned around and pointed frantically to the rear window.

"You! Now you must calm down a bit," urged the police officer who was sitting next to him, tired of Kauno and his drunken talk.

"Okay, great. Do not blame me, I am going to Berkeley," Kauno muttered dejectedly, insisting on pointing to the photo. "That boy is riding his bike over there, I saw him. I'm not that fucking drunk."

The police officers smiled and thanked him for the information, first they would transport him to a drunken cell where he could sober up in peace. With a bit of luck, he would get himself some hot food. Kauno, who just wanted to be helpful, sighed and looked out of the side window in disappointment as the police car turned left at the intersection of Vasagatan and Kungsgatan.

* * *

During the visit to McDonalds, Jacob ate his fill of a hearty hamburger menu, then went to the toilet where he washed himself. He really needed a good shower and room.

vain to lubricate themselves with. It still ached on some intimate parts of the body, despite folded toilet paper that lay in the underpants as protection against the butt.

However, it felt a little better after washing off the worst and getting some food. He still felt the salty taste after Lars and missed the fresh taste of toothpaste. The grotesque images were imprinted in his memory and etched themselves more into his bizarre reality. Ominous thoughts of revenge appeared, and he found himself thinking as Jimmy did before... Jacob sat down on the black toilet lid and began to cry.

"Mom! Dad!"

* * *

It was a little past nine o'clock in the evening when a measured Jacob cycled towards Norra Bantorget parallel to Vasagatan. Before that, he had wandered around Kungsholmen and accidentally passed the large police station, which led to him hurriedly cycling away.

As he rode his bike, he thought, "If the police station was over there, then the U.S. Embassy should probably be here nearby somewhere... too."

After a while, he had stopped and asked a middle-aged lady if there was an embassy nearby. The lady replied that there was an embassy nearby. It was found on Gjörwellsgatan in Marieberg beyond Rålambshovsparken, but she was unsure if it was the American embassy that was found there.

After two hours, Jacob found the Russian embassy.

Disappointed, he gave up his search and looked towards the tall newspaper building on the other side of Gjörwellsgatan. He decided to cycle back to Vasastan road Kungsholmen.

When Jacob arrived at Norra Bantorget, he cycled straight across the square and on onto Västmannagatan in the direction of Odenplan. Only twenty kronor remained of what he had received at Åhléns and he needed more money. Jacob began searching for a coffee mug in the trash cans he met along the way, but the mugs he found were either crushed or pigged down by cigarette ash and cigarette butts.

A dark blue Toyota Prius taxi from Taxikurir passed Jacob. The driver threw a coffee mug right out into the street so that the white lid fell off. Jacob stopped on the sidewalk and hurried to grab the coffee mug from the street while the blue taxi flashed left and disappeared into a side street.

Jacob noted that the mug was empty. He got on his bike and at the next intersection he turned left onto Rådmansgatan.

* * *

Ali stopped the taxi at Dalagatan 7 at the sex club Harem. In the back seat sat the twenty-five-year-old and incredibly attractive Yasmin, who was originally from Syria. Officially, she worked as a dancer if the question came up. It sounded more professional and professional in front of the public than openly declaring that you contribute your social livelihood by stripping and Pole-dancing.

"Call me tomorrow when you finish, I have a day shift and can pick you up," Ali said in Arabic, turning to Yasmin.

"I'll call an hour before I finish," she replied.

She opened the car door and was about to get out of the car when she heard Ali say, "Insha' Toh," while raising his right arm with a clenched fist.

Yasmin gave him an annoyed look. "Lay off!"

Ali studied her sexy body that moved sensually as she walked with determined steps to the gate where she disappeared in without turning around. It was a visual revelation that Ali was never measured on. She was one of the few women he could sacrifice his life for. Because he had a soft spot for sweets like Yasmin, he had an advantage as a taxi driver, namely free entry to the club. On several occasions he had sat as an audience during her performances, where men of varying ages had drooled and longed for her. These were men that Ali hated deep down, most of them were his livelihood, just like Yasmin's. They were allowed to exist for a while longer, even though the men were repugnant both to him and his Muslim world.

Ali droves slowly off in the direction of Norra bantorget. He looked in the rearview mirror and with a surprised look he saw a little boy coming riding his bike. The boy disappeared from time to time into the shadows of darkness where the glow of the streetlamps did not reach. Ali looked at the clock in the car that had just turned over to 22:00.

* * *

Jacob was extremely tired after the day's events and all the cycling. It was dark and quite desolate on most of the streets.

the towers on which he had cycled. All shops were also closed, which made Jacob's chances of begging for more money difficult. He had cycled past Sabbatsberg Hospital on Dalagatan when a large pink limousine slowly drove by. The limousine stopped at Dalagatan 7 where a group of dressed-up people got out and disappeared through a gate. Then came two taxis that stopped just behind. Several men got out and happily entered through the same gate.

He saw his chance. He would get a penny if he sat outside that gate.

He rode there and put the bike against the wall of the house, where he found a newspaper tucked between a downpipe and the wall of the house. He could use it as a seat pad while sitting outside that gate where most happy people seemed to enter.

Jacob unfolded the newspaper on the asphalt, sat down and placed the coffee mug in front of him. After ten minutes, another taxi arrived and stopped at the sidewalk. An older man and a younger woman got out of the car. They walked towards the gate but stopped at Jacob who showed off his charming smile.

"Damn! They are just everywhere," the man exclaimed, visibly annoyed.

"Give the poor boy some money," the woman urged charmingly with her foreign accent.

Reluctantly, the man tore open his wallet and was about to dig out some small coins from the coin compartment when the woman suddenly reached out and took a hundred-crowns note from the man's wallet, which she then handed to the boy. When Jacob was about to receive the banknote, the man tried to take it back, but was prevented by the woman.

"Nope! Not so. Now we'll give it to him, and I'll personally give you a little extra tonight, honey."

"But the money was meant for something completely different," the man protested.

"Well yes, don't think the girls in there would mind you giving a penny to this poor boy. You have hundreds of crown that you can put inside their panties. You have changed your mind after some thought?"

The man looked at the woman in surprise, and then at Jacob in annoyance. With a resigned shrug, he gave up. The woman smiled and handed Jacob the hundred-crowns note, while the man grumbled and disappeared through the gate with the woman.

It was a happy Jacob sitting with a whole hundred-crowns bill in his hand, but the feeling did not last. Out of the gate came a tall Yugoslav fellow named Ratko, dressed in a dark suit and burgundy sweater with a high neck.

He stood in front of Jacob and did not look the least bit happy. Then a taxi stopped, and three happy foreign men got out of the taxi and walked up to Ratko. They greeted each other in Serbian in an elated atmosphere. He escorted the men to the gate and then politely held the door open for them as they entered. Ratko was soon back and once again stood in front of Jacob, looking even more annoyed than last time.

"What are you doing here?" he hissed in a stern tone.

"Nothing," Jacob replied quickly.

"We don't want rabble-rousers here begging for money. You scare our guests."

"Do I?" replied Jacob in surprise, adding: You should look at yourself in the mirror first, but after reflection he decided not to.

One should not tease the bear standing in front of you and looking hungry," he quickly noted.

Ratko was a person of action, if you could not talk your mind into the young bastard, you had to scare it out instead. Ratko grabbed him and lifted him up with his bear labs to hands. He held him high in the air like a little rag doll.

On the Harem dance stage, Yasmin had let go of a bald head that belonged to an older man named George Skog. She had rubbed her genitals against him until the thumping music died out and George looked at her with lyrical eyes, to say the least, while he adjusted the glasses that had happened to end up a little on the sniffle during the show. He had just had his entire snout pressed against Yasmin's shaved vagina that smelled of strawberry. It may have cost five hundred crowns, but it was worth every penny.

Yasmin got up to leave, but then he grabbed her hand and offered more money in exchange for a more intimate existence. Yasmin smiled as she pointed out that there was a limit and instead suggested that he stay until he came home to his wife in Nacka. She picked up her clothes from the stage floor and then disappeared behind the stage curtain.

Inside the dressing room, she put on a velvet red dressing gown and sat down in front of the mirror to wipe her vagina with fragrant wipes. She had a break and was going to use the time to have a cup of coffee and smoke a cigarette. She put on a panty but let her bra hang on the hook. With pink slippers on her feet, she left her dressing room and went to the bar to get a cup of coffee.

With a cigarette in your mouth and a mug of black coffee in her hand, Yasmin walked out of the gate. Suddenly, she stopped when she saw Ratko holding onto a terrified little one fair-haired boy. Ratko was very rough in the mouth when he threatened the boy. It was quite clear that the boy had urinated on himself and accidentally Ratko had gotten a few drops of urine on his face while holding the boy up in the air. Yasmin became upset and hurried up to Ratko, who dropped the boy onto the asphalt and then chased him away.

"What the hell are you doing with the boy?" yelled Yasmin as she simultaneously grabbed his arm and pulled him to her to protect him.

"He's sitting here begging, Pitscha matreno, he on me!" hissed Ratko, humiliated by some baby urine that had dripped onto his rough-hewn face.

"Are you stupid for real! Of course, he peed on himself, he's terrified of you."

She took Jacob's arm and walked away with him.

"Idiot!" Was the last Ratko heard from Yasmin when she walked through the gate with the boy.

"You can't take him in!" protested Ratko, cheeks red, as the door slammed shut. A middle finger appeared for a moment inside the window.

Inside the dressing room, Jacob had to undress, and Yasmin pushed the clothes into a plastic bag from Ikea. She took out a bath towel, wrapped it around Jacob, and put him on a small, burgundy plush couch in the far corner of the lodge. Jacob lay down and placed his head against a colorfully embroidered decorative pillow. Yasmin smiled, then took the Ikeakassen and left.

Jacob fell asleep at once, despite the thumping background music playing from the bar and stage.

Yasmin was soon back with a glass of milk and a cheese sandwich. She stopped and looked at the boy who had fallen asleep on her couch. She gently set the glass down and the plate with the cheese sandwich on the table, then she went and sat down in the mirror to get ready for the next performance.

* * *

At 6:30 a.m. the next morning, Yasmin had changed into her own clothes and put on her makeup. She counted the money and had raised 1500 kronor. A girl looked through the doorway, and Yasmin handed her the money. The girl spotted Jacob sleeping on the couch and wanted to walk up to him but was stopped by Yasmin.

"No, let him sleep. You are silent about him being here with me," Yasmin whispered.

The girl nodded and made a zipper gesture past her mouth before smiling and disappearing.

Yasmin sneaked up to Jacob and gently woke him up. Jacob, who was not awake, stretched out both arms. He hugged her and mumbled to Mom, not being aware of it himself. He was exhausted.

She smiled as she got him up and tried to get him to sit up on the couch and not go back to sleep, then she dressed him in his freshly washed clothes. There was a knock before the door opened and Ali stepped in. He was surprised when he saw a little blonde guy sitting on the couch rubbing his eyes. Ali gave Yasmin a questioning look.

The worst morning rush hour wound its way towards Stockholm, so the journey towards Huddinge went painlessly. Yasmin sat in the back seat with Jacob who was lying with his head on her thigh. From the trunk, Jacob's bike stuck out, something that Ali was not exactly too fond of. Yasmin was assertive on that point; the bike was going along. It was neither the boy's nor her fault that Ali did not have a suitable car to transport bicycles in, she stated firmly.

During the journey home, there was an inevitable discussion about why she should take the boy home. Yasmin made it clear to him that you do not abandon a child on the street. There is a reason this boy was left alone and abandoned, and she would certainly find out.

Chapter 23
26 SEPTEMBER 2014

The morning was heavy and outside the kitchen window there was a foggy atmosphere. It was 7:30 a.m. when Linda was sitting in her nightgown drinking coffee at the kitchen table. She studied the almanac hanging on the wall and could see that they were on the fourth day of the search for Jacob. Neither she nor Chris had gotten a good night's sleep during those days. It felt more as if they had spent the nights in a kind of deep stupor, while the brain desperately tried to find a solution and answers to the growing number of unanswered questions. The atmosphere between them was both strained and tense, especially after meeting Detective Reneé two days ago.

Initially, there was hope, a small bright spot in their despair, when they stepped into Reneé's office in the police station. The police had seen Jacob flee on the bike, so far they were there. Why he fled from the police, however, they did not know. But... when Reneé spoke in more detail about the incident and that their son participated in a larger pedophile ring, it came as a fist bump. Information became too difficult to absorb, or even understand, the extent of. It was a world of evil that they had only followed in the media, and with disgust. That they would experience something so disgusting did not exist in their Christian world and the news came as a complete shock. At the same time, the picture became clearer as to why Jacob had not been in touch. He could not because he was a prisoner of a terribly obnoxious man, someone who outwardly had a highly regarded education as a doctor and a high social status. It was a thought and an image that could neither be imagined nor understood.

Chris came into the kitchen dressed in outerwear and with his briefcase in his hand and stood in front of Linda. He firmly set the bag down on the floor and spread his arms in front of his wife. A little embarrassed, she stood up and gave him a morning hug. He had to go to work because he stayed at home all day yesterday and was thus behind with the follow-up of his research program. In addition, he had a telephone meeting with Dr. Chan from the WHO.

A car honked outside, and Chris let go of Linda to walk over to the window. There was a taxi there. Linda would continue to be home if something new were to appear if Jacob were to appear. Chris gave her a kiss on the mouth and walked away. Soon after, she heard the front door close. She sat down at the kitchen table and grabbed her coffee mug. She looked at the mug and saw an image of Jesus blessing the people. Her invincible faith slowly began to weaken, and she questioned why God allowed this vile abuse to happen to her beloved son. Where was the mercy? Why subject children to these horrific abuses and violations? Why is Jacob not coming home? Linda dropped the mug and let it fall onto the kitchen table without trying to try to save her mug. The image of Jesus blessing the people broke into a thousand pieces.

* * *

Reneé was sitting in his office and had just hung up the telephone. She had had a conversation with Chris about going public with Jacob's disappearance to the daily press. After some reflection, he had asked to return, he first wanted to consult his wife about it.

Chris called back after ten minutes and gave his consent. Reneé himself thought that in terms of time, it would give the case more attention. The day before, the press management had released a release about the pedophile ring, and it was then possible to link Jacob's disappearance with that incident.

Reneé called the press department at the police station. An hour later, the major newspapers had received a press release about Jacob's disappearance with attached photo.

Chapter 24

26 SEPTEMBER 2014

Ummatī, qad lāḥa fajrun
"My land, a dawn is revealed."

It was 1.10 p.m. when Ali was standing with some colleagues talking inside the arrivals hall at Arlanda Airport. Some of them were Ali's compatriots who showed happy faces. Conversations outwardly were friendly with humorous touches as Ali's squeaky voice triggered volleys of laughter that were heard all over the arrival's hall.

At baggage claim stood passengers who had landed on a plane from Istanbul. One of them was a 45-year-old man who was in the background with an empty luggage trolley. Physically, he looked fit and nicely dressed. He had dark, short-cropped hair, brown eyes, and a mustache worthy of the name. The man's name was Mustafa Baykal and he was a Turkish citizen of Arab origin.

When Mustafa saw his suitcase coming riding on the baggage belt, he pushed forward and with a firm grip grabbed it and placed it on the luggage trolley. He walked off with the other passengers towards customs control. Mustafa showed no tendencies towards nervousness, quite the opposite. He had nothing in his bag that was not allowed to bring in through customs and his papers were perfectly in order. Should the question come up if a spot check,

Then was his reason for the visit to Sweden to visit relatives and friends for a week, something he had coverage for.

Ali stood with his colleagues and waited for his pre-ordered customers. When passengers came out to the arrival hall, all the taxi drivers held up a white sign with the customer's name or company. Ali's sign read M. Baykal.

Ali left the colleagues and walked closer to the exit, where he met Mustafa Baykal with his luggage cart. He greeted him politely and offered to take the luggage cart.

Together they moved on to the exit.

Arriving at the taxi, Ali loaded the suitcase into the trunk and then opened the passenger door for Mustafa, who thanked him and got in the car. Ali got behind the wheel and gave him a welcoming smile.

"INSHA'ALLAH!" said Ali with pride in his voice.

"Tohu Akbar," Mustafa replied firmly with a slightly delayed smile.

Ali started the car and drove off in the direction of Stockholm. During the journey, Mustafa wanted to make sure that everything was in order with the recruitment. The entire operation must be done painlessly and without any unnecessary delays.

"I'm going to pick up the last ones tonight," Ali replied.

"You know we have a timetable that can't be postponed."

“I know, I’ll do what I can to keep it. I had a minor problem with a female contact, but she has been punished and I expect an improvement.”

“If she creates problems in our organization, she must go,” Mustafa replied firmly, giving him a serious look.

“We can’t remove her; it would complicate the whole recruitment. I need her”Ali replied as he overtook some cars on the highway at the Rosersberg interchange. “Okay Ali, your problem, solve it.”

“The volunteers are they there?” asked Ali.

Mustafa nodded as he kept his gaze on the road.

“They undergo the education by the will of Toh.”

Ali looked at Mustafa with a respectful look, then a smile came.

After about twenty minutes by car, Mustafa could see that nothing had changed significantly since he last visited Sweden, which was two months ago.

“Where are we going?” he asked as Ali turned off at the Vårby exit.

“To Flemingsberg, we are offered food. Arabic my friend.”

Mustafa looked at Ali with a suspicious look as the blue Toyota turned onto The Forgotten Road in the direction of Huddinge.

Chapter 25

26 SEPTEMBER 2014

It was just after two o'clock in the afternoon when a lovely coffee scent spread in the kitchen. Yasmin took the last bite of the sandwich and washed it down with some apple-flavored Turkish tea. She straightened her dressing gown and was about to get up to clear the table when a hand patted her shoulder. It was her mother Fatma who thought she could sit while she cleared the table, and then set down a small gold-edged white coffee cup with Turkish coffee on the table with a small, wrinkled smile.

"Is the boy going to sleep long?" asked Fatma in Arabic as she went to the sink to set down the mug and cupboard.

"Mom. He is tired, let him ... Ouch!" said Yasmin with a subsequent brief curse in Arabic as she burned her tongue on the hot coffee.

"But my girl, I have to ask. Should I make him some breakfast?"

"Can you wait a minute, please," Yasmin begged to her inquisitive mother, stretching out her arms across the kitchen table as a prayerful mark.

The coffee had time to cool down a bit. Yasmin drank it and got up from the table when Fatma came and put away the coffee cup. With her brown eyes, she looked at her daughter and smiled lovingly.

Yasmin was her treasure, her only remaining child who had survived the war and fled to Sweden. Fatma straightened the shawl that covered her gray, white hair Then walked away with slow steps to the sink with the coffee cup. Yasmin looked at her mother with a little regretful look. She walked over and hugged her dear mother from behind.

"Look, my daughter," Fatma said, patting her arms that held her tenderly.

"I love you, Mom."

"I know. You must give your love to God. We have a lot to thank him for."

"I haven't forgotten about him. He has not forgotten me either," Yasmin replied as she felt a drop hit her hand.

"Are you crying?" asked Yasmin. Fatma nodded and tenderly clapped her daughter's hands.

* * *

Yasmin came out of the toilet and changed into grey sweatpants and a white T-shirt. She walked over to the bedroom door and opened it carefully. The door creaked, causing Yasmin to make a grimace and stop herself. Cautiously, she looked in, there Jacob lay sleeping. She crept over to her side of the double bed and crouched behind his back. Carefully, she put her hand on his shoulder and tried to wake him up. She nudged Jacob a little gently, no reaction. She made another attempt, Jacob whimpered and changed his sleeping position, the blanket sliding down from her shoulders. Yasmin opened her eyes when she saw bruises around her neck and the red whip stripes between her shoulder blades and lower back.

Jacob turned around and opened his morning-tired eyes. Yasmin stroked his blonde hair back and then caressed his red-flowered cheek with a small smile. He smiled and stretched out both arms and wanted a hug. On both upper arms, more blue-black bruises were visible. Instead of confronting him about his injuries, she gave him a warm hug. Jacob said ouch when she happened to touch his sore back. She let go a little and held her arms still so as not to get at the wounds and sore blemishes. With his head placed against her chest, Jacob held her tightly.

Yasmin tried to let go but he kept holding her tightly. He did not want to let go of the warm security he felt in her arms. Yasmin felt tears pierce the T-shirt between her breasts, then it broke. She let Jacob cry out in her arms as she slowly caressed his head. Saying something comforting had to wait. Jacob's hulking cry slowly subsided and turned into a rustling sound as he breathed. After a while, Jacob let go of her. Then she grabbed his chin and held up his head with her right hand. With her left hand, she wiped away the tears from his flaming red cheeks.

"Does it feel better?" she asked as she looked at him with tearful eyes.

He nodded gently and hugged her again.

"Are you hungry?"

Jacob nodded again, pressed his face even harder between her breasts, and curled up in her arms.

There was a knock on the door and Jacob saw an elderly woman looking in. Fatma saw Jacob curled up in Yasmin's arms on the bed. He seemed to be both sad and scared.

"Why is he sad? Why?" asked Fatma in Arabic.

Yasmin shrugged and at the same time made a slight grimace.

"Is he hungry?"

"Yes, can you arrange some?" asked Yasmin.

"Should I arrange some halloumi and foul?"

"No, just make some sandwiches and tea."

"But why not..."

"Mom!"

Fatma shrugged and was clearly disappointed as she left the room. From the outside, the mother could be heard complaining as she walked towards the kitchen. She stopped in the hall for a moment and straightened some shoes before moving on.

* * *

It was with a good appetite that Jacob ate his breakfast wearing one of Yasmin's t-shirts. She did not want to show the injuries Jacob had on his back to his mother. Did not want to remind them of the war and all the nightmarish events they once fled from.

Jacob had received two sandwiches with cheese and dried beef along with some Baba ganouj, in addition to a boiled egg that was then washed down with a few glasses of milk. Yasmin smiled when she saw the milk mustache on Jacob's upper lip. She pulled off a piece of paper towel and wiped his mouth then the tip of his nose. Then she held up his head with both hands and gave him a warm smile.

"Were you full?" asked Yasmin.

"Yes, it was delicious. Thank you very much."

"You're so cute," Yasmin exclaimed with a smile, gently pinching his right cheek.

Yasmin held out her arms and with a loving smile she asked, "Would you like a hug? I want one from you anyway."

Jacob stood up and threw himself into Yasmin's arms and gave her a warm hug. As she held him, she gave her mother a longing looks over his shoulder. Fatma felt tears in her throat as tears came to her eyes.

"Do you want to take a bath?" whispered Yasmin in Jacob's ear.

He let go of Yasmin, looked at her with an intense gaze, and then nodded with a smile. Jacob took her hand and wanted to go to the bathroom. This was a moment for which he had really longed. Yasmin got up, followed along.

The T-shirt ended up on top of the laundry basket as Jacob took off his underwear while the bathtub was filled with hot bath water. She sat staring with wide eyes at his bare back. The truth was there in front of her, half her back had red, horizontal marks and wounds. The buttocks had also suffered similar injuries as well as blue-black bruises that were also visible around the neck and thighs. Yasmin crouched down and held up his arms. She looked at his buttocks and saw that the boy was completely red inside the slit of his tail.

"Jacob."

He turned his head and gave Yasmin a pleading look as a drop of tear gently trickled down one of his cheeks.

"Do you trust me?" asked Yasmin with tearful eyes.

Jacob looked down at the floor and wiped away the drop of tears with his right hand. Then he looked up and met her loving gaze again.

"I want to trust you," Jacob said imploringly.

"Dear friend, I promise to be very careful. It can hurt a little."

Jacob nodded a little reluctantly and tense.

Yasmin gave him a kiss on the cheek and then gently parted his buttocks. Jacob grimaced for a moment. She saw that his anus was enlarged and that he was swollen. Yasmin began to understand that this was not a case of ordinary abuse, he had suffered more horrible acts than she had previously thought.

"Jacob, can you turn around."

He did as she said and at the same time looked down at the floor.

Yasmin grabbed his hands and held them gently. He did not want to be confronted with what had happened and tried to get out.

"Honey, look at me," Yasmin said with a slight smile.

Jacob slowly raised his gaze, but avoided eye contact with her and flicked his gaze.

"Shall we bathe together?" asked Yasmin.

She took off her clothes and left them in a heap on the floor and crouched down in front of him. With her index finger and thumb, she grabbed his chin and made him look at her. Jacob shook his head.

"There is no one here who will make you..."

Suddenly, Yasmin felt her feet getting wet and instinctively she looked towards the bathtub that was overflowing.

"Oh my gosh," she exclaimed as she stood up and hurriedly turned off the water taps.

Jacob began to smile and walked over to the tub. He felt the water and it was warm enough. Yasmin looked at him with a slight smile.

"Was it nice?"

Jacob nodded, stepped into the tub, and carefully sat down with a slight grimace.

"I was also going to go swimming; do you want company?"

Jacob stretched out his arms to Yasmin and she stepped into the tub. In a playful way, Yasmin tried to get Jacob to talk about what had happened to him. She took an empty shampoo bottle, put it in the water, and pushed it towards Jacob.

"A ship is coming loaded," Yasmin exclaimed with a smile.

Jacob looked with a bored look at the shampoo bottle sliding towards him, then a deep sigh came.

"I'm actually ten years old."

Yasmin was given things to consider. *What am I doing?*

"Sorry, friend. I just wanted to get you talking."

Jacob stood on all fours. He grabbed the shampoo bottle and crawled over to Yasmin and dropped it on her stomach. Then he turned around and sat between Yasmin's legs, leaning against her body as the bottle floated away with the help of the waves.

For an hour and a half, Yasmin sat with Jacob in the bath. It was time needed to make Jacob feel safe in telling him what had happened to him. Jacob had begun the story with how he met the man, Lars, at Sergeltorg and how he had then followed him home with the promise that he would sleep over and be invited to evening coffee. Yasmin naturally wondered why Jacob did not go home, but she never got an answer to that.

Jacob continued to tell how he would get five hundred crowns by undressing in front of a camera. There came the confirmation of what she had suspected and suspected from the beginning; Jacob had fallen into the clutches of a pedophile, a barbaric pig.

When Jacob began to tell in detail what he had to do, tears came. Yasmin hugged him while trying to hold back her own tears. There were tears of disgust, despair and hatred that were wanted out.

Jacob told me with such empathy that Yasmin could easily see bizarre images in front of her. How a rough male hand brusquely grabbed Jacob's blonde hair and inserted a penis into his mouth. How someone then pushed a penis into his ass while screaming for mercy. She closed her eyes tightly to remove the grotesque images while holding Jacob, who was crying in despair.

He ended his story by telling how he met Ratko who did not like children and how Yasmin came as a saving angel and protected him. Jacob turned and looked at her with tearful eyes. He hugged her and began to shake. She closed her eyes, held him, and shook her head dejectedly.

She gently wiped his back by dabbing with the bath towel. There were questions that she had not gotten answers to, something Jacob did not want to tell. He did not even want to say where he came from. Why? What was it that he did not dare to tell? Was there really anything worse that had happened beyond the horrific abuse he had been subjected to by this man? My God, what has happened?

Out in the hall, the doorbell rang twice in succession. Yasmin and Jacob heard Fatma walk past the bathroom door from the living room and at the same time shouted in Arabic to Yasmin that she was about to open.

"Okay!" replied Yasmin from inside the bathroom.

Chapter 26

26 SEPTEMBER 2014

During the afternoon, Croatian housewife Julia Novak had finished mangling the bed sheets and pillowcases. She had folded them neatly and neatly and put them in a pile up. Propped up on her forearm, she took the trot and walked to the hall. As she passed the front door, she heard male voices speaking Arabic from the stairwell. She opened one of the closets that was against the wall and started to pile in the bedding, then she heard the neighbor open the door. Julia closed the closet door and walked to the front door. She peered out through the peephole and saw two men standing in front of the elderly lady Fatma. Julia recognized the younger man; it was that taxi driver Ali with a front bite who was always hanging after Fatma's daughter Yasmin.

The older man who was in the company of Ali she had not seen before but he was Arab given the appearance. Behind Fatma, the daughter suddenly appeared along with a light blonde little boy. She had not seen the boy before, which gave her a bit of a headache. She stood at the entrance to the kitchen and looked questioningly at her half-naked Serbian old man, Rica, who was sitting in his underwear at the kitchen table studying this week's trotting coupon. Out of the corner of his eye, he saw Julia standing at the entrance and gave her a questioning look.

"What?" exclaimed Rica as he grabbed the coffee cup on the kitchen table.

"Come and have a look," Julia whispered, eagerly motioning for him to hurry up, then she disappeared back into the hall.

Rica put the trotting coupon on the table with a tiresome sigh, got up and walked to the hall. When he reached the front door, Julia grabbed his undershirt urging him to hurry to look out through the peephole as he heard voices outside in the stairwell.

"Damn woman! Do you have to be so fucking curious?" hissed Rica irritably.

"Look, do you recognize the boy and that Arab?" whispered Julia, pointing to the door.

Rica looked through the door binoculars. He said to himself that he had not seen any of them. Julia once again grabbed Rica's undershirt and then dragged him into the kitchen.

"Have you seen that boy before?" she asked.

"No, dear. Maybe it's a day child, Yasmin may have retrained as a nanny instead of showing her nipple."

Julia showed a particularly angry look when she decided to bring her husband down to earth.

"Show the snippet! Pisca Mattreno, you have been to that club and drooled. You've fucking driven Miss Dick there several times," she stated in a sharp tone.

"On behalf of the service, yes," he said, smiling contentedly. He loved to be a little provocative to his dear angel and wife.

“On behalf of the service! Pisca...” Julia exclaimed, instinctively raising her arm to give a flick to the top of Rica’s head.

Rica lowered her head and closed her eyes with a smile, a snappy blow hitting her head.

Rica laughed and said, “But Julia, I don’t understand why you get so upset. I’m a taxi driver, just like that Ali, or whatever his name is.”

“I get so upset when you say that about Yasmin. She is not going to do that. She is a good girl,” Julia protested loudly, then went to the stove to make yogo coffee.

Data from Säpo: In November 2014, 250 people had traveled to violent Islamist groups in Syria and Iraq, and in November 2015, there were data on 280 travelers. At the turn of the year 2015-2016, about three hundred people had travelled. More than 140 people have returned to Sweden.

Chapter 27

26 SEPTEMBER 2014

It was with skeptical eyes and a tight grip on Yasmin's hand that Jacob looked at the two men at the kitchen table. Ali recognized the taxi driver with a squeaky voice. The other muscular man, on the other hand, he had not seen before.

She noticed Jacob's uncertainty and stroked his head soothingly as Fatma pulled out both minced meat and onions from the fridge.

Yasmin crouched down in front of Jacob.

"Do you want to greet them? Ali do you recognize?" she asked with a smile.

Jacob regarded the two men with a certain suspicion. They smiled at him, and he grabbed her arm. The men's smile gave him a flashback to Lars' drooling smile. Yasmin stood up and stretched out her hand to Jacob.

"Come, I'll go with you," she said.

Jacob grabbed her hand and together they walked up to Ali who stretched out his hand to greet.

"Hey Jacob, you recognize me huh?" he said with a smile and in his squeaky voice.

Jacob nodded as he greeted.

"He's my mate, visit him too, he's kind," Ali said, pointing to the man.

Yasmin led Jacob to the other man who crouched over and stretched out his big hand to greet.

"What's the boy's name?" he asked.

"His name is Jacob."

Mustafa looked at the blonde boy who hesitantly took his hand and greeted quickly.

"Hi Jacob. My name is Mustafa and I cannot speak good Swedish," Mustafa presented in English.

Yasmin translated for Jacob but was interrupted. "I know English," Jacob enlightened.

With an American accent, Jacob told Mustafa:

"I understand English well. It's my second language besides Swedish."

Mustafa winced in surprise when he heard Jacob's brilliant English. Then he laughed and ruffled his hair with one hand.

"You are a surprising man," Mustafa said with a broad smile.

Jacob smiled as Yasmin stood by, trying to grasp the surprising situation.

"My beloved treasure, you know English great. Where did you learn that?" she asked in a spontaneous sense.

Mustafa was right, the boy really had unexpected qualities.

"School and my pap..." Jacob fell silent.

He glanced at her, then looked at Mustafa, who was still smiling. Yasmin crouched down in front of Jacob, stroked his hair gently, and gave him a warm smile.

"Friend, you don't need to have any secrets here. Tell me, has your father taught you English?" asked Yasmin.

Jacob nodded. "Yes, it's his native language."

"Okay, your dad is not Swedish. Where is he from?"

Ali translated the conversation between Yasmin and Jacob into Arabic for Mustafa.

"He's from Chicago," Jacob replied, looking at the floor.

Yasmin log.

"Is that your secret?"

He nodded and threw himself on top of Yasmin and hugged her with tears in his throat.

Ali winced and suddenly got a look that turned black as his smile subsided.

"The boy's father is a beast. An American boy from Chicago," Ali whispered to Mustafa in Arabic.

Mustafa smiled and nodded. He bent over and ruffled Jacob's hair.

"You're a nice boy. I understand, and I just want to say that you are among friends," Mustafa said in English.

* * *

Fatma had set the dining table for dinner with the fine China. After presenting two Loka bottles with lemon and pear flavors, Yasmin came with a platter of Syrian well-fried omelets seasoned with paprika, dried chili and onions. She smiled at Jacob and then went to get more food. Fatma brought a knotted breadbasket that had Liba bread and set it on the table. She returned with a pot of Dawoud basha. Fatma grabbed the ladle and stirred the saucepan, then nodded contentedly and left. Yasmin placed the saucepan on a coaster when Mustafa stood up and looked down curiously into the saucepan. He nodded, then smiled at Jacob who was sitting opposite with a curious look.

"This, Jacob, is delicious. My favorite dish," he said.

Jacob nodded and smiled as Yasmin sat down next to him. She stroked his cheek and gave him a kiss on the cheek. Fatma placed a pot of bulgur on the table and sat down next to Mustafa with some effort as the aching hips made themselves felt.

"These are fried meatballs with tomato sauce," Yasmin said, grabbing Jacob's plate while stirring the pan. She put a smaller part on the plate, then she put an omelet next to it and finally some bulgur along the edge of the plate. When the plate landed on the table, Jacob looked at the food and thought it looked inviting and took a bite.

"Is it delicious?" asked Mustafa in English as he took the napkin and wiped his mouth.

Jacob nodded and smiled, then took the next bite. When he swallowed, his throat burned and Jacob had a coughing attack. He hurried to drink water as tears streamed down his cheeks, and Yasmin gave her mother a determined look.

"Mom! I told you to be careful with the chili," Yasmin urged in Arabic as she took a piece of paper towel and began to wipe around Jacob's mouth.

Fatma did not like to be lectured by her daughter in front of the guests, especially when it comes to cooking. She glared irritably, and then replied in Arabic: "Bah! I only took half of all the spices for his sake."

Yasmin shrugged and at the same time held up her arms as a small protest. She turned to Jacob who had frequent cough. He looked at her with a smile and she gave him a kiss on the cheek.

Fatma looked at her daughter in disbelief.

"He's not the one who cooked the food," she said in Arabic, pointing to her cheek at the same time.

The laughter was not long in coming when Yasmin got up and walked around the table to give her a kiss on the cheek. Then she grabbed her mother's cheek and said in Arabic; "You are as grumpy and stubborn as an old mule."

The laughter around the table was further energized as Yasmin sat down in her seat. Then she translated the comment to Jacob, who then accidentally choked on the food.

After dinner, Fatma and Yasmin helped clear the table. Jacob was very full and became increasingly curious about Mustafa, as he saw similarities between Mustafa and Uncle Owen. The posture and manner of expressing oneself in fluent English were almost identical. It gave him a little sense of security. He could open and tell him what had happened, or would it result in the same mistake as that Lars? Yasmin was on his side as a loving mother, but he knew that.

Fatma placed small decorative coffee cups with accompanying dishes on the table. It was going to be real Turkish coffee. Ali blessed the coffee, just the thought of the hideous coffee soda served at Arlanda earlier today made him shudder. Jacob got a bottle of more with apple flavor instead of Turkish coffee.

It was inevitable that there would be discussion about the war in Syria and that they aired their differing opinions about President Assad. Mustafa had his Muslim views that he did not share. Instead, he made life a little easier for himself by agreeing with Fatma. Deep down, he could kill her without hesitation for her free opinions. A conflict would disrupt his mission and, in the worst case, lead to too serious complications, but when Fatma resorted to the sob waltz while invoking Toh for mercy, he simply had enough. He thought it was a bit rude to talk about war and misery in foreign languages when Jacob was sitting at the table, something Yasmin undoubtedly agreed with.

Jacob looked like a living question mark and naturally wondered what was going on. During dinner, everyone was quite happy, now the atmosphere was the opposite and the conversation sometimes sounded rancorous in the foreign language. Yasmin saw Jacob's confused facial expression. With a smile, she held him and caressed his red-flowered cheek. Mustafa smiled.

"We talked about the problems in Syria. We are talking about something else so you can join in," Mustafa said in English.

Jacob drank some of his Mer and nodded. Mustafa was about to say something when Yasmin said in English: "Can't you tell us a little about yourself? I'm really curious."

"May I stay if I tell you," Jacob asked with a pleading look.

She hugged him and gave him a kiss on the cheek.

"You are mine. I will never let you down or leave you."

Jacob looked at Yasmin worriedly. His lower lip began to tremble as he flipped the Mer bottle on the tablecloth. He did not really know where to start when Yasmin took his hand and held it. He began his story with Mom and Dad. That they had lived in Knutby and belonged to the Pentecostal congregation before moving to Upplands Väsby. My mother came from Uppsala and my father came from Chicago, USA. They worked at Karolinska Institute with infectious diseases in a bunker. No one was allowed in there because it was dangerous," Jacob added, looking at Mustafa, who followed his story with great interest.

"What's your last name," Yasmin asked with a smile.

"Sjogren-Lester. I'm going to change my last name."

"For what?"

"I want your and Fatma's last name."

Yasmin hugged Jacob and then gave him a kiss on the forehead. Then she held his cheeks and looked at him with a smile.

"Beloved friend. Have you run away from home?"

Jacob nodded and could no longer hold back the crying.

"Do you want me to call your mom and dad and talk to them?"

Jacob shook his head frantically and hurried out to the hall. Yasmin stood up with a questioning look and walked after. In the hall, Jacob put on his shoes while holding the doorknob. Yasmin crouched down in front of Jacob and held him.

"Beloved friend, don't be afraid. I'm not going to call." Jacob calmed down and then held her.

"Promise," he said with tears in his throat.

Yasmin nodded, thinking anxiously about what might have happened to him, given his strong emotional reactions and willingness to flee towards his parents. Together they went back to the kitchen.

Mustafa smiled and held out his arms. “My boy is back,” he said triumphantly.

Ali glared at him. What was he doing? The kid was an American, an unfaithful Christian demon whom he raised to skies. Mustafa saw Ali’s reaction and gave him a determined look.

Jacob walked over and gave him a hug. He could smell a strong scent of perfume from his clothes and stubble. He also felt Mustafa’s strong hands gripping his back. Mustafa let go, wanting him to sit down next to Yasmin. Jacob did as he was told and looked questioningly at Fatma’s tearful gaze. She shook her head and began to moan in Arabic.

Yasmin sat with one elbow on the table and let her head rest on her hand while she brooded. She did not understand Jacob’s reaction, why didn’t he want to go back to his parents?! She got up to leave and asked Jacob to remain seated while she went to get the cell phone from the bedroom in case someone called from work.

After a minute or so, she was back and started googling Knutby and soon she got more searches about the church than the town itself, which rattled in the wake of the news flow. The murders committed ten years ago were still at the top of the search lists, an event she recognized very well. She read some articles about the Pentecostal pastor Åbjörnsson and the bride of Christ: Moa Waldarud, who had previously had a connection to the Maranata movement. Yasmin found nothing that could be linked to Jacob’s parents. She looked up and noticed that she was not the only one searching for information through Google. Mustafa was sitting with his cell phone and was busy searching for something.

She got up and went to get the coffee pot. Offered Mustafa a refill, and as she filled his cup, she saw that he had searched for Chris-something. He turned the cell phone and gave her a black look. She at once turned around and left.

Yasmin thoughtfully placed the coffee pot on the stove, and then sat down next to Jacob and took his hand.

"Beloved friend. Can you tell me in Swedish why you do not want to see your mom and dad?" she asked gently, then glanced at the others around the dining table.

Mustafa and Ali were busy searching for information about Jacob and his parents. Why? Jacob looked at Yasmin with tearful eyes, his lower lip trembling when he tried to say something.

"I've killed someone. You must not hate me, that was not your intention. I love you!"

Yasmin pulled him to her lap and hugged him.

"But please, why do you say that?" she said in despair, as she noticed Ali whispering to Mustafa, who looked up from his phone with a surprised look.

"You wanted me to tell you," Jacob said, looking at her as he wiped away his tears.

"Do this. Take a deep breath, then you will tell me from the beginning," Yasmin begged, straightening his bangs.

Jacob began his story with how he was attacked by a bunch of schoolmates. How he then managed to escape with his bicycle and escape. How he hid in the bushes and tried to stop them from chasing him, by sticking a stick into the back wheel of Jimmy's bike and how Jimmy fell against a rock and died. There was complete silence around the table and everyone looked at Jacob in surprise. Yasmin was about to say something when Jacob realized that he forgot an essential detail in his story.

"Anna was going to pee on me as I lay there!"

Yasmin, with a particularly shocked expression on her face, raised both arms in the air and exclaimed, "Stop!

Now wait!"

There was silence again. Ali and Mustafa looked at Yasmin with surprised looks while Jacob sat on her lap. She gave Jacob a serious look.

"Is this really true what you have told us here?" asked Yasmin with some skepticism.

Jacob looked at her and nodded.

"It's true. The police are chasing me," he said with tearful eyes.

"Are the police looking for you?" exclaimed Yasmin, getting over her head.

Jacob nodded in horror with an inner sense of panic that produced pain in his stomach.

"That's why I have to hide. Mom and Dad do not want to hear from me after what I did to Jimmy. Jimmy's dad is also looking for me. I will never be forgiven."

Yasmin hugged him with tearful eyes and just shook her head.

Mustafa swapped places with Ali, then took Jacob's one hand and held it.

" Jacob."

Jacob turned his head and met his gaze and smile.

"I forgive you. All of us here forgive you. I swear to my God that I will protect you."

Chapter 28

27 SEPTEMBER 2014

It was stressful in Åhlén's clothing department during the morning, the summer garments would be sold out and the autumn and winter collection would be brought out. Cenela Charmer was unpacking bras and panties when she saw trainee Malin walking. She needed a coffee break and beckoned Malin to come.

Malin was an alert and smart girl, who showed her feet with her high pace of work and needed no further instructions on what to do.

"Hey, are you really cute and pick up the rest of the clothes?" asked Cenela with an irresistible smile.

"Sure, I can do that," she said, starting to unpack goods.

"Oh, thank you. I am just going to take a coffee break and take the opportunity to call. I will be back soon," Cenela said and left.

As she walked past a cart with stacked cardboard boxes, she turned around.

"Malin, don't forget these boxes either," she shouted, pointing to the cart before disappearing.

Cenela stepped into Café Å Lait and walked towards the cafeteria, where she passed Charlotte Grinder from the perfume department.

She sat at a table with the coffee mug in one hand and was busy with Expressen's middle spread. Cenela spotted the photo on the center spread and stopped.

She recognized the little blonde guy.

"It's the boy who sat at the entrance a few days ago," she exclaimed, pointing to the middle spread.

Charlotte interrupted her reading and looked up at her with an annoyed look.

"Aren't you going to get coffee?" asked Charlotte, who felt a little pushed.

"I will but isn't it him?" repeated Cenela as she leaned over the table and began to read.

Charlotte folded the newspaper and gave her a serious look.

"When you have picked up your coffee, there is a possibility that you can read."

Cenela was a little embarrassed.

"Sorry! I was so curious," she said, and then went to buy coffee and snacks."

When she returned, she sat down next to Charlotte, who had finished reading the article, and handed over the paper.

"It seems to be the same guy," Charlotte noted.

Cenela took a bite of the sandwich and started reading the middle spread. The boy was only ten years old and was named Jacob. The police searched for the boy in connection with a major pedophile ring in Stockholm.

"Oh my God! Poor child," Cenela exclaimed in horror after reading the article.

"It's damn bad that such pigs are allowed to go loose in our society," Charlotte said with a sharp tone.

"Did you read that? It says that it was a chief physician who had committed the abuse," Cenela said, pointing to the middle spread.

"And sitting in custody, yes I read that. Cut the cock off him, there is nothing to save on," said Charlotte, who was a mother of three herself, as she drank the last sip of coffee.

Cenela looked at her questioningly, then folded the newspaper and placed it on the table to pick up her mobile phone. "Should you or I call?" asked Cenela.

"It's not my kid. I just gave the kid a few bucks as I walked by. Do not know if I want to get involved in it..."

"It could be your kid, Charlotte. The boy is only ten years old and hiding somewhere. We have to call and tell him that we have seen him out there at the entrance with that Romanian old man."

Charlotte grabbed her hair with both hands as her conscience crept in. She certainly did not want to get involved in other people's problems, let alone ask the police.

"Do we have to get involved in that? What if you find the kid murdered and buried, then we can get shit for that. You know how authorities are doing it, they twist and turn everything and suddenly you stand there in a fucking courtroom and are suddenly complicit. I'm sure someone else has already called."

"I'm not going to carry that conscience. Think about the boy's parents, they must be sick with worry. I'll call."

Cenela keyed in 114 14. Charlotte took the newspaper, opened the center spread, and looked at the photo. She put two fingers on the photo and caressed it with sweeping motions.

* * *

Inside Kronobergshäktet on the second floor, Lars-Åke was once again in an interrogation room together with Reneé and George. Reneé studied his graying facial expressions seeking empathy and forgiveness. His gaze was flickering and dismissive as his brain feverishly sought a way out of the locked situation. LarsÅke had been assigned a defense counsel, named Lars-Olov Fridolin, in connection with the detention hearing. A lawyer who was seriously late this morning stretched the patience of the two detectives while waiting for him for today's hearing.

There was a knock on the door before it opened. In stepped a man dressed in a dark jacket, white shirt, and blue jeans. In his hand he held a document bag. His attractive face was adorned with growing stubble. The intense brown mottled eyes highlighted his youthful facial features slightly, even though he had recently passed forty-five. He smiled and at the same time apologized for his delay while greeting everyone present. Then he sat down next to his client.

Lars-Olov was able to set out, on the fourth day, that the fleeting period of detention had taken a heavy toll on his client. Karl had even lost weight.

"Then maybe we can start the interrogation with Lars-Åke," Reneé began, looking meaningfully at the clock.

"If my client feels ready, I don't see any obstacle."

"Good. Then Lars-Åke, we wonder if you know a man by the name, Hook?"

Lars-Åke looked down at the table and held his gaze. Then he looked up and replied that he did not know the name. George raised his arm to get Lars-Åke's attention.

"You have to remember that we have your computers and mobile phones. Then you should realize that my colleague does not ask any questions that are taken out of thin air", countered George kindly but firmly.

"Yes, but..." Lars-Åke managed to squeeze out before Lars-Olov interrupted him.

"Now it's probably like people in this circle don't go out with their true identities. It is natural, isn't it?"

"We have conclusive evidence that points to a connection, just as my colleague just mentioned," Reneé said, with a retaining look at Lars-Åke.

"I don't know anyone by that name," said Lars-Åke, whose eyes begged for credence.

"Pinocchio," George suddenly exclaimed.

Lars-Åke looked at George with an uncomprehending look.

"What did you say his name was?" asked Lars-Åke, straightening his glasses.

"Ass knuckle..." George managed to say intuitively before interrupting the sentence when he saw that Lars-Olov started taking notes on an A4 block.

"No, the man we just mentioned by name has an alias or username called Pinocchio," said George, turning his gaze a little awkwardly to

Reneé, who did not look happy. "Do you know the username, because Johan Hook doesn't seem to be familiar?" he added.

"I've had contact with a person called Pinocchio," Lars-Åke admitted, then looked fleetingly at his defender.

"So, you don't know his real name?" asked Reneé.

"No, we've only been in contact online and I've never met him in person."

"It was a shame... I mean you never had the opportunity to meet. Then you might not have sat here and instead fucked each other like real men and fucked the toddlers," said George sarcastically as he firmly gave Lars-Olov an unabashed look, who again began to take notes in his notebook.

"Is it your memoirs you are writing down?" asked George with a mocking smile.

Fridolin looked up but avoided answering and just smiled, then he put his pen on the notebook neatly and neatly.

"Maybe so, at least it's noted," the lawyer replied, running his fingers through his gray-brown hair.

Reneé's cell phone vibrated and spun to a quarter turn at the edge of the table. She took the cell phone and responded by introducing herself as the room fell silent.

"Yes hey, I'm sitting a little busy. What is the matter of? All right... When did she call? Had she seen the boy outside?"

Suddenly, she crouched down with her cell phone and pulled out a notebook from her bag that was on the floor. She rolled her eyes and crouched across the table, taking the lawyer's ink pen lying on her notepad. She began to take notes:

Åhléns, Klarabergsgatan 50, second entrance, Romanian beggar, 25 September. 24th Did the boy deviate from *Valhto Road?* <u>*One day diffs*</u>.

"What was the name of the caller?" asked Reneé, writing down *Cenela Charmer 076-179418*. "If more tips come in, I want the calls to be connected directly to the department. Thanks for calling, Bye" Reneé ended the call.

She looked at George with a serious face and then said with a smile: "We've caught up with the boy."

George gave Lars-Åke a determined look, leaned back in his chair and marked by putting his arms together against his chest.

"It's starting to take shape," he said with a mocking smile at LarsÅke.

Reneé began typing in a phone number while reading the inside of the notebook.

"Please excuse me, but I need to make a phone call about this."

She lifted her phone to her ear as she walked out and closed the door.

"Hello! My name is Reneé Grahn and I am calling from the police... yes exactly, that is why I am calling. Are you at work now? Good, we will come as soon as we can. Can I have your phone number, sorry I have that, Bye" she concluded.

She opened the door to the interrogation room and entered. With her firsthand the table, she sat down and looked intently at Lars Åke's questioning mine.

"Yes, what were we... Well, what do you think this boy who left your apartment will tell us? As you can imagine, it is only a few hours before we find him," Reneé added.

"Nothing that will improve my situation," Lars-Åke said a little unclearly.

George could not help but laugh. "Nope! Think... Neither do we."

"You have admitted that you had met the boy and also had him at your house. What did not come out clearly enough was whether you had a sexual relationship with this underage boy," Reneé said.

"Nor if there were more people who shared this relationship, like Pinocchio," George added.

Lars-Åke shook his head and showed a clearly remorseful face.

"Do I really need to go into intimate details?" asked Lars-Åke as he fixed his gaze on the tabletop.

"It's not something we wish for right away..."

"The prosecutor, on the other hand, wants it," interrupted George.

"However, it can be an advantage for you in purely criminal terms, depending a little on what you have to say," Reneé said. "It's in spite of everything little difference between sexually abusing children and committing aggravated rape of children," she added firmly.

Lars-Åke looked questioningly at his lawyer and then turned his gaze to Reneé.

"I'd love to consult with my defender anyway," he said.

"Absolutely, it might be a good idea. We will stop the hearing now, and you can speak in peace. We are a little anxious to get away," Reneé said, rising from the table.

"The pen!" Lars-Olov said as he held out his hand and snapped his fingers at Reneé.

"Oops! Sorry. I forgot it was your pen. Thank you for the loan," she said, handing it over.

Chapter 29

27 SEPTEMBER 2014

IT HAD PASSED half past two in the afternoon when Linda drove on Almungevägen in the direction of Knutby. A feeling of being a bad mother had haunted her at times, which made her unable to think clearly. She felt a depression knocking on the door of her conscience and needed to talk it out with someone. Chris was no longer a given sounding board, perhaps because he had chosen the job as a refuge instead of being at home and getting more involved in Jacob's disappearance. There were additional hidden reasons that contributed to his preference to be at work. A thought that was increasingly reinforced given his recurring disinterest in closeness and intimacy, for which she longed. A thought and suspicion of infidelity that she would rather ward herself off.

On the other hand, the consequences would be catastrophic if Chris could not conduct his mission for the WHO. No, it was not something she wanted to continue her conscience and felt guilty just by the thought. Linda turned into Lunda liv's parking lot and stopped. She convulsively kept both firsthand the steering wheel, then leaned her body over the steering wheel and cried in despair.

The car was idling while tears dripped onto the steering wheel hub. Suddenly, the car honked and frightened her. She leaned back in horror with both hands outstretched to the steering wheel. She quickly wiped away her tears as she looked around to see if anyone else had reacted.

In the parking lot there was only a young man dressed for work and a little further away stood an older man with a white jacket who was unlocking the driver's door of an old white Volkswagen 1300 of unknown model year. None of them had even cared.

Linda backed out of the parking lot and drove on towards Knutby. She did not have to sit crying outside Ica, she needed to talk to someone who listened and cared. Someone who could give her comfort and understanding. A pastoral counseling could purify her soul and help her regain her faith in God.

Just over two hours ago, she had called Moa and it was not an easy decision. After a while, the conversation with Moa became confidence-inspiring, almost loving, which led them to decide to meet, before God's presence. An encounter that made Linda think of something else, something that could cure her depression and be able to understand something clearly at last again in the paralyzing, bottomless darkness that she groped in.

The white Mercedescombi turned right at Almunges church and onto road 273. Linda read on one road sign, Edsbro 27 and on the other sign underneath it said Knutby 13 where she felt a tingling sensation in her stomach area.

When she arrived at the address, she drove slowly to the turnpike and parked in front of the garage of Moa's house. She turned off the engine and wondered if it was really the right decision to go here, to the bride of Christ. What would she do if Moa made any sexual advances? She pushed that thought away, instead grabbing her purse, and getting out of the car, without making a final decision on the matter.

Linda stood at the front door and was about to ring the bell when the door suddenly opened. They stood at Moa, as attractive and beautiful as ever. She shone like a sun and stretched out her arms as she walked over and hugged Linda.

"Hello and welcome Linda," she said next to her ear.

"Thank you," she replied, and with some hesitation she answered the hug.

"Come in, I've set out some coffee," Moa said, letting go of her.

Linda smiled and walked in, closing the front door.

She sat down at a set kitchen table. Moa fetched the coffee pot while Linda studied her body and could see that she had not aged one bit. God! What should I do? she thought embarrassedly, casting a glance out the kitchen window. Then she felt the warmth rising across her cheeks as Moa filled the coffee mugs with coffee. As she walked back with the coffee pot, Linda studied her firm but with a slightly curious look. So solid is not mine.

Moa sat down opposite Linda and stretched out her left hand across the table while she drank some coffee. Linda responded to the gesture by extending her hand and Moa happily accepted it.

"Nothing new about Jacob?" asked Moa worriedly as she let her thumb caress Linda's hand.

"No, nothing since we talked on the phone. Moa, I need to talk to someone before I break down completely. I can't take this anymore."

"I can tell you that I have some contacts within the police that I have contacted with following Jacob's disappearance. I hope that we will have more insight into what is happening and what is happening. Just wanted to tell you. How is Chris?" asked Moa, a little dismissively. "Do you talk to each other; do you pray together?"

Linda shook her head and crouched across the table to squeeze Moa's hand.

"Chris... He has a lot to think about in his work. Increasingly often he feels like he is blaming me for Jacob's disappearance, he does not say much either. It feels more like a forced presence when he is at home. Honestly, I'm not entirely sure he loves me anymore."

"Beloved Linda, I am convinced that he loves you. I can't think of anything else."

"He barely touches me, we don't pray together, and we haven't..." Linda interrupted, looking at Moa with a look that lacked closeness, love, and intimate touch.

"Sex," Moa added, smiling with her whole face. Linda nodded and looked down at the table embarrassedly.

"I always thought it was an important detail in men, but apparently not for Chis," Linda said. "I get the feeling that our marriage has become a substitute for something else."

"Beloved Linda, sex is important to all of us," Moa reminded as she reached out her right arm and grabbed Linda's hand.

Slowly she began to massage her middle finger with caressing movements. Linda met her intense eyes that bore as she felt a slight shiver pass through her body. Moa got up and walked around the table to stand close behind Linda's back. She grabbed her shoulders and began to slowly massage gently as she crouched over and kissed her neck. She again felt a pleasant shiver from her touch. Moa let go of her shoulders and methodically let them find their way down to Linda's chest. She was about to stop her but hesitated, instead turning her head and meeting Moa's lips. The kiss became increasingly intense as the tongues familiarized themselves with each other. Linda got up from her chair and grabbed Moa's waist.

Moa took her hand and led her out of the kitchen. It carried up the stairs to the upper floor while she eagerly unbuttoned Linda's blouse from behind. Linda felt an ardent desire and a hot longing for her warm, sensual body. Now all earlier biblical and moral barriers and doubts were blown away. Not even God could stop her from being seduced by the bride of Christ when her blouse ended up on the doorpost into the bedroom.

Arriving at the bed, Moa quickly removed her upper body and just had time to throw her bra on the floor when she was pushed onto the bed. Linda threw herself on top of Moa and kissed her intensely as she breathed faster and faster with arousal. Linda took off her bra while Moa drilled her face in between her breasts. She caressed them and Linda shuddered so that her nipples stiffened like ripe wild raspberries. Moa closed her lips around one nipple and let her tongue rotate uninhibited while her hands massaged both breasts.

Linda got up from the bed to take off her clothes. Moa was quickly up and let her jeans fall on the floor, then stood in front of Linda and started caressing her. Linda pulled her panties down to the folds of her knees and began to gently caress the inside of her thighs, further up to her shaved vagina. Moa bounced with a smile.

She laid Linda on her back the crumpled bedspread straddled her and continued to caress her. Linda closed her eyes in pleasure, just that feeling that someone was touching her excited body was magical. Her imagination made her shiver with pleasure. Suddenly, she winced when she felt Moa's warm breath find its way between her legs and the fantasy became reality.

Suddenly, Moa's mobile phone rang down from the hall. Moa leaned over Linda's face so that her soft hair fell over her.

"You don't have to," Linda said as she met Moa's surprised gaze.

"I have to," Moa said reluctantly, standing up as Linda moved with a heavy sigh.

Moa hurried down the stairs and to her mobile phone on the kitchen table. It had stopped ringing and out of curiosity she looked at the display. Linda approached behind her and wrapped her arms around her waist.

"Who was it?" asked Linda as she gently kissed her neck.

"Don't know, it was unknown number."

"Come, bring your phone and we'll get up," Linda said, letting go of Moa.

The cell phone rang.

Chapter 30

27 SEPTEMBER 2014

Reneé showed his annoyance towards George as they left the office. On her way to the elevator, she took the lead to mark for her big-jawed colleague who was walking just behind. She stopped at the elevators and flicked the elevator button with her palm before looking at George with a look that could trap everything in its path. He did not seem completely unmoved; he knew full well that he was making a fool of himself during the interrogation. At worst, this could lead to internal consequences, as he was aware.

The elevator stopped, and the doors opened and Reneé stepped in decisively and turned around demonstratively. George stepped into the elevator and kept his eyes on the floor, like a shamed dog, and stood at a safe distance from his colleague. He inserted a key into the button panel and turned it over. The elevator started going down towards the parking garage.

"Can you stop sulking now? I apologize for my crude choice of words. Besides, that lawyer sat and challenged me with his damn notes. You saw that for yourself," said George without sounding particularly credible.

Reneé turned to face him. "Who the hell do you think you are, Gunvald Larsson? Did you behave like that towards your wife too?"

"That hurt," George replied.

Reneé bit her tongue as she stepped out of the elevator.

They got in the car and Reneé put the mobile phone between Front seats. She turned on the radio while staring out the side window to avoid eye contact. George started the car and gave her a look.

"I didn't mean that, you know that. That was fucking stupid said by me, sorry," she said as she looked out the side window.

"There you see. It is not so easy to be humble and show understanding for a person who has committed serious sexual abuse of young children, Reneé. Think of your do..."

"Nope! Lay off!" interrupted Reneé with a powerful mark. "It is sick people who commit these abuses, and it is not our job to judge them. We have courts that manage it," she said, grabbing her cell phone. "You're keeping my daughter out of my job," she added.

"Both you and I know what's going on behind the scenes."

"George! Your wife has left you and I have apologized for what I said. Concentrate on traffic instead."

"Worried?" asked George with a small smile as he turned right onto St. Eriksgatan after a while.

"Not one bit," Renéé said. "I came up with another thing, if the boy is at Åhléns when we arrive and he sees you. What happens then?"

"What, should I stay in the car while you look for the kid? If he sticks, we'll have a run."

Reneé looked at George questioningly. "In all seriousness. Should we chase the kid inside Åhléns? Is that what you are saying?"

"Why are you getting so fucking dramatic? It will be you who walks up to him if he is sitting there. I'll stay close if he pulls."

Reneé was about to say something but was interrupted.

"One more thing! You cannot come forward with that look. You even scare me," said George and at the same time pulled a little on one corner of his mouth.

Reneé smiled, feeling while the tension between them had released.

"Is it that bad?" she asked, showing a smile.

George gave her a quick glance and then looked forward again with a smile.

"What do you think yourself?"

Reneé shrugged and a peaceful silence settled in the car. There was even silence on the police radio. When George drove straight across Vasagatan, he started looking for something with one hand by patting the outside of his jacket pockets.

"It's ringing, where the hell is the phone?"

George tore open his mobile phone and answered.

"George ... Yes, hello... Having a bit of a tough time talking now... is on his way to Åhléns for a business matter. Can I call a little later? Exactly... Can I come back a little later? Thank you, hello."

George put his mobile phone back in his jacket pocket while he concentrated on traffic. Reneé looked at him questioningly.

"That conversation sounded very cryptic to be you," she said, smiling.

"Sometimes I don't understand women. There must be something genetic about you to constantly be curious and question everything you do."

"Are you referring to me now or is it general?" asked Reneé with a short smile.

"No, on the person who called," he said, falling silent for a few seconds before adding, "you should have your fair share too." George turned into a parking garage at Mäster Samu elsgatan and parked.

"Okay, shall we split up like you said? I take the elevator up to the ground floor so you can walk around and meet me at the last entrance. You can take the opportunity to call that secret madam while you leave," Reneé said as she got out of the car.

"We keep in touch with the mobile. Don't be in a hurry, I've got some way to go from here."

"Well, it might be a long conversation," Reneé said, starting to walk towards the elevators. "Don't fucking forget me," she added before disappearing out of sight.

George came out of the parking garage and started walking towards Åhléns while he flipped out the phone number for Christ's bride.

* * *

The white Mercedes was speeding at Almungevägen in the direction of Upplands Väsby. With both hands firmly on the wheel, Linda drove as fast as she dared. Next to her sat Moa, holding the handle convulsively and praying to God in a whispered sound. A speckled cat came from the grassy ditch on the right side and walked calmly across the roadway. Linda, who caught sight of the cat, honked her horn and the cat stopped and looked at the cabin. She turned onto the opposite carriageway and passed at high speed. The cat turned around and ran back to the ditch.

After passing Upplands Väsby interchange, she began to drive more calmly and Moa was finally heard. Linda, who had always focused on driving, had forgotten about Chris. She must call and tell me. With a guilty look, she looked at Moa who met her gaze.

"What is it?" she asked, taking Linda's hand.

"I have to call Chris, but what should I tell him? I must tell you that I have met you..." This wasn't very well thought out by me."

"Why?"

"Why? You are here with me. He will of course wonder why I have met you when he comes to Åhléns."

"You can say that we met there by chance at Åhléns, nothing strange about that."

"I can't run at Åhléns while our son is missing, can I?" said Linda as if that were impossible. "He will question this; no, it is not possible."

Linda keyed out the phone book on the car's dashboard, marked Chris, and then pressed dial. Linda put her index finger in front of her mouth towards Moa.

"Hey honey," Chris said as he answered. "Hello?" "Hey, I just wanted to call and let you know that the police have called." "Have they found Jacob?" he exclaimed with joy.

"A woman who works at Åhléns has met him and I'm on my way there."

"Are you picking me up? Where are you?"

"I'm almost there. Can't you take a taxi, please?" she begged to gain some time while telling an emergency lie.

The white Mercedes combi passed by the Sollentuna interchange.

* * *

Reneé got off the elevator at the entrance level and looked around but did not see Jacob among the crowd. Instead, she started walking towards the entrance to see if he was there. He had a bicycle, she recalled, pulling her mobile phone out of his jacket pocket. She called George to find out where he was, after two signals a female voice was heard announcing that the subscriber was busy in another call. She stopped at the entrance, but Jacob was conspicuous by his absence there as well. Just a female beggar wrapped in colorful veils sat on some pillows with a paper cup from Seven Eleven in front of her. Soon after, George came through the entrance and walked up to Reneé.

"Have checked towards the central station and along Karlbergsgatan. Could not see any kid with our description. Not even a blue children's bike."

"I'm not really sure this is the right entrance. Should we go to this Cenela Charmer and she can show us where she saw the boy?" asked Reneé. "We need to talk to her anyway," she added.

"Yes," sighed George and looked embarrassed. "Which plane are we going to?"

George and Reneé started walking towards the elevators.

"Plan four."

Inside the elevator, George could afford a small smile. He was once again able to conclude that he was fortunate to work with Reneé, who was a loyal colleague and friend. Through the mirror, Reneé could see that he was on second thoughts and smiling.

"Now you get everything to share! What is so funny?" she asked, starting to laugh.

"No, it's nothing. Just generally happy," he replied, laughing embarrassedly when the elevator stopped.

They stepped into the clothing department for ladies. A short distance away, a younger girl stood and took apart boxes while an older woman in her forties stood at the checkout and took payment from a customer. Reneé walked up to the checkout as the customer walked away. She and George showed their police IDs to the woman.

"Hi, we're looking for Cenela," Reneé said as she put her ID back in her jacket pocket and held out her hand to greet.

"Hi, it's me," Cenela said with a warm smile and greeted them over the checkout counter.

"George Lindmark", George introduced himself.

"Is there a staff room where we can talk a little undisturbed?" asked Reneé.

"Sure, come along here," Cenela said and started walking.

Cenela walked past the younger girl and asked her to take care of the cash register while she was gone, then continued through a door with the police officer.

The staff space was not large. A small kitchenette with a table and four chairs as well as a walk-in closet. Behind a curtain was a toilet. Reneé and George sat down when Cenela offered to make some coffee, but they declined. Cenela sat down next to Reneé who showed a photograph of Jacob and placed the photo on the table. Cenela took the photo and looked at it.

"Was this the boy you saw?" Cenela nodded, then placed the photo on the table.

"It's him, poor thing," she replied dejectedly.

"Where did you see him? Did you talk to him at any point?" asked George.

"Out at the entrance closest to the central station. He sat there with a coffee cup and begged for money. I gave him some money but it never occurred to me to talk to him. I wish I had."

"There was a little guy begging for money, why didn't you react? Was he alone?"

"No, he was sitting with an older man. You know, one of those Romanian beggars who usually sit there every day. I should have reacted more than I did, but there are beggars outside our entrances every day so you do not react in the same way.

If, on the other hand, the boy had sat by himself... yes, you see."

Reneé nodded in agreement. "Can you show us where you met the boy?"

"This Romanian citizen is he sitting there today? I assume you have not seen the boy today?"

"I haven't been out today, but I can show you," Cenela said, rising from the table.

***

Linda turned left from Vasagatan onto Mäster Samuelsgatan and then drove into Åhlénsgaraget. During the drive, they had agreed that Linda would tell it like it was about why she had visited Moa, even though Chris would have a negative opinion about it. The fact remained, it was not about who Linda hung out with but about finding their son, period.

The risk that Chris would have a reason to believe that Linda had had an intimate relationship with Moa was highly unlikely. Linda parked the car and while they ran to the elevator picked Linda out her mobile. They got into the elevator and went up to the ground floor.

* * *

Outside the entrance at Klarabergsgatan 50, a young girl was sitting on a blanket. Judging by the colorful attire, she was Romanian. Her name was Perla and she had semi-curly, center-colored hair. Next to her, she had handmade wooden spoons that she was trying to sell, and in front was a plastic box with some small coins and some banknotes.

A woman stopped and contributed a few crowns to the plastic box while the Roma girl humbly thanked with a flawed Swedish.

Perla looked towards the glazed entrance doors, hoping that more people would come out of the store, and saw a woman stop inside the doors and point to her. Soon after, another man and a woman stopped and looked at her. Perla perceived that they were talking about her because they were both looking and pointing at her while they were conversing. She sensed something was going on. It was social work... she had time to think when she caught a glimpse of a gun inside the man's jacket. No, these people were not from any social welfare office, rather they were police officers or even worse mafia. Except for the first woman who worked in the department store, something that the nameplate clearly showed.

Now they come," she said as the two women and the man stepped out of the glass doors.

Reneé stood in front of the young girl, hoping that she could make herself understood in half-Swedish or in best case in English.

George stood next to her and looked around but did not see a boy. Cenela chose to stand in the background.

Reneé was about to crouch down when George's mobile phone rang. He picked it up from his jacket pocket and saw who was calling. A little untimely that she would call right now, he thought as he walked away.

"George."

"It's me. We are found on the ground floor here at Åhléns, by the elevator. Where are you?"

"Where am I? What are you doing here if I may ask?" hissed George and felt panic creeping in. He looked back as he walked to make sure Reneé did not hear the call or go after. "Moa, now listen to me. The fact that I supplied some information about the kid does not mean that you or you should interfere in my job. Don't you understand that you put me in a penile situation? Go home for hell... For God's sake."

"You swore, George."

"Yes, and I corrected it in the same sentence. Do you have a mother with you?"

"Of course, the mother is there," Moa replied.

"Well, you're not supposed to be here anyway."

"Is it your colleague talking to the girl outside the entrance?"

Reneé looked towards the glass doors and saw something she did not want to see. Surprised, she saw Linda come out in the company of another woman. They looked with questioning glances at the Roma girl sitting on her blanket with her wooden spoons. Reneé now recognized the woman who was in the company of

Linda. It was the bride of Christ from the Knutby drama, what was she doing here?

What was the mother doing here? She thought as she tried to remind herself of the real name of the bride of Christ.

George, who had returned, frantically tried to produce a solution to the situation while smiling at Reneé's surprised expression.

"Now we are in good company, just missing that the Pentecostal pastor has received permit from Kumla," Reneé muttered ironically. She sighed when she realized that it was just to confront a problem head-on and beckoned Linda to come.

When Moa had visited George, Reneé discovered that something was not right. It was in a distanced way, as if they did not really want to touch each other and George gave the appearance of worry in his eyes. She followed Linda's gaze as they walked away and stopped a short distance away.

Linda walked up to the Roma girl and was about to crouch down to greet her when Reneé came up and grabbed her.

"Now I want you to listen to me. I want to manage this conversation and the investigation myself," Reneé said in a firm tone.

"Oh, sorry. It was not meant to... I just wanted to greet her," Linda excused herself and took a few steps back.

Perla tried to take advantage of the situation by stretching out the plastic box.

"Thank you. Thank you very much. Hello."

Reneé began to look in his pockets for small coins and turned to George when she could not find any.

“I’m sure you have some small coins to spare,” she said and began to search for George on the outside of his clothes.

He backed up two steps and looked at her in surprise.

“What are you doing? Are you going to search for me? I am fucking don’t have any small coins.”

“You have all sorts of things in your pockets, feel it,” Reneé ordered.

Without commenting, George began to feel in his pockets and suddenly pulled his hand out of his trouser pocket. In the palm of his hand were car keys belonging to a BMW, two ten crowns, one five crowns and two one crowns. Reneé grabbed the car keys and held them in his hand. She then nodded at the Roma girl who smiled and rattled her plastic box.

“Should I give her my parking money?”

“Yes, either that or Madame here becomes a proud BMW owner. For me, it doesn’t matter.”

George grumbled, walked over to Perla, and put the coins in her plastic box.

“Hello. Thank you, thank you very much,” she said with a smile.

“Sure, no problem,” George muttered as he turned around and took two steps up to Reneé and stretched out his hand.

Reneé smiled teasingly and handed back the car keys. So, a grindstone should be drawn when it comes to men and I am not done with you yet, Reneé thought to herself.

“Now you have passed the intake test. Let us see if you can hear the woman without being rough in the jaw while I talk to Jacob’s mother a little,” Reneé said in a low-key tone, nodding at Linda.

George looked questioningly at her and then at Perla.

"Isn't it better that you talk to her? You have more talent for languages than I do, and I will also be better able to keep these ladies as objects of protection," suggested George and nodded discreetly towards Linda and Moa.

Reneé gave him a look that simultaneously said a thousand words and nothing. She shrugged.

"Okay, then you can make sure they leave so we can work alone," she said and started walking towards the Roma girl.

When she arrived at her, the girl made another attempt to beg for more money. Reneé brought Perla's arm down to the pavement and she dropped the plastic box.

"Can you speak Swedish?"

Perla was about to grab the plastic box again but was stopped by Reneé.

"No, no money now. You do not know Swedish, is that so?" Perla looked at her and nodded while smiling.

"Can you speak English; do you speak English?" repeated Reneé.

The girl shook her head and then said hello in Swedish.

Does she speak Swedish or not? she mused. Reneé did not want to be taken by the nose by an EU citizen trying to get away because of a simulated lack of language skills. In such a situation, you could get good aid and support from a colleague like George. Reneé stood up and looked at him as he stood and tried to persuade Linda and Moa to leave and walked up to them.

"Let's try to get an interpreter here," she said, interrupting him mid-sentence.

"Doesn't she know Swedish poor girl?" asked Linda.

"Can you make sure we get an interpreter here?" repeated Reneé to George and then turned to Linda with an irritated tone. "No, obviously not."

"Can't we take her to the station? It must be better than standing here," George suggested. "We have a car," he added.

Reneé looked around.

"Okay, we'll do that. Get the car and I will take care of your obvious slight problem," Reneé said, handing over the car keys.

George gave a thumbs up and without saying anything he took the car keys and disappeared through the glazed entrance doors.

Chapter 31

27 SEPTEMBER 2014

THAT THERE WAS a lot of traffic on Sveavägen, especially during the lunch rush, was common knowledge, not least for Ali. The customer sitting in the back seat was in a great hurry from Karolinska Institute to Åhléns in Stockholm city, he thought as he gave the customer a tiresome look in the rearview mirror. He drove a few meters and then came to a standstill again. There was Åhléns much closer to Karolinska Institute, he thought, and began fingering his bracelet to keep his calm.

The queue slowly continued towards Kungsgatan and Sergel Square. Of course, it was red at the intersection at Olof Palmes street.

Ali recognized the man's face but could not recall where he had seen him. He was also remarkably like that cheeky doctor in the TV series Mash. It turned green and Ali drove slowly forward.

Doctor... It is him! Ali stopped at the next red light right at the entrance to Sergel the garage. Discreetly, he began to Google with his mobile phone between his legs. Pressing the letter C on the search box revealed all earlier searches on the letter C, including Chris Sjögren-Lester. He pressed the name and suddenly a picture of Professor Chris Sjögren-Lester, an expert on pandemic diseases and viruses, appeared.

Oh my God, he is in my car. It is not possible, he thought triumphantly as his face looked like a birdhouse with overbite. This is what I must tell Mustafa.

"Can you drive, please, it's green and I'm in a bit of a hurry," Chris urged after looking up from his plane ticket and seeing that the driver was sitting like a birdhouse staring in the rearview mirror.

Ali turned right at Sergel Square onto Klarabergsgatan and stopped at the second entrance to Åhléns. Chris handed Ali his American Express and driver's license. While taking down the plane ticket and some documents in his briefcase, Ali took the opportunity to take a photo of his driver's license with his mobile phone.

Chris looked towards the entrance as he put the cards back in his wallet. He saw Linda talking to Reneé and to his surprise, he also saw Moa standing next to his wife. He accepted the taxi receipt and together with the briefcase he hurried out of the car to catch up with Linda and Moa who were about to leave.

Ali drove off at high speed in the direction of the centre. There he stopped at a taxi rank, took his mobile phone from the passenger seat, and began nervously browsing the photo gallery. With a gesture of victory with his left arm, he noted that the photo of Chris's driver's license turned out well. Now he would just make an important call and inform.

* * *

As Chris approached the entrance, it felt like he was a dollop of honey near a wasps' nest. He got the feeling that Linda, Reneé and not least Moa had all locked their eyes on him.

"What's going on?" he asked, glancing questioningly at the young Roma girl Perla.

"I can enlighten you on that. While my colleague was arriving in the car, I wanted to get rid of these ladies who, by a strange coincidence, turned up here. The same goes for you," Reneé said.

"You can tell me what this girl has to do with Jacob's disappearance, right?" begged Linda.

"For investigative reasons, no. We are going to bring this young lady and talk a little. Could you please go now?"

"Does she have any connection to our son's disappearance?" asked Chris, spotting Cenela standing next to Moa. "Who is she?"

"We don't really know what this girl knows. We are looking for an elderly man of Romanian origin," Reneé replied, then pointed to Cenela. "Cenela is her name. She is one of the witnesses who has seen Jacob."

Chris walked over and greeted Cenela and thanked her for getting in touch.

A dark grey VW Passat stopped at the pavement. George got out of the car and walked over to Reneé.

"Interpreters are on their way. Is your phone turned off?" he said.

Reneé took out his mobile phone and found that the battery was dead.

"Yes, it's off, must have forgotten to charge. Have you tried calling?"

"Among other things. A female priest named Christina Grenholm had called. She is a chief theologian of Hedvig Eleonora parish. Isn't it enough to have a professional title as a priest or bishop without arguing it all up by proclaiming a title that no bastard can spell?" said George and shrugged. "At least she's read the article and says she met Jacob away at Hedvig Eleonora church in Östermalm two or three days ago. I have her number," he added.

"Good, we'll call her later. Come on, try to take this young girl to the car without having to call the task force."

They walked up to Perla. Reneé motioned for her to get up as the girl took her plastic box and again began rattling it. They helped her get up with one arm each. They walked slowly towards the car and Perla was allowed to take a seat in the back seat without any major protests. She had her plastic box with the money with her and she was also in a police car, it could not be safer than that.

George picked up the blanket and wooden spoons from the pavement before going to the car and putting them in the trunk. Linda walked over to Reneé, who was standing by the police car with the back door open.

"May we come along?"

Reneé looked at her and then at Chris and Moa without answering.

"I promise we won't get in your way or disturb you. It feels like you are close to a breakthrough and I have a desire to be present as a mother if you find Jacob today," Linda added with a prayerful tone of voice and tears nearby.

"You, now I'm starting to feel sorry for you. We have nothing to go on now. This investigation is much bigger than a lost boy. How you and your friend found your way here when we are here is a mystery to me. The same goes for your husband who just shows up in a taxi, but I will have to solve that riddle later. The answer to your question is still no. We will contact you as soon as we have something to tell you. So now, go home."

Reneé turned and waved to Cenela as she walked around the car and sat in the driver's seat. George jumped into the back seat and joined Perla, who was in her own world, with her plastic box. The dark grey VW Passat drove off with a flying start.

Linda watched as the young girl in the back seat turned around and looked at her with a small smile before she and Chris walked over to Cenela and Moa.

"I want to thank you so much from the bottom of my heart that you reached out to the police," Linda said with tearful eyes.

Cenela smiled and hugged Linda.

"I have two boys myself and I'm really keeping both my fingers crossed that you find the boy."

Linda nodded as she let go. They said goodbye to each other, then Cenela disappeared through the entrance among shopping people.

Chris turned to Linda and Moa. "Understand me right now Moa," he said before turning to Linda with a serious look. "Linda, is she with you for any special reason?"

Linda looked at Moa with imploring eyes, and then at Chris.

"I have lost my faith in God, something that has never happened before, I ..." Linda managed to say when Moa interrupted. "Linda came to my house and we spent some time pastoral care and prayer time," she innocently explained.

Chris held Moa with his gaze for a moment, then he looked at Linda who flicked her gaze as conscience wanted to reveal her secret. The first obvious question Chris was asked was: Why did she look so guilty?

Chapter 32

27 SEPTEMBER 2014

A FREIGHT TRAIN PASSED and made the yellow house just outside Sparreholm vibrate slightly. In the living room, Mustafa was kneeling on a hand-knotted rug with a small compass sewn on one end. In the middle of the carpet was an embroidered mosque at sunrise. In front of him, two girls and two dark-skinned boys were kneeling and praying with their new leader, Mustafa Baykal. The purpose of the prayer was two, the ordinary prayer that began at 12:54 and the second prayer that included a wish; that Toh would guide them and the white boy to a better world and a true eternal faith.

Just over an hour ago, he had received a call from the leader on a portable satellite phone. Mustafa had produced an idea that he presented, a plan that grew and became increasingly sophisticated when he googled Professor Chris Sjögren-Lester.

* * *

The interpreter arrived as promised. It was a woman who grew up in Bucharest before fleeing to Sweden during the revolution with the former dictator Nicolae Ceaușescu. The revolution had had a bloody course, which meant that Ceausescu's head finally became the people's trophy on a riding tank.

A bizarre media image that spread like wildfire across the world's newsrooms.

Perla had had to spend her time in an interrogation room. Locking her up in a detention cell was not considered necessary because she was not suspected of any crime.

Reneé managed to arrange for the girl to have a hearty lunch. Hopefully, it would lead to the girl becoming more benevolent to tell who this man was that they were looking for, as well as where he was.

* * *

At Linda and Chris's house, they sat with Moa at the kitchen table and drank coffee while the atmosphere was pressed. The reason was primarily Chris's frustration that he did not get a straight and honest answer as to why Moa had become increasingly embroiled in Jacob's disappearance. Linda, in turn, was upset by the news that Chris and a helping assistant would fly to London tomorrow at such short notice and without her knowing it. What upset her the most was the female assistant. Chris was going to the Royal Free Hospital where nurse Audrey Limpton was to arrive from Sierra Leone. Moa tried to mediate in the name of God, which was outright rejected by Chris.

* * *

Inside the interrogation room, the interpreter had sat down next to Perla. Opposite them sat Reneé and George. A tape recorder on the table was set in motion.

"Ask her if she knows where she is?" asked Reneé the interpreter.

The interpreter repeated the question in Romanian. Perla nodded as she replied, "Police" and nodded to Reneé.

"In the place where you were sitting, there has been an elderly man sitting with a little boy. We believe that this man is a compatriot of yours. Do you know him?" asked Reneé.

The interpreter translated it into Perla. She pondered and then looked alternately at Reneé and George. Perla made signs with her fingers that she wanted money.

"Tell her I'll give her a penny if she tells me," Reneé told the interpreter.

"The man you are looking for is called Gabor, she does not know her last name. He usually sits at the Åhléns entrance, which was his place. She does not know of any boy. The man apparently lives alone."

"Where is the man now?" asked Reneé.

Perla gestured with her arms as she explained.

"He lives at the same camp as her. He is supposed to be there, he is obviously sick," the interpreter explained.

"Is there a fair-haired Swedish boy in that camp?" asked Reneé. "Where is that camp?"

Perla looked questioningly at Reneé, then stretched out her arms and shrugged as she explained in surprise.

"She doesn't know what it's called. There is an industrial area and a forest hill nearby."

Reneé looked at George with a questioning look. "What she describes can basically be anywhere around Stockholm," said George.

Reneé nodded and turned to the interpreter.

"Can she show us where the camp is?" Perla showed a little irritation when she nodded and replied.

"She can show but she loses a lot of money helping you," said the interpreter.

Reneé watched as George clenched his fist in pure frustration on the table and with an angry terrier look he was about to say something when Reneé intervened.

"My colleague has just declared that she will be compensated through compensation."

"We need to find this boy and Gabor," George said as his terrier-like gaze slowly subsided and he gathered himself to endure.

Reneé stood up.

"Let's go now, and she'll show the way. It would be good if you could come along, we probably need more help from you when we arrive at the camp."

The interpreter nodded and stood up with Perla. Everyone except George left the interrogation room. He stood up slowly, frantically searching for mental strength while the tape recorder stood on the table recording. He turned it off and removed the cassette.

While Reneé was putting on her jacket in the corridor, she met prosecutor Bjorn Elofsson, who stopped her for a moment.

"There you are, Reneé. How is it going? Are we making any progress on the boy's disappearance? He is an important witness in our case," said Björn.

"We're going off to a camp where we think a man named Gabor can stay," she said.

"Possible. We know that he has met the boy at Åhléns. Reasonably he should know a little more that can help us further with the search."

The prosecutor looked at Perla and the interpreter standing behind Reneé while George came behind and stopped at them.

"Okay, we'll have a briefing tomorrow. Call me if there is anything special," Björn said and left.

Reneé looked at George.

"Let's do this, you arrange reinforcement and the interpreter and the girl can go with us," Reneé suggested.

George nodded and walked away while calling the radio center. After the call, he came back and walked past Reneé.

"We can go down to the garage and meet up with the colleagues who are going along," he said as he walked towards the elevator.

Reneé explained to Perla and the interpreter what would happen next. Before Reneé and the party could arrive, George had already entered the elevator and shouted: "I'll go ahead and prepare a little."

Chapter 33

27 SEPTEMBER 2014

With some irritation after spending hours in queues on the E4, Ali approached Sparreholm in his taxi. Thoughts drifted as to why Mustafa had to meet this late afternoon. It had been important and taking it over the phone was out of the question, so Ali had to get in the car and drive there. He could at least rejoice that he had more information about Chris Sjögren-Lester, something Mustafa would certainly appreciate.

Suddenly, Ali had to brake sharply so as not to miss the entrance to the yellow house that was on the right side. He parked behind a dark Mercedes 500, a slightly older model and got out of the car. When he heard Mustafa's voice behind him, he jumped terrified.

"Good that you came, let's go in," Mustafa said, walking towards the house.

After placing the children's downstairs in the basement, they could sit down on the sofa in the living room. Mustafa informed Ali that Hadishe was no longer there but had gone home. Instead, it was a younger girl from Iraq who took over the care of the children. She was currently in the kitchen making Arabic coffee to serve with some snacks, and Mustafa wanted to hold off on the meeting until she had served them.

When Flowing, Hadish's replacement, had served coffee and Mutabbaq, a bread filled with Mea, she had to go down to the children in the cellar.

"Tomorrow we'll pick Jacob up and bring him here," Mustafa said, taking a sip of his coffee. Ali looked at him in surprise.

"Wait, I need to tell you. I got Jacob's father as a customer today and drove him from Karolinska Institute to Åhléns in Stockholm city. He is a fan professor and has worked for the U.S. Army. He can pay well, if you know what I mean," Ali said, showing the photo of his driver's license with his mobile phone.

Mustafa looked at Ali with a serious look, then a slight smile came.

"Good job. I have also done research on the father, a remarkably interesting man I must say. We will have use of him."

"Ah, you're going to take the boy hostage," Ali said with a mocking smile.

Mustafa shook his head.

"No, not really. We will recruit him to the fraternity. He will be the first Christian brother of Islam on earth. He will understand."

"Now I don't understand," Ali said before taking a bite of his mutabbaq.

"The most important thing is that Jacob understands my mindset and my action."

"Is he going to be a soldier and a faithful Muslim, is that what you're saying?"

"I will tell you more in a while. Drink up the coffee while it is still hot. When does Yasmin start work tomorrow?"

Most of the individuals who come to Sweden and beg on the streets are already marginalized by society, regardless of whether they had stayed in their home country, ended up in another European country or come here to Sweden. A substantial proportion are Roma from Romania and belong to one of society's most discriminated and marginalized groups, individuals who do not have basic civil rights even in their own country. For them, begging is a desperate attempt to support themselves and the families who often remain in their home country and live well below the poverty line. Children and family are often left behind in their home country.

Chapter 34

27 SEPTEMBER 2014

George drove behind a police car out of the garage. With him sat Reneé, Perla and the interpreter. In the police car in front were two uniformed colleagues. From St. Eriksgatan you turned onto Fleminggatan in the direction of Kungsbron. George and Reneé saw that some kind of discussion was taking place between the police colleagues in front of them. When they turned left onto Kungsholmsgatan towards Klarabergsgatan, Perla told them that she could not find her way to the camp by car because she had only taken the commuter train there. Reneé called the colleagues in front and told them that there had been a slight problem and that they needed to stay.

Both police cars drove into the parking lot at the entrance to the train station and stopped. Reneé turned to Perla and her interpreter.

"You can stay here while we go out and talk to our colleagues," Reneé said and got out of the car with George.

They met the police colleagues who looked dejected. Reneé had to explain that the Roma girl could not show where she lived because she had only taken the train and got off at a station she recognized. From there she had gone to the camp.

She had never travelled by car to and from the camp.

"Well, what the hell are we doing now?" asked George, looking at Reneé with a surprised expression on his face.

"Obviously, someone has to ride the train to camp with her," Reneé noted.

The two police colleagues held up their arms in protest. They did not intend to travel alone with the girl and the interpreter, neither by commuter train nor by subway. That was out of the question. Reneé sighed with the sudden realization that the police academy needed to cull a little harder during the admissions. You must find people who at least want to work. She turned to George.

"No, forget it. I am not going to go..." George managed to say before Reneé took the floor.

"We'll go with both of them, then one of these gentlemen will drive our car," Reneé said, pointing to his colleagues.

Reneé walked up to the police car and asked Perla and the interpreter to get out. Together with them, she walked up to George who shook his head. He handed the car keys to one of his colleagues, who accepted them with a small smile.

"I don't want to see that fucking grin from your head again," said George and started walking.

Reneé and George walked just behind Perla and the interpreter down the stairs towards the subway.

"Well, then it will be an exciting trip underground," said George to break the silence.

Reneé did not answer, but just gave him a serious look.

At the security guard, they showed their police IDs, informed them that they were on business and that both ladies were in company. When they arrived at one of the platforms, it turned out that they were going to take the green line T119 south. Reneé called his colleagues.

"Hey, we're going to Farsta. It is just for you guys to go. I'll call when we get to the station."

Reneé hung up when a train stopped at the platform. At the front train carriage, George and Reneé sat down and straightened their jackets to hide the service weapons. Perla and the interpreter sat down opposite them.

When they had stopped at eleven stations and approached the next station, Perla got up. She looked at George and Reneé, who also stood up. They got off at Högdalen station and Reneé took out his mobile phone to update his colleagues.

After going through the centre of Högdalen, they were heading towards the industrial area where Perla turned off onto a small gravel road.

Reneé called his colleagues and gave them detailed instructions on how to drive. According to the interpreter, there were only about a hundred meters left to walk up to the camp. After fifteen long minutes, they saw the lights of two cars driving towards them. After a request from Reneé, Perla and the interpreter got into the police car while George and Reneé got into their police car.

"So, this is where they are," said George as he looked out the side window and saw a subway train leave a subway depot behind the edge of the forest.

"The camp should be along this forest road," Reneé replied as George drove slowly after the police car in front.

She got to see the outline of the camp, which was lit up by two campfires. It was a sight that made her lose concentration for a moment.

"Oh my God, is the boy here?" she exclaimed with a single breath.

The camp consisted partly of old dilapidated caravans, self-made wooden sheds whose building materials came from the nearby recycling station. Even an old crew shed on wheels stood in the center of the camp and was partly lit up by the glow of the campfires.

George and Reneé got out of the car at the same time as their colleagues, Perla, and the interpreter. Two elderly women dressed in worn clothes approached Perla and the interpreter. George and Reneé walked over to introduce themselves. When the older women realized that these visitors that Perla had dragged with her were from the police, loud complainants came in varying tones. Perla was soon seen as the odd one out in the presence of the moment, something that made everyone in the camp come forward.

The uniformed police began to walk around the camp to search for Jacob. Reneé and George approached Perla and asked her to show him where Gabor lived. She walked through the crowd towards the old crew shed, stopped at the door, and pointed. George walked up to the door and knocked. Inside, a loud coughing was heard that turned into a hoarse husky voice calling out in Romanian; "Who the hell is that?"

Perla shouted that the police wanted to talk to him. There was complete silence in the crew shed. The silence was interrupted by a squeaky bed, then a few stacking footsteps stopped at the rotten wooden door. It slowly opened and a shard of glass from a broken window fell to the ground. A rickety old man appeared in the doorway with tired and worn eyes. From inside came an unpleasant smell. George backed up two steps as Reneé walked up to him and the doorway as she motioned for the interpreter to come forward.

"Ask if he's seen this boy?" asked Reneé as she held up the photo.

The interpreter turned nervously to the man and translated Reneé's question. Gabor stepped forward and looked at the photo in surprise. He nodded while pointing frantically at the photo.

"That sling tried to take over my territory," he said in a hoarse voice before another coughing attack came.

The interpreter translated for Reneé and George, while the camp residents gathered behind them in a semicircle.

"Is the boy here?" asked George.

"No, no. I have sold him to the wolves," Gabor said with a twinkle in his eye, showing a toothless smile.

The interpreter looked at him in horror and then translated. George quickly became annoyed with Gabor and his grinning, snatched the photo from Reneé's hand and walked up the step. He grabbed the torn flannel shirt with his fist and held up the photo with his other hand in front of Gabor's face with a particularly black look.

"We'll take this one more time. If I get the wrong answer, can you ride with us in the trunk, understood? Where is the boy?"

"How am I supposed to know? I chased him away from the store, since then I have not seen him. Tell the bastard to drop my clothes, or it will be a shopping trip at Dressmann and his wallet will foot the bill," Gabor said, giving him a toothless smile with bad breath.

The moment the interpreter was about to translate, a teenage boy came rushing with an axe at the ready from the pitch-black darkness that surrounded the camp and was heading towards George.

George pulled out his service weapon and aimed at the boy who stopped abruptly and slowly lowered the axe to the ground. Reneé kept a firm grip on the butt of the gun and was prepared to pull the weapon.

"Good that you stayed," George informed the boy and gave the interpreter a quick glance.

Terrified, she frantically rattled off the translation as two police officer walked over and took the axe from the boy. Gabor gave the boy a tired look, and then shook his head.

"Let's try again. Has the boy been here in the camp?" asked Reneé.

Gabor shrugged and shook his head.

"The boy has never set foot here, I swear by my mother's grave," he said, putting his right hand to his chest. "I didn't really understand that the boy was missing when I made fun of myself at your expense. I apologize," he said with a downcast look.

Why does a little suburban kid have such a head start? What is it that makes him flee and hide? How can a child just disappear? Reneé thought.

A little girl, barely four years old, strutted a little unbalanced up to Reneé. The girl raised her arms to her, wanting to be lifted. Then she lowered her right upper arm to wipe the snot from her nose and a yellow quivering string fasting to her shirt sleeve. Reneé crouched down to lift the girl up when Perla suddenly came and lifted the girl into her arms and backed up two steps. She gave Reneé a serious look that made her lose her smile and meet Perla's serious gaze.

"Money can't buy everything," Perla said.

Reneé held Perla with her gaze as she took out a piece of newsprint from her pocket and wiped the snot off the little girl.

"But my God, I would only lift her up because she wanted to. I am not going to buy her," Reneé said, finding the situation both abstract and embarrassing.

"Anything else you wanted?" asked Perla, staring at Reneé and George.

Reneé shook his head. "No, we're done here. Gabor has probably told me what he knows about the boy we are looking for and I trust him."

"What happens now? Will you come tomorrow and chase us out of our home?" said Perla, making a waving gesture of powerlessness.

Reneé looked questioningly at George and then at the two uniformed colleagues standing next to the teenage boy.

"Neither I nor my colleagues will make any kind of eviction or complaint against you so that you are forced to move. But I would like to inform you that the landowner or the municipality can request aid from the Swedish Enforcement Authority and then you will have to move. We are done here now," she said informatively.

Reneé headed for the car and George walked right behind along with his two police colleagues. Behind them, all the camp's Roma followed, except for Gabor. He stood there watching with a victorious face. He understood very well that this would not be the last visit from the authorities.

Reneé's hopes of finding Jacob had been dashed, but she could not help but smile at the thought of Jacob competing with Gabor for public money. She shook her head when she thought about it, what a cheeky boy anyway. When she reached the car, she turned around and waited for the others.

George was less amused by this visit to the Roma, it felt a little uncomfortable with the peloton walking behind him, where there was a little giggle and short conversations in Romanian. As usual, he thought. His thoughts turned to another hypothesis when he began to analyze the facts that had appeared in this case. Something was not right. There was no doubt that the boy's parents were very much in the minds of the Pentecostals from Knutby. Moreover, Moa engaged in some way given her presence, he thought. Wait, was there another sexual theme in this investigation? If you looked back at what happened in Knutby, it turned out that that priest had ravaged both nannies and neighbor's wives in God's name before it became locked up for life at Kumla. A sweet tooth that priest, who undeniably had strong dominance over the sect. Then there was Moa, who inherited the entire clergy after Pentecostal pastor. She, too, cuckooed like a rabbit, he thought and smiled as the memories began to clear up in his mind.

Could it be that the kid had been sexually abused before he met this fucking chief doctor? Possible. If so, was that the reason the boy stayed away and sought out men, to whom he sold both his body and soul? To find the boy, the truth must be told, either in an interrogation room or during a confession, he said when he arrived at the car.

Chapter 35

28 SEPTEMBER 2014

During the night it rained continuously. It continued into the early morning, making it even harder to get out of bed. Chris noted that he had woken up before half an hour and let his tired gaze rest on Linda as she lay next to her with her back to him. He stretched out his arm and let it rest over her waist, waiting for a reaction.

Linda, who was already awake, took his arm and pulled it up to chest height, then put her arm over his and hugged it. She had an enormous longing for Jacob and a longing for Chris' physical and mental closeness that long loomed in her mind. She felt the marriage showed a tendency to crumble with Jacob's disappearance. It was a guilt she was carrying, considering she let Jacob go that morning. A guilt that Chris also burdened her with through silence and an increasing rejection of her. The desire to express herself freely about her bleeding feelings, to scream swearing and use coarse power expressions that make the hair on the back of our neck stand up on our creator, was within her. It was a rage that had to be let out. In addition, she had also sinned in God's presence so badly that the damage was already a fact. Any profanity to or from was irrelevant given her earlier dealings with Moa.

"Are you awake, honey?" asked Chris with a yawn.

"Do you have to go to London?" asked Linda.

"We must seize this opportunity. What if the girl has developed antibodies after surviving the worst crisis? We have a mutual agreement on who would be home. It worked," Chris noted.

Linda pushed his arm away and got out of bed.

"Work takes precedence over our son and me," Linda said bitterly. "What else is going before us?" she added, turning to Chris who had gotten out of bed.

"We must not think like that. God has given us two trials of life that we must solve. And you know I will come as soon as something happens. Jacob is alive, which means God is with him. He is in someone's house, I am absolutely convinced of that," he said without any hesitation.

"Oh my God! Now, if he is at someone's house, why is no one calling? Why isn't Jacob calling?" asked Linda in despair. "Do you have any fucking idea how painful this is?" she exclaimed, biting her tongue hard as she blamed herself for her verbal abuse and profanity.

Chris gave her a glance. Without saying anything, he left the bedroom.

"No, sorry I didn't mean..." Linda excused herself and rushed after.

Not much was said during the drive to Arlanda. Linda, who was driving, looked alternately at the road and at Chris who was sitting next to her, fingering the plane ticket. The noise of the road and the silence between them suffocated her and her thoughts. They passed by the Märsta exit. The rain had once again begun to patter on the windscreen when a yellow 020 taxi overtook it.

* * *

Ali stopped with his taxi at terminal five at Arlanda. After taking payment, he got out of the car and during the passing he opened the back door to the customer before opening the tailgate. He picked up an empty luggage cart that was standing a few feet away. Just behind, a Mercedes had just stopped and a light blonde woman got out and walked around the car. From the passenger side, a tall, slender man got out of the car while the woman took out a smaller suitcase from the back seat and handed it to the man.

Ali walked with the luggage cart to his taxi where the customer was waiting. While loading two large suitcases onto the baggage cart, he looked at the couple standing by the white car. He got the impression that there was a chilly relationship between them. He wished the customer, who was on his way with the luggage trolley towards the terminal, a pleasant trip. He stayed standing and saw the couple standing and hugging. When the man turned to walk away, he recognized him. There is the American man I drove from Karolinska Institute to Upplands Väsby, it was his son who had disappeared, Ali thought and shrugged. He got in the car and was about to leave when the white Mercedes combi drove by.

* * *

Linda felt within herself that this parting with Chris was uncomfortably cold when she started driving. Anxiety stuck in my throat. It was that feeling that made her look towards the entrance for a moment and see her husband hugging a woman. She had to look at the road again, but after passing a yellow taxi parked, she looked towards the entrance again and braked. Now she saw that that woman was his assistant

Nettan Gustavsson, why should she? she thought as the yellow taxi honked behind her. She reacted at once, made a strong start and drove away.

So, the little sensual Miss Puma is going with her to London ... with my husband. Not a word had he said, not even a shred of it. You do not have to be a rocket scientist to understand that it was not just about antibodies.

As she approached the Stockholm slip road, she flashed right but changed her mind when she saw the sign Almunge and instead drove straight ahead. When she reached the roundabout, she turned left and drove towards Trosta. When she passed Lake Arlanda, she looked at her mobile phone. Would she send a text or just call? Say what?

* * *

Reneé was lucky when she found a vacant parking space on Storgatan just outside Hedvig Eleonora church during the morning. She had seen the main entrance to the congregation as she drove past and knew where to go. When she arrived at the entrance, she looked at the large brick-colored church. It was there that Jacob had stayed when the chief theologian Christina Grenholm had met him, she thought as she walked through the entrance to the parish office.

She entered a hall where Christina met her, dressed in the usual priestly robe and a warm smile. Christina led the way to her office, which was to the right of the hall. When they had sat down on either side of the desk, Reneé was once again greeted by a smile from Christina.

"Great that you could come. I was worried when I read the article in the newspaper and of course called right away," she said as she put her hand on her chest. "Have you found him?"

"No, unfortunately, but after the newspaper published the article, there have been some tips, including your observations.

You said it was the twenty-fourth you met him?"

"That's right, four days ago. I had a brief little errand at church when we bumped into each other at the entrance to the church hall. A cute boy," she added, smiling.

"Then what did he say?"

"Oh, the little modest kraken apologized that he accidentally collided with me at the doorway. Then he asked for a toilet and we went here to the congregation."

"How long was he here?"

"He was in the toilet for a long time and after reading this gruesome article, of course I understand why. It is terrible what has happened. You really mean you have not found him?"

"I think my visit should demonstrate that. Did he get anything to eat or drink? What did he say before leaving?"

"He said he would go to our church and pray. He had been subjected to ... yes what did he say... atmospheric disturbances," Christina said, laughing. "Absolutely wonderful boy. Can also say that our caretaker had to try when there was a stop in the toilet. The boy had accidentally flushed down quite a lot of paper napkins."

"Wow!" said Renéé, laughing. "Did you see him anymore after he left?"

Christina shook her head. "No, he wasn't at church when I went there."

Reneé stood up and thanked him for the information. When she reached the doorpost, she turned around, walked over to Christina, and handed over a business card.

"Take this in case he reappears. The boy is a believer and there is a possibility that he might turn to you again."

"Thank you. Yes, absolutely, I'll get back to you right away if I see him."

Reneé smiled and thanked me. She walked away as she took out her phone from her jacket pocket. There was nothing to go on here either, the boy was plastered.

Chapter 36

28 SEPTEMBER 2014

Yasmin sat at the kitchen table dressed in cozy clothes and flipped back to the center spread of yesterday's paper. She had read the article about Jacob's disappearance and got it confirmed that he had been the victim of a vile pedophile, and that the police were looking for him about it. What was said nothing, however, was the fatal death of the boy. Had she missed it? She read the body text one more time, but no, nothing. She folded the newspaper and hid it in the bottom of a paper bag filled with newspapers and advertisements.

I do not think Jacob made that up with the dead boy. She got up and went to the living room. There on the couch Jacob sat curled up, dressed in his new pajamas with teddy bears and watching television. She sat down next to him and wrapped a light blue blanket around them. Jacob leaned against her chest and gave her a hug while his concentration was partly directed at the television screen.

She gave him a kiss on the forehead and hugged him tightly. What should I *do now, should I contact the police? Wondering if Jacob will find his way back to the address where Lars lives?*

Yasmin clenched her left hand under the blanket.

Jacob looked at her questioningly. "You believe in God, don't you?"

Yasmin let go of her thoughts and smiled, "I believe in my God, Jacob."

"Can you change God if you want to? Just to give it a try, I mean."

Yasmin hugged him and smilingly caressed his head.

"Of course, you are allowed to do it. That's up to you."

"Okay! Then I want to believe in the same God as you."

Yasmin looked at him with an intense gaze as she held his cheeks with both hands. "Jacob, I love you so much," she said in a broken voice, trying to hold back tears.

Jacob hugged her tightly as a few tears streamed down his cheek.

"I love you too," he said, unable to hold back the crying.

Yasmin continued to hold him and cried. She had found herself in a new world when Jacob came into her life. A child she was willing to sacrifice herself for if necessary. God had blessed her by giving her the gift of life because she could not have children of her own after that fatal miscarriage while fleeing to Sweden.

She lifted his chin and gave him a warm and loving look.

"Would you like lunch?"

Jacob nodded. Yasmin stood up and reached out to him. He took it as he stood up and stood in front of her with a questioning look as he pulled out his pajama shirt with both hands.

"Yasmin. I am ten years old and about to turn eleven," Jacob muttered, a little embarrassed.

Yasmin closed her eyes as she closed her mouth with both hands to hide her smile while holding back her laughter.

"Oh sorry, honey. I did not think twice. I just wanted to..." She shrugged and together they went to the kitchen.

While she was pouring water into a saucepan, the cell phone on the kitchen table rang. She quickly set the pan on the stove to the highest heat before hurrying to the kitchen table and answering.

"Yasmin."

"It's Ali. When should I pick you up?" "I'm not going to work today," she replied.

"Why? You work all the time, why don't you work today?"

"Why do you ask?"

"I'm just wondering," he replied with a spontaneous tone in his voice. "How is Jacob?"

"He's fine," she replied, starting to get suspicious.

"Is that why you don't work?"

"You ask too many questions."

"Your mother, is she okay? Is she home?"

"What are you after?" asked Yasmin irritably.

"Nothing Yasmin, nothing. Why are you talking so hard to me? I want you as my wife and mother to my children. Are you going to work tomorrow? I can drive you."

"I'm going to work tomorrow. You can pick me up at one o'clock."

"I'm coming to the boom, are you sure you're going to work tomorrow?"

"It was a lot of nagging," Yasmin said, hanging up with a deep sigh.

She looked at Jacob who was sitting at the kitchen table and had followed the conversation with Ali. He looked like a small question mark. "Jacob, may I ask you something?" asked Yasmin.

Jacob nodded with a smile.

"Do you remember where this Lars lives?" she asked as she leaned over the kitchen table and took his hand.

"129 The Shepherd Road," he replied with an anxious look. "Could it have been Valhto Road 129, maybe?" asked Yasmin.

"Yes! That is how it was called. It was a long park with parking in the middle," Jacob explained.

"Thank you, honey, you're my treasure," she said, giving him a kiss on the forehead.

* * *

At a roadside barrier in Flemingsberg, a taxi was parked. In the car, Ali was sitting with Mustafa, and both looked pensive. The news that Yasmin had suddenly taken time off work was not what Ali had expected when he put away his mobile phone.

"Well, are you going to drive her?" asked Mustafa.

"There was a little change of plans. We must do this tomorrow," Ali replied, feeling a little stupid after promising a little too much.

"Changed plans! What is going on?"

"She's home today with the boy. Going to work tomorrow and have ordered me to pick her up at one o'clock tomorrow afternoon."

Mustafa thought and tried to change his planning. He gave Ali an annoyed look as he took out his cell phone to make a call. During the conversation, it appeared that the person he was talking to could spare another day, which saved Mustafa's schedules and he became very humble in tone.

"Okay, I've bought another 24 hours and we have to get there by one o'clock in the afternoon the day after tomorrow. Everything must come together. Have you had contact with Hadishe?"

"Everything is ready. I'm going to Märsta tonight and pick up two more."

"I'll go with you," Mustafa said firmly.

"But, you don't have to..."

"No buts, I'll go with you."

Ali shrugged, started the car, and drove away.

"Tomorrow we'll pick up the bus," Mustafa said.

"I don't know if it'll be ready then," Ali excused himself nervously.

"Tomorrow it's ready. It is your job to make sure of that," Mustafa clarified firmly with a serious look. "The day after tomorrow, the container will be fully loaded and everything in place. Have you got hold of Remeron?"

"Have put a pack in the house," Ali replied as he drove.

"Good. Call Hadishe and tell him we're on our way."

Chapter 37

28 SEPTEMBER 2014

IT WAS A concerned Reneé sitting at her desk looking at the missing child cases on her desk. All but one were refugee children and in some cases some of them disappeared just days after being placed in the detention centre. She noted that refugee children had disappeared earlier, but not to this extent. Was it organized? By whom and in what way? They had no passports, which meant that they had been smuggled out of the country.

There was a knock on the door that opened instantly. George stepped in while straightening his bangs. He sat down in front of the desk and placed one leg over his lap.

"I've talked to Chris Sjogren-Lester on the phone. He is in London and cannot take part in any interrogation tomorrow."

"Do you really think Jacob is staying away from his dad? It feels so far away," Reneé said as she looked up from the folders.

"Don't forget the statistics, Reneé. Most child abuse occurs within the family or by close acquaintances. A bit rough actually," George stated.

"He is committed and emotionally affected by Jacob's disappearance. The same goes for the mother. You must not forget that they are believers and involved in church activities", recalled Reneé with a faint feeling that she could be wrong. "I've talked to some of the Pentecostal church in Upplands Väsby, who confirms that the parents are very concerned about Jacob and basically do everything for the boy. But, as you are trying to Imply, it is no guarantee that there has been nothing improper within the family," she added with a resigned gesture with her arms.

"You forgot an important detail, namely the Knutby gang. That is what made me a little curious about my father. He, like our man in custody, is a doctor. In addition, you can add another piece of the puzzle, namely Moa, who seemed incredibly involved in Jacob's disappearance. A little too committed may seem, if you ask me."

"In theory, I can buy to suspect the father of sexual assault. But to suggest or believe that half of the Pentecostal movement in Knutby is pedophiles, then you really must shake out convincing evidence that can support it. The fact that they then jump into bed with each other when liking arises is not illegal unless it is sexual assault. It is more of a question of a moral report," Reneé said.

"I have taken a closer look at the closed case regarding the nanny and the barge Ragnar, and talked to the colleague who investigated the matter in Uppsala. Yes, we worked together then. There were two essential factors in this matter, namely sex and power play under the banner of God's will. Who were the main players in that gang, yes - Ragnar and Moa", George stated.

"What about the nanny?"

"Some of Ragnar's trophies in God's will. He was on every wife in the whole district and the younger age the more exciting it became for him. Moa had or has similar inclinations except that they were young men who, in the legal sense, if you ask me, had passed the age of fifteen, anyway. Of course, it is evil tongues that spread the rumors, I am fully aware of that", said George with a sarcastic smile.

"Your theory, then, is as follows; Jacob may have been involved in yet another pedophile ring before Lars-Åke came into the picture, were

The father and Moa may have a strong connection as main actors. This is fucking far-fetched."

"It's a theory worth spinning on. This is one of the reasons why Jacob hides and at the same time seeks out men with money to survive and get a roof over his head. Men who get hallelujah moments with the kid for payment... What is your theory?"

Reneé showed seven photos, six children with a foreign background and one with a Swedish background, then presented the photos on the edge of the desk. George studied them and then looked at Reneé.

"Do you really think there's any connection between these kids and Jacob?"

"The only thing I know is that they all disappeared in the space of two weeks," she replied with a sigh. "But as I said, it's not impossible that there's a connection."

"I can agree with the trafficking theory when it comes to these children," said George and held up photos of all the children except Jacob. Reneé nodded.

"We are talking about children who are without identities and virtually risk-free to sell in the prostitution market or in the illegal labor market. Jacob, on the other hand, is a White boy with an identity. Placing him with a bunch of dark children is a huge exposure and quite a risk. Take a white chess piece and place it with the opposing side," George said, reaching out to Reneé.

"You're talking about exposure and risk-taking. So, it is less likely to sexually assault a 'White boy' within Sweden's borders?" asked Reneé.

"The answer to that question is yes. Here, the children are manipulated and the abuse usually takes place within the family or in closed company, like what exists in Knutby. There is no transparency and the times when the abuse occurs in the public sphere.

Light is when victims have talked or been found worm-eaten in a grove of trees."

"Sometimes you're so charming with your verbal expressions," Reneé sighed. "After all, there is a risk in these cases as well."

"Yes, of course it is, but the risk is significantly smaller. Let us take a particularly good example like the Catholics in Vatican City. There they put on the whole boys' choir. The abuse took place under God's presence and forgiveness and was then leaked to the media and the public. The Pope..."

"Stop! Now you are out spinning," Reneé protested.

George smiled when he found her pain threshold as he leaned against the backrest of the chair.

"Don't be so damn sensitive. I was not going to say that the Pope puts children on, I just wanted to mention that he has heavy millstones resting on his shoulders. On the one hand, he will sort out this scandal internally and, on the other, try to mitigate the damage that has been inflicted on the Catholic Church and its office since the rumors."

George got up from his chair. "Should we take the father in for questioning when he comes home from London? Or should we let our London colleagues arrest our doctor before he gets the brilliant idea to go to that Julian Assange at the Ecuadorian embassy?"

"Nope! Do not start anything now. How long have you been laying on these wild speculations? Do you sleep at night?" asked Renéé.

He pulled on his smile and walked towards the door. "Well, by the way, I asked Chris when he thought he could show up at home, something he had trouble answering," said George and raised his eyebrows.

He opened the door and walked out then turned around, gave Reneé a glance and smiled before closing the door shut. Out in the hallway, he shouted, "It was just purely informative, Reneé."

She gave the door a glance when the phone rang.

Chapter 38

28 SEPTEMBER 2014

The fog had settled over the fields when a dark blue taxi whose light tried to penetrate the fog in the darkness slowly traveled on Kolstavägen at Arlanda. Ali had previously visited the area and selected a suitable pick-up point about two hundred and fifty meters from the escape facility. It was in the old premises of the rescue school that they conducted operations and at the same time-shared premises with the Attunda fire department. The meeting point was at a radio mast station belonging to the Civil Aviation Administration and was found on a dirt road. Beyond was a forest glade and on the other side of the gravel road was a red old abandoned wooden house where the fire brigade had their fire drills.

As Ali and Mustafa approached the entrance to the escape facility, Ali pointed to the building and continued onto a small dirt road. They drove through a small farm and followed the road into a sparser forest glade. There were some detached houses that were not blacked out.

"Is this?" asked Mustafa, looking at the lighted houses where people were home.

"No, we're going further away," Ali said, slowly driving on.

The road continued past some older houses before arriving at the turnpike at the radio mast station. Ali made a U-turn and stopped. Outside, it was completely pitch black except for the lighting at the airport terminals several hundred meters away. Mustafa looked around but could not perceive any movement in the dark. One perfect setting for an unexpected ambush, he thought with a slight shiver.

"No one is here," he said impatiently.

"They're coming," Ali said. "Wait."

Ali got out of the car and disappeared into the darkness while Mustafa looked after him. After about two minutes, he saw some movement away at the old, dilapidated house. The back doors opened and two underage girls wearing face disguises got into the car. Behind them was Hadishe urging them to get further into the back seat so that she could fit in. She pulled the car door shut with a bang. Ali had gotten behind the wheel and now hurriedly turned around and glared angrily at Hadishe.

"You're not in some fucking market square in Baghdad. There are people living here idiot," he hissed.

Mustafa looked up at the roof of the car with a resigned look and at the same time stretched out his arms. Then he slapped Ali. "Run for fuck!"

He started the car and drove away slowly. After driving past two houses, Ali turned right onto another small forest road that led right into the woods.

"Why this way?" asked Mustafa.

"It's better and faster to the highway," Ali said as they were about to pass a lonely house on the right with two parked cars and a rear loader.

Ali stopped and looked in amazement at the elderly man who appeared in the car's headlights with one hand raised as a stop mark. The man started walking towards them along with a dog. Ali turned off the engine but left the dipped beam on.

"Keep him busy," Mustafa said, disappearing silently from the car.

Ali hoisted down the side window a few inches. A rough-hewn face appeared and had a strikingly angry look. The little girls in the back seat moved closer to Hadishe and pressed themselves against her.

"This is not a fucking public road. The road is mine!" hissed the man, his breath reminiscent of an old liquor factory.

"Sorry, I've gotten a little lost. Can I get out to the main road from here?" asked Ali with a strained smile as he tried to see where Mustafa went.

"You should not drive..." The man did not have time to say more before a gurgling sound rose from his throat and blood oozed from his mouth. The tip of a knife stuck out through his throat.

Ali looked at the grinning expression on his face in horror. The man's eyes were about to leave his eye sockets before he collapsed next to the car with a loud thud. Ali turned and looked at the girls who were huddled together. He looked out the side window, hoping to catch a glimpse of Mustafa. Instead, he watched as the body was pulled from the car and disappeared across the road in the dark. He heard footsteps stopping. Seconds later, another dog whined and it became deathly silent.

Diagonally in front of the car on the left side, Mustafa stepped out of the darkness and stood like a demon in front of the headlight. Demonstratively, he held up the man's head with his right hand and sneered before throwing it in the direction of the house. Mustafa crouched down and wiped his firsthand the grass next to the road before walking to the car and sitting on the passenger side. The car door closed again gently, only a slight popping sound was heard.

From the house, a creaking and squeaking sound could be heard from a door that opened. In the dim outdoor lighting, an elderly woman looked out.

"Martan! Do not get in. Where is the dog?" she shouted.

Suddenly, a black Labrador came up to the woman and licked frantically over her snout. The woman crouched down and discovered that the dog's nose and neck were permeated with something. With the palm of her hand, she rubbed her nose, then looked at her hand. It was fresh blood mixed with saliva. She stood up and looked questioningly out at the road and darkness.

"Martan. I think the dog has found some animal; he is completely smeared with blood. Where are you?" the woman shouted.

Mustafa folded up his butterfly knife and placed it on the floor mat before looking towards the back seat. The girls and Hadishe sat paralyzed and looked at him with horrified looks.

"When she goes in, you drive," Mustafa said, showing the direction with one hand. "Insha' Toh," he added.

They saw how the woman herded the dog into the house and how the door closed behind her. Ali started the car and silently rolled off on the dirt road. Hadishe looked out the car window and saw in the car's headlights the silhouette of his head lying on his side in the overgrown grass. She understood what Mustafa was going for with his grotesque display. It was a clear marking that no one in the car could misunderstand.

Mustafa passionately believed that sometimes a verbal exhortation was not enough to tighten up. You had to use some more tangible methods to get your message across. Where the very purpose of the deed could not be interpreted as anything other than a powerful marking. Sometimes you must be a little realistic, something Ali could sometimes ignore. It happened that you could obviously lose your head for a moment, Mustafa thought with a discreet sneering smile.

The Bible rejects homosexual behavior. The Bible says in Romans 1:26-27 "Therefore God gave them up to degrading passions. The women exchanged natural intercourse for unnatural intercourse, likewise men abandoned natural intercourse with women and were aroused by lust for each other, so that men fornicated with men. In doing so, they themselves incurred the proper punishment for their error."

Chapter 39

28 SEPTEMBER 2014

THE CLOTHES WERE scattered across the lacquered wooden floor in the bedroom. In bed, Linda was lying on her back with her hair spread across the pillow. In her right hand she held her panties and could not stand up. The body needed rest. Every now and then, tremors pierced her body, causing her skin to Knott again. Her stiff nipples were still sore. She looked to her left and found that the bed was empty. She must have fallen asleep for a while and not noticed when Moa got up. She saw a white remote lying on the bed next to the compressed duvet. She pressed the button on it and let her gaze rest on the TV that was sitting on the wall right in front of the bed but nothing happened, no picture, nothing. Instead, it began to buzz softly and vibrate in bed. She pressed the button again and the buzzing stopped. She pointed the remote straight at the TV and pressed the button again. The red light under the TV did not go out, but the buzzing began again. Linda put her hand under the covers and pulled out a vibrating dildo. She turned it off and was embarrassed because it reminded her of what they had done together. She changed position and felt pain in her lower abdomen. She looked at the turned off and nudged it. "This is your fault," she thought, smiling.

Out in the hall, she heard the toilet door open and a few tripping footsteps were heard. Immediately afterwards, Moa appeared in the doorway. She was dressed in a white, see-through negligee and her hair was still badly bruised. Linda studied her naked body through the white negligee.

Moa smiled as her head was tilted against the doorpost. She walked over to Linda, bent over her, and kissed her, finally nibbling on her lower lip. A warm, tingling sensation went through her body.

"I'm so sore," Moa said, kissing her again.

"Mmm, right for you," Linda replied, ending the kiss with a smile.

Moa knelt over Linda as she took off her negligee. Gently she sat over her belly and Linda spread her legs. She pushed the away and slowly began to massage Moa's breasts. Moa slowly leaned forward, over her, curling her breasts while letting her lower body slide down between Linda's legs. Slowly she rubbed against Linda's genitals and felt her teeth bite the nipple.

The Royal Free Hospital (also known simply as Royal Free) is an important teaching hospital in Hampstead, London. The hospital is part of the Royal Free London NHS Foundation Trust, which is a member of UCL Partners' Academic Health Sciences Centre and runs services at Barnet Hospital, Chase Farm Hospital, and several other locations. The Royal Free Hospital has a high-level isolation unit equipped to treat many infectious diseases such as Ebola virus. In 2014, British nurse William Pooley was successfully treated for Ebola virus at the unit. In December 2014, a British health worker named Pauline Cafferkey, diagnosed with Ebola in Glasgow, was taken to the unit for treatment.

Chapter 40

28 SEPTEMBER 2014

THE FLIGHT TO Heathrow went painless and since Chris and Nettan only had hand luggage with them, all that remained was the walk to the train terminal to take The Express Train to London. Taking a taxi from the airport would be unnecessarily costly, even if the WHO footed the bill. Chris instead chose to take a taxi from Airport Transfers in London when they arrived.

During the train journey, Chris sat across from Nettan. She looked through the window at the surroundings passing by while Chris studied her surreptitiously. She was an extremely attractive and attractive young lady with body shapes that even Tony Irving would fall for, despite his disposition. There were many hours of training with both gymnastics and martial arts behind her forms. That she was aware of her appearance was clear in her tight and challenging attire.

As she bent down to take a pen and notebook out of her bag, Chris could glimpse that she was wearing a thin, black lace bra. It was hard to take my eyes off the goodies, but the candy store closed again when Nettan stood up. She reached up to take her small suitcase off the shelf, and Chris's gaze fixed for a moment on her jeans-covered abdomen and thighs.

He took out his mobile phone from his jacket pocket to keep his brain busy with something other than his erotic fantasies when Nettan sat down and opened his suitcase. It was not really thought out to bring her along. She was an irresistible woman who was even considered lethal to men.

I must call Linda; he thought as he pulled out the number and put the phone to his ear. There were four signals without answer, the fifth signal did not sound out until someone responded with a quick, labored breathing, and then a groan was heard. Chris quickly looked at the display and realized that it was indeed Linda he called and put the mobile phone to his ear again. As he was about to say hello, he heard Linda whimper between breaths and it sounded like... as she would get one... orgasm! In the background, Moa's voice could be heard speaking in tongues and then shouting, "Come now, give me, give me your love for General. Oh!"

Chris sat with his mouth wide open and his eyes as big as saucers. He interrupted the conversation, wondering if he had really heard correctly. Where Is It Possible? Would Linda cheat on him? he thought when he suddenly felt a hand on his knee. He let go of his thoughts and looked at Nettan who was leaning forward towards him.

"Chris, has anything happened?" she asked with her hypnotizing blue eyes.

Chris squeezed out a smile that quickly subsided.

"Honestly... I do not know. My wife is having an affair," he said with some hesitation.

The train slowed down and a male voice announced that they had arrived at the Paddington terminus and the train stopped at the platform. Chris and Nettan got up, grabbed their hand luggage, and stepped out onto the platform.

Nettan came out through the main entrance and saw a black London taxi drop off a passenger. She rushed up to the driver and the car was indeed free. She put the bag in the back seat when Chris came out of the entrance with his bag. He looked around and saw Nettan waving to him from Taxi. He asked the driver to drive to the Holiday Inn Camden Lock Hotel.

* * *

Chris came into his hotel room, threw his hand luggage on the bed, and then sat down on a chair. Would he call Linda back? Why did she answer in the middle of a sex act? If it was, that is? Did she have sex with... Moa? Or was there a man in that sex? He did not hear a man's voice; it sounded more like it was her and Moa who lost themselves with each other. If that were the case, that she had sex with another woman, Moa to top it all, would he accept it?

The room phone rang. He turned and looked at it questioningly before answering. It was Nettan who wanted to remind him to call the Royal Free Hospital and at the same time suggested a late lunch before they left for the hospital. They agreed to meet downstairs at the reception in five minutes. After the call, he called Dr. Margret Johnson at the hospital. He was given a brief review of Audrey Limpton's continued overly critical health condition. They also went through the sample analyses that had been done and decided to meet in one and a half hours at the hospital.

At the reception, Chris and Nettan decided to skip the hotel restaurant and instead chose a smaller restaurant that was about five minutes' walk from the hotel. As they ate, Chris noticed that Nettan was studying him with a curious look. Just the thought of what could happen between them in a hotel room became tantalizing and enticing. She took two arugula leaves from the plate with her fingers and put them one by one in her mouth which she then chewed slowly, very slowly, while her secreting saliva moistened her lower lip before the tip of her tongue swept it away. Chris responded by taking two pieces of bacon with his fingers and putting them one by one in his mouth while chewing slowly. A little yolk happened to end up on the lower lip, which was then swept away with the tongue. Their eyes were etched on each other. Nettan smiled and turned a little embarrassed. Chris smiled as he stuffed a piece of rösti dipped in yolk into his mouth.

"We're here and now Chris," Nettan pointed out as she took off one shoe under the table and caressed his shins.

"I'm married," Chris reminded with a heavy sigh. "Besides, we have a job to do."

"I'm engaged. My guy should meet your wife. He has also been unfaithful at least a couple of times, they may have something in common. I heard that conversation and you couldn't misinterpret what was going on even if you tried."

"It was with a woman," Chris excused, as if to elicit a forgiving argument for the incident.

"And that would be an exception under the rules of infidelity, you mean?"

Chris took the last bite and put it in his mouth before putting the cutlery on the plate.

"Are there exceptions when it comes to fidelity and infidelity rules?" countered Chris as he chewed his food.

"Let me ask a counter-question instead. Is there a difference between having sex with a penis or with a dildo? From a moral perspective, I think," she asked with a twinkle in her eye. What did she want to get out now? Of course, there is a difference ... Or?

"I guess there's a difference," Chris replied uncertainly.

"Is it? Does your wife have a dildo?"

"Do I have to answer that question?"

"I have a dildo that I play with when the urge comes in," Nettan replied unabashedly.

"Okay, okay, there's an anonymous dummy in our bedroom." Nettan started laughing so that she had tears in her eyes.

"That sounded like her dresser is mined," she said as she grabbed a napkin and wiped the tears from her eyes. "Usually, she use it when you are not available as now, I mean the dummy then, loose, Nisse from Manpower?"

Chris gestured with his arms that he was fully aware of what she was referring to while looking around the guests embarrassedly.

"Stop, thank you, I understand what you're referring to. Well, at least I think she's used it."

I think, he says, it was good. You do in the church my dear Dr. Chris Sjögren-Lester. Wondering if the doctor's inhibitions are dropping in bed? He might be a real beast, this Hawkeye Pierce from M.A.S.H. Think how similar he is.

"We have to go now," Chris said. The clock became his salvation from the embarrassing topic of conversation.

"No, wait! I would like an answer to my question. Is it okay for your attractive wife to have sex with another woman?" repeated Nettan.

"There may be extenuating circumstances in that matter," Chris replied, rising from the table.

"Are there extenuating circumstances if you jump into bed with me?" asked Nettan, smiling.

"I never said that. Come, we'll have to take a taxi to get there on time."

* * *

The condition of Audrey Limpton was indeed critical inside the high-risk ward of the Royal Free Hospital. The latest values showed slightly better results than the earlier test, although marginally. Dr. Margret, Chris and Nettan passed through the security gate, each dressed in a certified class 4 safety suit. After them, two specialist nurses came and went through the same procedure.

Inside the high-risk room, Audrey was in a so-called security chamber consisting of a transparent security tent hanging from a white metal scaffold. The chamber itself had three pairs of plastic arms that were inserted into the arms to be able to collaborate safely with the patient. Next to it was a white worktable with similar security tents. Incidentally, the room gave a sterile impression. Even the ventilation was a closed system where the air passed through several special filters before being released into the open. The air pressure in the room was also high to avoid the spread of various infectious agents and to keep them at a low level in the room.

Chris and Nettan walked up to Audrey. Her face paint had a grayish-white tint and her lips a faint bluish color. Her eyelids began to move slightly, then her eyes slowly opened and looked straight up at the ceiling.

"Like I said before, it's very difficult to take samples because her veins don't hold," Margret said.

Chris nodded. "I need six tubes of blood plasma." "We managed to get two tubes and then we were lucky," said Margret.

"And no antibodies?" asked Chris.

Margret shook her head. "We also lose our body temperature."

"I suggest that we..." Chris said, then fell silent in thought. "No, we'll try below the neck," he added, tucking his arms into his protective sleeves.

He gently grabbed Audery's hand and held it. "Audrey, can you hear me?"

She turned her glassy gaze to him and nodded slowly.

"My name is Chris Sjögren-Lester and I'm from Sweden. I am going to stab you below your neck to hopefully get some blood out of you. You're very hard to sting."

Audrey squeezed his hand weakly to show that she heard, then she released her grip.

"Can I have a short cannula?" asked Chris, one of the assistant specialist nurses.

Nettan got ready by opening a smaller aluminum bag on the worktable next door. Chris pulled the cap off the needle and with one finger he felt Audrey's neck. Slowly he inserted the tip through the skin and the needle slipped in.

No blood came.

The statistics of the Finnish Immigration Service show that of all
In 1898 children who absconded in 2010-2015, only 12 percent were girls. However, the proportion of girls has decreased over the years; In 2010, girls accounted for 17 percent of the total number of absconding, but since 2012, the proportion of girls has been around 11 percent (9 percent in 2015). At the same time, more unaccompanied boys than girls apply for asylum, so in terms of the number of arrivals, an equal proportion of girls abscond as boys; a proportion corresponding to 3.5 per cent of the girls who have been asylum seekers and 3.6 per cent of the boys who have been admitted.

Chapter 41

29 SEPTEMBER 2014

It was eight o'clock in the morning when Linda was sitting at the kitchen table with a mug of coffee looking at a photo of Jacob. Her anxiety about his disappearance was always in her mind. Now the concern had increased even more about her husband. Why did she answer her phone in the middle of a sex act and let Chris hear what was going on? What was the purpose, to give back for infidelity? *What evidence do I have for that?* It was an innocent hug between two work colleagues who met at the airport. Chris had a cuddly personality; it was his charming way of welcoming people. The shame began to show its countenance when she came to the realization that she had no concrete evidence that Chris was cheating. It was a bout of jealousy based on Chris not having mentioned that Nettan was coming with him to London. If he then hugged her in public at the airport, he would be punished.

Linda placed the mug on the table and took the mobile phone. Suddenly, she realized that she had unknowingly given her husband a thorough reason to cheat on the handsome Nettan, given what he was told on the phone. He never called yesterday or last night either. She dropped the cell phone on the table. With a defiant attitude, she put her elbows down on the table and let her head rest on her hands. A remorseful, deep sigh was heard, and she just wanted to scream for help.

She glanced at the cell phone that was next to one of her elbows. Would she pluck up the courage to call him? Or even be honest and tell her that she suffered from a jealousy that was unfounded and then apologize for it? But if it turned out that Chris had had an affair with Nettan, would she accept it? She took the cell phone and called him.

Shortly thereafter, she put her cell phone back on the kitchen table and frowned. Chris's cell phone was not even turned on, only the answering machine was heard and she avoided leaving a message. *Did* he take such offense *at this stupid conversation that he does not want to talk to me, or is he sleeping with Nettan?* She looked at the clock that showed a quarter past eight. Could he and Nettan already be on a plane on their way home?

The phone rang. The display showed *Unknown number*, but Linda decided to answer anyway. "Linda."

"Good morning Linda, it's Detective Inspector Reneé Grahn. Am I interfering?"

"No, I sat in my thoughts as usual. Anything new about Jacob?"

"Sorry. I was going to ask you if Jacob has any friends who are foreign-born, from school or privately?"

"Not someone he hangs out with privately, but there are children who are foreign-born in the class," she replied, becoming a little pensive about the question. "Why do you ask?"

"No, we are looking for a possible connection between Jacob's disappearance and other missing children that we have on our table.

We are therefore toying with the idea that there may be a common explanation for these disappearances. All the children are in the same age group as Jacob with the difference that Jacob is Swedish-born and the others are foreign-born," Reneé said.

"Would it have any connection with Jacob's disappearance?"

"It may have. At least that's one of the hypotheses we're working on."

"What are the other hypotheses?" asked Linda.

"We can get into that a little bit later. I thought we would meet for some supplementation. Your husband is out of town, from what I understand."

"He's in London," Linda replied.

"When is he coming home?"

"Today or tomorrow. Why?"

"I just thought we could take this when your husband gets home," Reneé replied, getting the feeling that Linda was getting a little suspicious. Could there really be a chance that George was on the right track?

* * *

Shortly after ten, George came into Reneé's office and stood at her desk.

"We have a murder out at Arlanda. Technical is in place," he said.

Reneé looked up in surprise.

"I just received an email from my Arlanda colleagues about a report about two girls who had disappeared from a refugee facility near the airport. They did not mention anything about murder," Reneé noted, pointing to the computer screen.

"Okay, but I got information about the dark-skinned little girls who disappeared on the night the murder was supposedly committed. The body had been found early this morning about three hundred meters from the facility," said George.

"Are you trying to say there's a connection?"

"Not entirely unrealistic. Shall we go?"

Reneé got up from his chair and put on his jacket.

"I've also talked to Linda a bit. It feels like she is trying to hide something as soon as you mention her husband. Either way, she'd get in touch when he gets home."

George opened the door and walked out with Reneé. As they walked towards the elevators, he said, "As for Chris, I know he's on his way home. Lelle had checked it out."

"We're not going to meet him at Arlanda, we have other things to do now," Reneé said firmly, pressing the elevator button.

"It was just a thought that struck me," said George when the elevator doors opened.

"George, Gunvald, Lindmark," Reneé said with a bit of irony in her voice as she walked into the elevator.

"We don't need to go into superficialities," George replied and he stepped into the elevator.

"Lay down."

"You need to find your way to Jesus," commented George a little ironically as he put the key in the lock on the button panel and turned it over.

George turned off at the exit towards Arlanda Airport. After passing over the motorway and following the roundabout, they turned onto Kolstavägen. Arriving at the Attunda fire department and the escape facility, the road was cordoned off. At the entrance stood several curious children and young people.

"Well," said George as a uniformed policewoman walked towards their dark grey VW Passat.

She nodded when she saw George's service ID printed against the side window and walked over to lift the marking tape so that he could continue towards Kolsta farm.

Arriving at the crime scene, Reneé and George got out of the car. They looked around and could see that there was an older red dwelling house inside a worn and partly broken wooden fence. On the other side of the road was an open meadow field next to a planted spruce forest. A white tent had been set up about ten meters from the road out on the meadow, where the technicians were working at full speed. Reneé and George went there to gather more information.

George folded away the tent flap and looked inside. There, a technician squatted down and put something in a small plastic bag. Next to it was a body covered with a black tarpaulin. George asked the technician to lift the tarpaulin while Reneé stuck his head in it. They saw a body missing its head and was dressed in a brown woolen cardigan as well as a bloody flannel shirt and camouflage pants.

"Have you found the head?" asked George as he grimaced at the mere sight of the severed throat. He backed out of the tent to let the technician out.

"It's on the other side of the road to the house," the technician said, pointing to the house as he stepped out.

Reneé took two steps to the side as the technician came out of the tent. "Is this the crime scene?"

"No, we believe the crime happened on the road about eleven yards from here," the technician replied. "We have found a large pool of blood where we believe the victim was killed. Then there are larger blood trails as well as trails along this stretch."

"Are there traces of any kind of battle?" asked Reneé, taking three steps forward and looking into the tent.

"What we have found so far suggests more that the victim was probably taken by surprise. There are no stab wounds on the body itself or the clothes, no gunshot wounds for that matter. There are no skin fragments or other traces on either fingers or hands. However, the head has been cut off here and moved to the other side of the road. There are footprints of bloodshed that show that this may have happened."

Reneé walked up to George while looking around the surroundings.

"Was it the wife who found him?" asked the technician.

"She had gone out with the dog in the morning and found the head, the body we found. In the case of the dog, we found traces of blood on the fur and around the nose. We also found paw tracks and dog hair by the body."

"No injuries to the dog in general?" asked Reneé.

"No, no injuries. The dog was somewhere else in the surrounding area when the victim was attacked. Then the dog found the body lying there and probably tried to wake the victim by licking the body. We have found saliva on the body and on the head. Given the cut around the neck, it has been done with a sharp object or knife, like a scalpel but with thicker and longer knife blades. The coroner will have to clarify this." Reneé made a grimace as she looked away for a moment.

"Is the woman here?" asked George, looking towards the house.

"She's on her way to the hospital by ambulance."

"Should we look at the next body part?" asked George Reneé.

"Don't know, is it necessary do you think?"

"I don't need to see it. I have a clear picture of the situation," he said.

"Then we'll move on. Thank you," Reneé said to the technician, who shrugged and walked into the tent.

As they walked towards the car, they met a colleague from the Sollentuna police who came on foot and stopped at the company car to wait for them. The police colleague greeted them and introduced himself as Detective Inspector Jan-Ove Sandberg.

"So, you're already plugged in?"

"Initially, yes," Reneé replied. "We have talked a little with the technicians and have got a reasonable picture of what has happened."

"Then I don't need to mention that we found the head..."

"We are informed about that," said George. "Are there any other tracks?"

"The victim's wife mentioned that she had seen the taillights of a car going down there," Jan-Ove said, pointing to the dirt road. "In addition, a car has been parked on the road next to a large collection of blood."

“No license plate number or car make?” asked George.

“No, no license plate number or car brand. It was last night and it was dark when she saw the car between ten and eleven o’clock. She had called out to her husband just before, but only their dog came. Soon after, she found blood on the dog, but thought it had eaten some dead animal.”

“Probably that was the time when the victim was killed,” Reneé noted.

“We have secured car tracks from a passenger car so far.”

“I have a feeling that this is not some madman’s work, rather a pro, or what do you think?” said George to Reneé.

“It looks like that. The perpetrator sneaked up on the victim from behind and cut the aorta in his throat. Then he dragged his victim out into the meadow and removed his head from his body with two cuts. It is what I believe,” Reneé said,

“He?” said Jan-Ove, a little questioningly.

“Given the victim’s body size and height, there are few women who can do this physically,” George noted as he looked at Reneé.

“We have to make a joint effort on this. Send me a summary when you are done here”, Reneé told Jan-Ove. “We have to move on.”

* * *

Margaret Samuelsson, head of department at the refugee facility at Arlanda, was almost distressed after a personal meeting with the Migration Agency’s case officer. Two little girls from Sudan have disappeared from the ward. Hadishe had also disappeared in connection with it. This was the second time children had disappeared from the refugee facility within a month, which made the conversation with the Migration Agency's case officer even more difficult compared to the earlier visit.

The case officer from the Swedish Migration Agency had discovered by pure chance that Hadishe had substituted in both disappearances, which is why questions arose that Margaret could not answer. Now there were also police cordons in the immediate area due to a murder that had taken place on the same night as the girls disappeared. The murder meant that all children had to be kept under surveillance, and a curfew was decided as a safety measure.

There was a knock on the door. Margaret looked at it wearily and shouted at the visitors to come in,

whereupon George and Reneé stepped in. Reneé stepped forward and pre-while George was content to show his official ID.

"Sit down," Margaret said, trying to keep a good face as she made a hand gesture to the visitors' chairs in front of the desk.

"You know the reason for our visit, don't you?" said Reneé, pulling out a notebook.

Margaret nodded with a serious grin.

"The girls who disappeared yesterday," she replied.

"What time did they go out? Did they go out alone, or did they have some staff with them to watch over them?" asked Reneé.

"There was an assistant substitute called Hadishe who went out with the girls and it was around eight o'clock in the evening." "And where is she?" asked George.

"Don't know. She does not answer the phone and she is not here either, as she should be," Margaret said worriedly.

"So, she disappeared at the same time as the girls?" asked Reneé.

"All three are gone," Margaret said, shaking her head helplessly. "Could this have anything to do with that murder that happened last night?"

"Not what we know right now. It may be that they have seen something," said George and changed his sitting position.

"You don't think the girls committed the murder, do you?"

"There's nothing to suggest that anyway," Reneé said.

"This assistant, where does she live?"

"I think she lives somewhere in Skärholmen," said Margaret.

"She was a substitute, that's what you said, right?" asked George.

"Yes. Normally, she works at the refugee facility in

Fagersjö."

"Fagersjö! Children have disappeared there too," said Reneé.

Margaret nodded.

"In almost all cases in Fagersjö, Hadishe has worked. At the time of one of the disappearances, Hadishe had been out with the children and the boys had gotten lost at a subway station. At least that was her explanation, from what I have heard," she said.

"The children here, how were they dressed?" asked Reneé, pressing the tip of his pen against his notebook to write.

"One girl was dressed in a black robe and burqa and the other girl was dressed in almost the same costume, though the color was more brownish with a black burqa," Margaret explained, adding; "Do you want photos of the girls and names?"

"We already have. If you think of anything else or hear something, I would be grateful if you would get in touch," Reneé said and stood up.

"That also applies to murder," George added.

"Absolutely, if I hear something, I will of course get in touch."

Reneé and George thanked them and left.

***

George drove out onto the highway and gave Reneé a pensive look.

"Do you think the same as I do, about this Hadishe?" asked George as they passed Märstapåfarten towards Stockholm.

"In all the cases before me, Hadishe is named, except in Jacob's case. I find it hard to believe that it is due to coincidence."

"I think that Hadishe is a little mole. She supplies some person or gang with cubs that are then fed to pedophiles or other scum. At least she is involved because she has disappeared without a sound," George said as he winked for overtaking.

"I have a feeling that this bestial murder has something to do with the girls' disappearance. Both events took place at the same time and immediate area," Reneé noted. "I'm hungry," she added as she looked at the clock that showed a quarter past one in the afternoon.

George smiled. "Crap food at Donken up here, or should we afford a hearty lunch later on?"

Chapter 42

29 SEPTEMBER 2014

Chris and Nettan were in the plane that was on approach to Arlanda and had passed Stockholm hidden by clouds. While Nettan slept, Chris sat in deep pondering over the phone call with Linda during the morning. Already at the beginning of the conversation, he heard that it was not the same lovable Linda to which he was talking. Instead, he talked to an incredibly quiet woman and got the feeling that she was about to leave him.

Nothing new about Jacob had arrived and the police wanted to have a supplementary conversation with them when he got home. She did not have much more to say than that, and Chris had an uncomfortable feeling that she was deliberately withholding something. A feeling that was new to Chris. It may not have been a proper time to bring up her intimate engagement with Moa, it would rather wait until he got home. Linda also did not think she asked about Audrey's state of health. The conversation ended with Chris informing me when he would land at Arlanda but was not given any clear information on whether she would come and pick him up at the airport.

Since he did not get answers to all the questions about his wife's thoughts and actions, his thoughts instead turned to another problem, namely Nettan. After working with Audrey, they had visited a pub near the hotel and the evening had ended in an intense making out between the beer glasses on the table.

In his drunken state, Chris thought he had valid reasons for jumping into bed with her, but afterwards he was filled with guilt.

Nettan grabbed his arm as the plane began to descend for landing. He looked at her as she closed her eyes and waited for the plane to make ground contact. Chris smiled and looked out of the window.

When they came out with their bags to the arrival's hall, Nettan's boyfriend met her. He hugged her and gave her a kiss on the mouth, something she wanted to avoid. Chris and Nettan agreed that they would meet tomorrow. By then, the blood plasma would have arrived at Karolinska Institute K4.

Nettan and her boyfriend walked off together towards the exit, and Chris saw her annoyance at her boyfriend's clinging. Just inside the entrance, Linda stood staring at him. She did not bother to greet Nettan who waved to her as she walked past and out the entrance with her boyfriend. Chris walked up to her and gave her a hug but she stood like a cold figurine without hugging back. When he was about to give her a kiss, he was rejected. She turned and walked out through the entrance.

During the drive home, there was a tense atmosphere in the car. Chris tried to start a dialogue by telling Audrey how Audrey's blood collection was going and mentioning a little about her critical health condition. Linda did not even look in his direction, but her gaze was locked out through the side window. The meeting with Nettan had given her unwanted pictures of a meeting between her and Chris in an anonymous hotel room. Her contempt for Chris supplanted the desire to talk to him and she therefore added deaf ear to. Chris understood and decided to wait until they got home.

Back home, he wanted to have a conversation after taking off his outer clothes. They sat down in the kitchen and stared at each other. The marriage castle had begun to crumble. Linda did not need an explanation, she immediately felt Nettan's perfume on Chris's clothes.

"Let's take this from the beginning," Chris suggested as she looked down at the kitchen table. "I want to know if you're dating anyone else, given that conversation."

Linda nodded and got over her head. Lies would only make her fall even deeper into her sense of shame and betrayal. Chris swallowed the lump in his throat that only grew.

"Can you tell us how it happened and why? I heard Moa in the background and somehow I got the impression that she was the driving force. Did you have sex with that man who was hiding upstairs at Moa's house when we came to look for Jacob?"

Linda looked up with an extremely surprised and questioning look.

"Nope! It was just me and... Moa," she said with a little thought, and was embarrassed.

Chris stared at her with a shocked expression on his face.

"There was no male partner in that game. Why did you answer the call? You must have seen that it was me calling," Chris asked, not knowing what to think.

"Nope. I had sex with Moa and we were at her house. ... I responded to give back."

Chris spread his arms across the kitchen table with a surprised expression on his face, and then shook his head.

"Give it back? Because what if I may ask? What have I done?"

"I watched as you hugged Nettan at the airport terminal. You had not mentioned anything about her going with you to London. Do you hug at work behind my back too?" asked Linda at last indignantly.

"It was just a hug between colleagues and she hugged me because she was grateful that she was allowed to come with her to the Royal Free Hospital for a more practicing purpose."

"Did you sleep with her?" asked Linda, straining her gaze at Chris.

Chris put his palms together and then placed his elbows against the table. With a deep sigh, he looked down at the table.

"I don't want to lie to you, but yes it was after I heard you having sex with someone else and naturally wanted to give back."

Linda began to cry. She had lost everything, first Jacob and then her husband. The biggest blame was her own because Chris was right in what he said. It was not a lie to escape infidelity, he chose the truth and the possible consequences of marriage. A truth that had turned Linda's reassuring world completely upside down.

"God, how stupid I feel! How could this get so crazy? You must not get angry with Moa; it was I who took the initiative this time..."

"What?! Have you had sex with her before?" Linda nodded.

"Ten years ago, before Jacob was born. You were at a medical congress at the time. I want to put all the cards on the table. I have seen your and all the other men's thirsty glances at Moa at every meeting and service. She is extremely attractive and sensually alluring. God can attest that I felt the same."

"But... Why haven't you told me this sooner?"

"I didn't want to give you a pretext or valid reason to jump into bed with her," she said, swallowing her tears. "How many times have you fucked Nettan? Yes, I do not care about my choice of words just knew," Linda added.

"That was the first time," Chris replied as he tried to put the pieces of the puzzle together to get a clear picture of the situation. "I was jealous because I thought you slept with a man."

Linda gave him a determined look. *Was there a difference between sleeping with a man or a woman? What did he want to achieve with this?*

"I needed it. She made me feel whole again. My hope was that I would experience something spiritual. Instead, I got to experience something completely different, an erotic adventure that I never thought could happen to me. We got apart increasingly, with Jacob's disappearance. Our world is one great disaster, not even God pleases to help us."

"How are we going to put this behind us and move on?" asked Chris, extending his hand with a look of shame. "Will you meet again? Do you want a divorce?"

Linda looked at Chris for a long time with tearful blue eyes. Then she reached out both hands, grabbed his hand, and caressed it tenderly.

"I love you and I always will. We must find our way back to Jesus."

Chapter 43

29 SEPTEMBER 2014

ALI SAT IN his taxi and waited for Yasmin to show up. He looked at the clock and could see that it showed a quarter past one. Women simply could not fit times, he thought frustratedly. How hard could it be? And why didn't the human answer when called?

When he looked up at the clock, he saw her walking towards the car. She was dressed in a challenging outfit that exposed her sexy body. A sight that became increasingly irresistible to Ali, the need to have her grew ever stronger and he hoped to gain some support with Toh's blessing.

"Why did it take so long?" he asked irritably as she got in the car.

"Mom was making a fuss," she replied as Ali backed away and drove away.

"What's the fuss?"

"I didn't want her to leave Jacob home alone when she went shopping."

"What, the boy is big. He can manage on his own."

"She'll keep an eye on him while I work, period," Yasmin replied succinctly, losing her temper.

"Okay, okay," Ali said as he drove out onto Huddingevägen in the direction of Stockholm.

He became increasingly irritated by the deadlocked situation. He must create a reason to stop to call Mustafa who was waiting near Flemingsberg. He could not call when Yasmin was in the car. At the intersection of Huddingevägen and Ågesta road, he turned onto OKQ8 to refuel and, with objection from Yasmin. She saw that he refueled the car for SEK 100 before he went in to pay and borrow the toilet and followed him with his eyes as he stood at the checkout and then disappeared out of sight inside the gas station. She felt that his behavior was not normal. You did not refuel for SEK 100 when you had a customer in the car. You tried to do that with toilet visits between runs, she thought suspiciously.

* * *

Ali locked the toilet door around him. He pulled out his cell phone, hurried to put the headphones in his ears, and then called Mustafa.

"Where are you?" he asked when Mustafa answered. "Flemingsberg city centre."

"Yasmin's mother is at home. She is going shopping. If Toh is with us, she leaves the boy at home, it is risky to have the boy with her to the store because he is wanted. Yasmin tried to tell me something else. Keep an eye on the mother and you'll see."

"Okay," Mustafa replied, then hung up.

When he got in the car, he smiled at Yasmin who looked annoyed. He started the car and then drove out onto Huddingevägen towards

Stockholm. She looked at him questioningly but did not say anything. After a minute or so, he looked in the rearview mirror and felt some concern that Yasmin was staring at him.

"What is it?" asked Ali nervously.

"I wonder that too," Yasmin replied. "What was this about?"

"What?" howled Ali, trying to play innocent.

"What you just did."

Ali looked at her increasingly questioningly through the rearview mirror as he drove.

"You saw! I refueled and at the gas station. Damn woman, I'm a man."

The cell phone rang and Ali put one earpiece in his ear. He did not have time to introduce himself until he heard Mustafa's voice.

"Is Yasmin with you?" asked Mustafa in a firm tone.

"I have a drive to Stockholm," Ali replied nervously.

"They has gone and is by themselves," Mustafa said, breaking the conversation.

"I'll call when I get free," said Ali, who pulled the earpiece from his ear and slipped it into his jacket pocket. He glanced quickly at Yasmin who was looking fleetingly out the side window.

Yasmin felt an indescribable anxiety growing stronger within her. She was sure that Ali was hiding something from her, which he normally would not do. His sudden interest in his mother and Jacob was not true either. Ali's friend Mustafa was a person to be incredibly careful with, she noted, without really having anything concrete to go on. However, his authority and posture spoke volumes. She had previously faced dangerous men in Syria, especially during the flight to Sweden. Men who understood only one language: US dollars and the woman's vagina. The alternative was death.

"Ali! I have changed my mind. Instead, drive me to Valhto Road 129," she said.

Ali turned around in surprise for a moment.

"Aren't you going to work?"

"I'll probably have to change drivers. Either you drive me to Valhto Road or you drop me off here," she said in an irritated tone almost aggressive.

"Yasmin, my woman! Why are you doing this to me? I'll drive you to Valhto Road, okay."

Yasmin took out her phone and then started browsing the menu without commenting.

* * *

A playground in the middle of Flemingsberg with children of varying ages and with different ethnic and cultural origins was not the ultimate lookout post for Mustafa. However, it was good camouflage in front of the public when you would think that it was a father who was out with his child reading a newspaper, no oddities and no questions that could cost his life.

A little girl with snot running from her nose wanted to sit on Mustafa's lap while her mother stood a short distance away and was busy talking to friends. The rescue could not be timelier when he saw Yasmin's mother step out of the gate and start walking towards the center. He lifted the girl, carried her to the sandbox, and then set her down with the other children.

He quickly walked away, hoping that the girl would not start screaming. He turned around for a moment and was able to see with reluctance that the girl was eating sand in the sandbox, when someone tapped him on the back. Mustafa turned around and came face to face with the girl's mother.

"What are you doing with my daughter?" she asked grimly.

Mustafa pointed to the girl.

"I think you'd better concentrate on your daughter sitting there chewing sand, right?" said Mustafa, showing off a tattoo on her arm.

The woman was appalled when she saw the tattoo, rushed to the sandbox, and lifted the girl up to her arms. She turned around staring as Mustafa calmly walked away.

He looked around before stepping into the gate. There he could smell food as he went up to the top floor. Now he really hoped that Jacob would open the door, otherwise all that remained was to try to persuade him through the mailbox.

When the elevator stopped, he stepped out and walked to the door. He turned around and looked suspiciously at the neighbor's door. It was a door equipped with door binoculars that he did not feel comfortable with. He looked around and saw an information note from HUGE housing taped to the elevator door. He piled up the tape on the note and then crept to the neighbor's door to put it over the door binoculars before returning to Yasmin's front door and ringing twice in quick succession. He listened carefully through the front door and could hear the television from the living room.

Jacob sat on the couch watching movies in the living room.

He heard the ringing of the front door and turned down the volume on the TV. There was another ringing and he got up to walk to the door.

"There's no one home," Jacob said.

"Jacob, it's Mustafa. Is Yasmin home?" asked Mustafa in English.

"No one is home," he replied in English.

"Not Yasmin's mother either?"

"Nope. It is just me. Yasmin's mother is shopping. I must not open the door for anyone."

"It's good Jacob, that you are careful. I must call Yasmin. The police are on their way here and it's urgent."

From the door, Jacob heard Mustafa speak quickly in Arabic in a serious tone. Jacob got scared and looked around the apartment, he did not want to climb down from the balcony again. Jacob put on his shoes and tore his jacket from the coat rack. He opened the door and there stood Mustafa with a smile as he put his phone in his jacket pocket. He held out his hand, and hand in hand they walked up to the elevator. Mustafa grabbed the handle to open the elevator door when the elevator suddenly disappeared down.

* * *

Ali turned left onto Erik Dahlberg Street and made a leaf out onto Valhto Road again. He drove two blocks before stopping at Valhto Road 129 while an elderly man stood at the gate.

"Should I wait here?" asked Ali.

"Yes, you will. Wait!" stressed Yasmin before hurrying out of the car and to the gate.

Ali watched questioningly as the older man let her into the gate before he himself entered. Where is she going? he thought, shaking his head.

* * *

Rica had locked the taxi in the steel cage down in the garage before he went to the elevator and pressed the button. While he waited, he could with a satisfied face note that he had driven in 3500 SEK and was particularly pleased with that day's cash. When the elevator came down, he opened the door and stepped inside. Just as he was about to press the button, the elevator went up. When the elevator stopped, Rica discovered that he had come to the right floor and was about to open the door when it was suddenly torn open.

In the stairwell stood a moustachioed man with a small blond boy holding his hand. With a surprised look and a spontaneous hello, he barely got out of the elevator before the man and boy had rushed in. As the elevator door slammed shut, he could see the man's hate-filled gaze and a glimpse of the boy's terrified face as the elevator disappeared down.

It was with a strong discomfort after meeting the man and the boy that Rica unlocked the front door. Before he was about to enter, he looked at the neighbor's front door and saw that it was slightly ajar. He walked to the door and shouted hello, but all he heard was a faint sound from the television. He shouted again, no answer.

"Julia!" cried Rica as he entered the apartment and locked the front door.

She came out to the hall from the kitchen with a tea towel in her hand.

"What is it, Rica?"

“There’s something wrong with the neighbor, I have to call the police,” he said, upset.

“But Rica! What has happened, old man?”

“I met the boy who lives with Yasmin with that fellow that Ali had dragged here a few days ago, remember?”

She nodded. First they left the front door open then the man and the boy were in a great hurry with the elevator, I barely made it out of the elevator.

Julia suddenly disappeared into the kitchen and soon returned with a newspaper. She flipped through the middle spread and showed the article about Jacob’s disappearance. Pisca Matreno!

* * *

On the name board in the gate there was no Lars listed, but an abbreviation of a double name, L-Å, on the second floor, Yasmin noted. She hurried up the stairs and caught up with the elderly man who lived on the first floor. She ran past him up to the second floor. When she got up, she read all the name badges on the front doors and found the door that belonged to L-Å Rosén.

She was about to turn around when a neighbor opened the front door. It was a middle-aged woman who came out with a garbage bag. She stared at Yasmin.

“There’s no one home and it’s bound to take some time.” “Has anything happened?” asked Yasmin.

“It’s safe to say that” the woman replied as she returned to her door. “The police have been here to pick him up. I hope they never let out such a monster,” she added before entering the apartment and closing the door.

Ali watched as Yasmin hurriedly came out of the gate, ran to the car, and got inside.

"Go!" she said as she pulled the car door shut.

* * *

In a dark Mercedes 500, Mustafa and Jacob travelled along The Forgotten Road in the direction of Vårbyallé. He smiled and ruffled the hair of Jacob who smiled back with some relief. Suddenly, he braked and looked serious. Jacob looked ahead and saw two police cars standing by the side of the road. His heart almost beat a free-volt, and his lower lip began to tremble with fear. Mustafa drove slowly past the police checkpoint without being stopped and they were able to breathe again. A moment that Mustafa took the opportunity to take advantage of.

"You see, they're going to set up roadblocks here," Mustafa said with a serious look.

"Thank you for picking me up. Where are we going?" asked Jacob as he turned and looked back for a moment.

"Now we are going to a secret hideout. It is outside Sparreholm," he said, giving the officers a quick glance in the rearview mirror.

"Is Yasmin coming?" asked Jacob.

"She's coming. You are going to meet Muslim kids who are there now," Mustafa said.

"My bike!" exclaimed Jacob, horrified.

"Calm Jacob, we'll work it out. Yasmin can take it with her when she arrives," Mustafa said.

The dark Mercedes drove onto the motorway in the direction of Södertälje.

Chapter 44

29 SEPTEMBER 2014

INSIDE THE OFFICE, Reneé, George and Lelle were busy in a planning meeting. Reneé had decided to call for staff reinforcements from his colleagues at Söderort. She wanted to be relieved of the ongoing pedophile ring that only grew in scope.

Reneé wanted to devote all her time and focus to the disappearance of the children and the murder at Arlanda. She decided that Lelle would take on the murder in the first place and focus on checking up on the victim, partly in the criminal record and partly in his social circle. In addition, Reneé thought it would be a clever idea to start a cooperation with his colleague Jan-Ove from the Sollentuna police. A later interview with the victim's wife would provide more useful information for the initial investigation, which was in an important phase. Time must not run out so that everything gets cold, as the good criminologist G.W. Persson used to put it on television.

"Are you still of the opinion that the murder of this man is related to the disappearance of refugee children?" asked Lelle.

"The crime scenes and timing speak for it. One hypothesis could be that this man had seen something that he should not have seen," Reneé said. "Just found out that he is originally from Russia and had shared citizenship. Something that may well change my hypothesis," she added. He ended up getting a head shorter for some reason," George said with a slightly sarcastic smile.

"The search area will be extended towards Kolstavägen and the radio mast. There is an abandoned house there that might give something," Reneé said.

"Should we go to Skärholmen and see if we can find that Hadishe? I have found my current address," said George. "Good, what was that street address?" asked Reneé.

"Äspholm's road 7, close to the centre of Skärholmen."

Reneé drank the last splash of coffee and got up from the table.

"Let's go. Lelle, you call me or George in case of uncertainty," she said, taking her jacket.

Lelle and George got up from their chairs and left the room. Reneé pushed his chair into the desk and was about to leave when the phone rang. She was not going to answer, but her sense of duty got the better of her and she reluctantly picked up the phone.

At the other end, a man named Rica Novak called from Flemingsberg. He explained very matter-of-factly how a light blonde little boy had been abducted from an apartment at the diagnostic path 5B in Flemingsberg. Reneé began frantically taking notes on a college block. A family from Syria lived in the neighboring apartment seven floors up, where the boy had stayed for a few days before he was abducted. Reneé was given a description of the man, about 180 cm tall, short-cropped hair, brown eyes, moustache, fit and with two gold chains around his neck. Then came a detailed description of the boy that Reneé recognized. She wrote down a mobile number and the conversation ended with her promising to get in touch.

"Lelle! George! Come here," Reneé shouted as she picked up the phone again.

* * *

Rica knocked on the neighbor's door and waited, no answer. He felt the doorknob and noticed that the door was still unlocked. He opened, stuck his head in, and listened. He shouted but no one was home. Curiosity wanted to enter the apartment, but he closed the door and turned around. There, Julia stood at the doorpost with a worried look. Rica hurried into the hall and quickly put on her outerwear and shoes.

"Where are you going now?!" asked Julia anxiously.

"I have to find Yasmin," he said, and went outside to push up the elevator.

* * *

In a dressing room at the Harem sex club, Yasmin had just changed into a red transparent negligee with matching panties and hip holders that held up the black mesh patterned nylon stockings. She had been getting ready for the first performance of the evening on stage.

The song Love to love you baby by Donna Summer roared out through the speakers when Yasmin entered the stage, dancing to the beat of the music. As she lay on her back on the stage floor, she spread her legs apart and began to touch herself outside of faith.

San in front of the men sitting at the stage. Suddenly, she felt someone grab her thighs and a rude, bearded face pressed against her hand. She looked up in horror and saw Bullen Dahlin together with his colleagues from the contracting company Frestania AB. Bullen was a tall man with cropped hair. He would show himself on the tightrope in front of his colleagues by making the motorboat between the seductive legs of the stripper. He raised his head with a satisfied grin as Yasmin gave him a sharp slap across the cheek. At the same moment, Ratko came to the rescue and dragged Bullen away with his bear labs to hands. He had the firm opinion that this man should be allowed to play motorboat with Ratko out on the street.

* * *

Rica stopped the taxi at Dalagatan 7. He got out of the car and hurried to the gate the moment it opened, and Ratko came dragging out a bearded, tall man who swore loudly under huge protests. Ratko took a firm hold of the shirt of the Bull while with the other hand he gave him such a powerful slap that he went out headfirst. Rica at once had to back off two steps to avoid being hit by her compatriot. Then Ratko politely held open the gate door for Rica, who hurried past and thanked him.

He showed his taxi ID to the entrance host, a young pretty girl with a bare upper body, and hurried to the bar and asked for Yasmin. The bartender pointed to something behind Rica's back and turned around. There, Yasmin came running with her mobile phone to her ear, talking loudly and indignantly. She stopped at the bar and told the bartender that she had to go home, then continued communicating loudly on the mobile phone in Arabic and then interrupted the call. Rica saw that Yasmin was crying with despair and stood in front of her to comfort her. He could understand Arabic words but understood so much of the phone call that she had talked to her mother. Rica grabbed her arm.

"Come, you can go with me, we are in a hurry."

Yasmin wiped away the tears from her cheekbones and looked at Rica with a surprised look.

"What are you doing here?" asked Yasmin.

"Picking you up. We must go, now!"

Rica grabbed her arm and dragged her with her towards the exit.

With Yasmin in the passenger seat, he drove at high speed towards Oden Street. In the meantime, he told them what had happened and that he had also contacted the police after seeing the article in the newspaper. Rica turned onto St. Eriksgatan in the direction of Fridhemsplan and gasped. Out on Drottningholmsvägen, they were overtaken by a dark grey VW Passat with flashing blue lights with two following police cars in emergency.

"Yasmin, what have you done woman?" exclaimed Rica when he saw another emergency police car drive past at high speed. Pisca matreno! Now the cooked pork is fried, Rica thought as he swung out onto the Essingeleden.

Chapter 45

29 SEPTEMBER 2014

CHRIS KEPT CLEARING the kitchen table after dinner while Linda was in the bathroom. At least they had agreed over dinner that there was no question of divorce, but that they would instead try to strengthen the marriage and its family ties. A decision that Chris felt a sense of relief about. The feelings were with God's presence, now it was just a matter of finding the last piece of the puzzle, Jacob.

Thoughts about where he might be intruded as he put the butter and milk in the fridge. Chris was convinced that Jacob could be at anyone's house at night, even strangers. But why did no one call and tell me where he was? Some adults must be around him who, over time, should question.

Chris began to think about the chief physician who had abused Jacob. Was it a coincidence that their paths crossed? Or was it Jacob who made the contact? For money? Jacob was sitting outside Åhléns begging for money. Jacob must have been lured with money by this man, he thought as Linda sat down at the kitchen table and placed a pharmacy bag on the table.

She looked out the kitchen window and noted that autumn had made a serious entrance. The birch tree out on the plot had already released a covering carpet of its colorful foliage on its lawn. Out there somewhere was Jacob, terrified and unable to get in touch. Now the question was...

Linda took a pregnancy assessment out of the pharmacy bag and placed it on the table. Chris stood at the kitchen faucet, writhing out of the dishcloth when he saw the test on the table. He threw the dishcloth on the counter and walked over to Linda.

"Have you taken a pregnancy test?" he asked, smiling.

Linda nodded and handed over the test.

"My period has not appeared. Now I know why. I am pregnant," she said with disappointment in her voice.

Chris stood behind Linda and placed the test on the table before hugging her.

"You don't look happy?" he said, putting his hand on her stomach.

"What does this mean? Have we lost Jacob forever?"

"No, honey, you must not think like that. We will find him and at the right time we will be four in the family," he said with a sneaky smile.

"I don't even know if I want this baby," Linda said with an anxious look at the test. "I think some dark power is trying to punish us."

Out in the hall, they heard Linda's cell phone ringing. She hurried to answer.

"Linda," she replied as she heard an emergency siren in the background.

"Hi, it's Reneé Grahn. We are currently on our way to an address in Söderort where Jacob has been seen until recently."

"Oh God! Can we get there?" asked Linda, swallowing a lump in her throat.

"Absolutely not! This is a sharp situation, which means that the task force will soon be there and cordon off. If we find the boy, we will of course take him to the station and call you."

"Sharp location! Task force! But..."

Chris came running and took the cell phone from Linda.

"I'll take it Linda. Hello! This is Chris, Jacob's dad, what is going on?"

"I just wanted to let you know that we may have found Jacob at an address and we are on our way there," Reneé said succinctly.

"You talked to my wife about real life. Does that mean Jacob's life is in danger?"

"We don't know yet. As I said, I'll get back to you when we know a little more, goodbye."

The call was interrupted. Linda looked questioningly at Chris as he handed over the phone.

"They're on their way to an address where Jacob might be," Chris said.

"Yes... with the task force, Chris!" exclaimed Linda in horror. "This is just getting worse and worse. We have never dealt with the police before. Now it feels like you carry a feeling where our son has become a gangster that everyone is chasing and we stand behind the scenes and watch."

Chris hugged her, feeling the same resignation and powerlessness as her.

"They will call as soon as they know anything more," he said.

Linda let go and tightened her eyes in him.

"Come, let's go," she said, hurrying to her outer clothes.

"Going where?" asked Chris in surprise and followed. "We'll go to the police."

The National Task Force (NI) is a task force within the Swedish police authority intended to manage difficult and dangerous situations when people's lives are in danger, including cases of terrorism, hostage-taking, kidnapping and the like. Members of the National Task Force previously served only part-time in the force, having two weeks of training and then two weeks of regular police work in a government agency. Nowadays, all police officers work full-time in the force as they usually have a lot of training and many assignments.

Chapter 46

29 SEPTEMBER 2014

RICA BACKED THE car into the steel cage in the garage while Yasmin ran to the elevator. He was short in stature with a little excess weight around his stomach but moved smoothly when he hurried out and locked it with a rolling steel gate. When he arrived at the elevators, Yasmin was missing and the elevator was on its way up. He pressed the elevator button and saw that the elevator had stopped on level seven. Suddenly, he heard a car stop outside the closed garage door. There were car doors that opened and closed, at the same time voices were heard that fell silent. The engine of the garage door began to buzz when the door opened and four men dressed in black with automatic weapons rushed in. They stopped when they saw Rica standing by the elevator and showed a hesitant smile.

Yasmin rushed into the apartment while shouting at her mother. She heard some words of pleading in Arabic from inside the living room and ran there. There she sat on her knees and prayed to Toh for help and mercy. Yasmin nudged her to get her attention and was met by a pair of tearful eyes surrounded by the wrinkles of age. She felt that her mother had aged even more in the few hours they had been apart.

"Mom! What has happened? You must tell me," Yasmin said pleadingly, and at the same time got down on her knees. "Sorry I yelled at you," she added.

"I have prayed to God for help," her mother said sobbing.

"Okay, you have to stop now and tell me what happened instead."

"Don't know! When I got home, the door was unlocked and the boy was gone. His clothes were also gone," she noted, pointing to the hall at the same time.

"Where have you been?" asked Yasmin.

"Shop my dear girl, I've just been to the store shopping," she said, showing off a cheek egg she held in her hand.

"Why didn't you bring him? You promised."

Fatma stared wide-eyed at her daughter and shook her head.

"Yasmin! You have not thought right. Jacob is wanted and appears in all the newspapers. I cannot even with God's help take him to the store. I may go to jail my dear daughter," she said, gesturing with her arms to prove the seriousness. "I don't want to go there again."

The front door rang twice in quick succession. She felt chills that made the hairs on her neck stand up. Fatma got up to go and open but was stopped by Yasmin.

"Stay here, I'll open it," she said firmly, and walked to the hall.

She looked through the peephole but it was black. It rang twice and someone knocked on the door while the last ringtone died out.

"Open! It is the police," a powerful male voice came from outside the stairwell.

Yasmin was paralyzed by fear as she stood next to the front door. Strong memories of war-torn Syria appeared and clung to her. Images she thought had been erased appeared like demons. The longing for Jacob burned in her heart as she slowly unlocked and opened.

* * *

Marina Novak was about to drive into the garage on the diagnostic path when two uniformed police officers stopped her. They informed that the area was cordoned off during the ongoing police emergency. Marina was about to reverse the car when she saw two men from the task force walking with Rica between them. From the opposite direction, a woman and a man came running. Marina stopped the car and hurried out while a white dog rode around in the back seat barking. She managed to get past both police officer and rushed to Rica. One of the police officers pointed his automatic weapon at her and yelled at her to stop! Then Reneé came and said he was going to lower the gun. Marina hugged Rica and was completely beside herself.

"What's happened? Where is Mom?" she asked in dismay.

Rica smiled slightly as he used to when his stepdaughter Marina was upset and tried to calm her down.

"Marina. Mom is home and right now I think... that she sets the kitchen table for food."

"But Rica! What are the police doing here and why have they caught you?"

"No, they haven't taken me, look here, no handcuffs or plastic ties," Rica noted with a smile as he showed off his wrists, then shrugged. "They're going to surprise our neighbor, you see."

"What? The Syrian family, Yasmin, and her mother?" she exclaimed in horror and started looking for the cigarettes in her jacket pocket.

Reneé and George stood by and let them talk it out, hoping that Marina would calm down.

"Hello. My name is Reneé Grahn and I am from the Crimea," Reneé introduced herself when she greeted Marina and then Rica.

"Oh, it's you I was talking to on the phone when I called about the boy," Rica said.

"Rica!" exclaimed Marina, horrified, gesturing with her arms. "What boy?"

Reneé and George could not help but smile when a call was heard on the radio.

"Your father has observed a missing boy," Reneé explained matter-of-factly, trying to downplay the whole situation as she reached out to George to answer the call.

"Do you have a boy at home?" asked Marina, then looked at all the police officers stationed at the garage entrance.

"No, Marina, the boy has been staying with Yasmin," Rica said.

George pointed to the residential area.

"Reneé, the apartment is secured and two people have been found. Shall we?" said George and started walking.

"See if we can bring it..." Reneé interrupted when she could not think of the first names and instead pointed to Rica and Marina.

"Rica, my name is Rica. This is Marina, my stepdaughter," Rica pointed out.

George made a call request and was told that it was possible to let the residents into the stairwell.

A dark blue Toyota Prius from Taxikurir suddenly appeared and swerved behind Marina's Mercedes that was parked in the driveway.

The taxi reversed and drove away slowly, while Marina and Rica looked for the car with surprised eyes.

"He had just driven the wrong way," Reneé told Rica and Marina and started walking.

Rica turned and looked pensively at the street where the taxi had just disappeared out of sight.

Chapter 47

29 SEPTEMBER 2014

Ali was in a cold sweat and completely pale, as if he had looked death in the eye, as he drove towards Huddingevägen. There was really no doubt that the police were there for the boy, but why the big police operation and why had they arrested Rica and his daughter? How did it go with Yasmin and her mother? Have they been arrested? But... Yasmin was at the club, right?

Ali took out the cell phone from his jacket pocket but then hesitated. Could it be so bad that the police had taken Mustafa? I will send you a text message instead, he thought as he turned off towards Huddinge center from Huddingevägen.

After parking at Huddingecentrum, Ali sent a text message in Arabic with the text: *God is great?* He waited impatiently for an answer as a run appeared on the screen. Would he accept the run? Ali declined, and a text message came with a ringing sound: *A dawn appears,* the text read.

Ali felt a little relieved. Everything had gone according to plan. Now only one problem remained, was Yasmin still at the club or was she arrested with her mother? He called the sex club Harem and got to talk to the bartender. Pretty soon it became clear that Yasmin had left the club. He had no idea where she went, but Yasmin had been terribly upset when she disappeared. Ali thanked him and hung up.

Calling her or texting her was not even on your mind. Was there really any cause for concern at all? What would she say about him? Nothing, he noted as a new run blipped onto the screen.

* * *

It was a particularly upset Reneé who stood and scolded one of the task force's men for notes at Yasmin's house. It was with such aggressiveness that George chose to back off a few steps but still be present in the room. Now that colleague was in a bad position, he thought.

"What the hell were you thinking now? Think you are in Auschwitz, huh?"

"I went by the rules," the colleague replied with an embarrassed expression on his face.

"Went by the rules! You see for the hell that there are two unarmed women kneeling with their arms over their heads, as if they were prisoners of war. Did they resist at all when you stepped in? What?"

"No," the police colleague replied, glancing at Yasmin who was trying to comfort her mother, who was completely beside herself with fear.

The acting chief operating officer, an elderly man dressed in safety equipment, came to the rescue.

"What's the matter?"

"I'll tell you that. Your boys cannot analyze a risky situation in a humane way. I found this man standing here holding his fucking

MP5 aimed at the women while they were on their knees with their hands over their heads. What fucking nonsense is that?" said Reneé in a way that could not be misunderstood.

"He did his job," defended the chief operating officer. "We're not doing kindergarten; I thought you knew that."

Reneé looked at his boss colleague with a serious look. One more word than it will slam, Reneé thought and bit down. Instead of responding to her colleague's arguments, she turned around and shouted at two female police officers to come. She glared angrily at her colleague before going to Yasmin and her mother.

"Can you speak Swedish?" asked Reneé.

Yasmin nodded.

"I know Swedish, she can't," Yasmin said, pointing to her mother.

"Good. We do this now; we go to the station and we can talk a little more about this in peace and quiet. Come, you can go with my nice colleagues," she said, nodding towards the female police officers standing on the sidelines.

When Reneé came out to the stairwell, George came out of Novak's apartment.

"Well, that's where you were. We can take this family to the station," Reneé told George as Yasmin and her mother walked past and got into the elevator, escorted by the two female police officers.

"Thought I did better there. I have talked to Rica and his wife. We should have stopped that damn Gay Express from the taxi courier that turned down by the garage. The guy who drove is called Ali and is familiar with the women who now go down with the elevator. In addition to the fact that this desert robber is studded with Yasmin, he also has a friend who has been popping up here in the last few days and is remarkably interesting. It was the guy who came with the boy when Rica ran into them here in the stairwell, or rather the elevator."

"Any name?" asked Reneé.

George shook his head. "Just have that Ali. Shall we go?"

Chapter 48

29 SEPTEMBER 2014

Bāqiyah wa Tatamaddad

"Remain and expand"

Outside Sparreholm, Jacob stepped out of the black Mercedes while looking at the yellow latticed wooden house with a worried gaze. Mustafa smiled as he got out of the car and put his hand on his shoulder.

"Now, Jacob, you are safe for the time being. You're going to meet the other kids who live here and are in the same tricky situation as you."

"Why are there grilles on all windows? Is it a prison?" asked Jacob worriedly.

"No, my boy. Do you really think I would put you in a prison?" laughed Mustafa heartily and added. "The bars are just a shelter so no one can get in. There's been a lot of burglary here and it's good protection for us, Jacob."

Jacob showed a smile, stood in front of the car, and looked out over the lot and the railroad that was below the property line.

"Shall we?" asked Mustafa, gesturing towards the house.

They walked up to the porch and Mustafa knocked on the front door. Jacob heard that there were children inside the house giggling and shouting something in Arabic. The door was unlocked with three locks before a young girl dressed in Black with a Burqa opened the door. She backed away at once and pushed the curious children away. Mustafa and Jacob entered, and Mustafa closed the front door and locked.

After a call in Arabic from the black-clad girl, the children lined up. Mustafa's disciplinary demands had paid off, and he was satisfied. He asked Jacob to come over and greet the children. Jacob first introduced himself to the black-clad girl Flowing, and then greeted the boys, who greeted back politely and correctly. When it was the girls' turn, they greeted each other respectfully with a little modest giggles and curious glances.

Mustafa looked at the clock and could see that it was 17:00. He gave Flowing a look that made her walk away with the children lined up in a disciplined order. With a slight smile, Mustafa gestured for Jacob to follow. Jacob did as he was told, and Mustafa followed with both firsthand his shoulders. It was time for afternoon coffee before the Magrib prayer was to begin at 18:37.

After coffee, consisting of tea and Arabic syrup-dipped biscuits and cardamom worm sticks with sugar, Jacob tried to socialize with the other children despite the language problems that arose. Mustafa kept watch and carefully studied the behavior patterns of the children, especially Jacobs.

At 6:30 p.m., everyone gathered in the living room. Flowing had cleared away the living room furniture so that there was enough floor space to lay out twelve small prayer rugs. It was time for prayer. Mustafa, who was their imam, helped Jacob with the washing ritual called wudhu. Then everyone stood at their respective mats and began the ritual. Since Jacob did not know the Quran, he was allowed to pray in his own way to Toh. He mimicked the children's movements to the extent that he kept up.

Mustafa assessed Jacob's learning ability as good and it was an excellent quality for the future. His loyalty to God would certainly ease the conversion to Islam itself. How strong his loyalty would be to his new leaders and people remained to be seen. Given all the abuse the boy had endured, it should be easy to get him to go against his current Christian faith and people. There must be a hidden hatred in his subconscious, it was just a matter of picking it up and controlling it.

During the evening, Mustafa sat and told the children what was going on in Iraq and Syria. It was with empathy that he went into details of how their people suffered and suffered because of the war. It was a bloody power game fought between faithful Muslims and Christian Western allies. Mustafa avoided mentioning the greatest enemy of them all, namely the United States. It was a sensitive subject that had to be dealt with carefully and patiently, especially in the face of Jacob because there were strong blood ties to the country.

There was evening coffee that ended with a prayer. Mustafa had decided that Jacob would spend his first night with Flowing in his own room. He had seen Jacob's close relationship with Yasmin, and when she was not here, they had to resort to a surrogate who could give him the security he needed.

After Flowing put Jacob to sleep, she waited for five minutes, then carefully left the room. She sneaked over to Mustafa's room and went inside. A small table lamp spread a faint glow of light in the room. There Mustafa was lying on his back in bed with a duvet pulled up just above his waist. Flowing understood what to expect and began to undress. Mustafa stretched out his arm and turned off the light as he waited for Flowing to crawl under his covers. He felt her warm hands begin to caress his hairy chest and then systematically find their way down to the more intimate parts of his body. Flowing lifted the covers and his head found its way in. Mustafa saw the bump on the quilt moving slowly as he felt her warm breath against his skin. He reached contentedly and closed his eyes as he felt her lips touch his thighs stretched out his arm and turned off the light as he waited for Flowing to crawl under his covers. He felt her warm hands begin to caress his hairy chest and then systematically find their way down to the more intimate parts of his body. Flowing lifted the covers and his head found its way in. Mustafa saw the bump on the quilt moving slowly as he felt her warm breath against his skin. He reached contentedly and closed his eyes as he felt her lips touch his thighs.

Chapter 49

29 SEPTEMBER 2014

INSIDE THE RIKSKRIM there were divided opinions between Reneé and Linda, which finally made Reneé almost lose his temper. At the same time, she gave herself a lesson, that you should give the hell to call the parents before you had anything concrete to produce. George would have been quick to complain about this if he were not in such a hurry to the bathroom suitable enough. She would later mention the issue of admitting relatives to the ward at the next meeting. It was not proper no matter how they begged and prayed to get their way.

"There's a police investigation going on!" Reneé had finally said to Linda as it fizzled out.

Since a supplementary interrogation of Chris and Linda had already been planned, Reneé could do nothing but send them out to the coffee room. There would be time left after she had interrogated the Syrian family as soon as an interpreter had arrived, and when George wanted to come out of the toilet. Thankfully, her daughter Yasmin was almost fluent in Swedish, but it was worse with her mother's language skills. On the other hand, who said this job would be easy?

* * *

Inside a conversation room, Yasmin paced back and forth. The thoughts were many and unanswered and contributed to the approaching headache. What would she say? Where was Jacob? What would Mom say? Why didn't she contact the police when she met Jacob already at Harem? What was she really thinking? The door opened and Reneé came in, closing the door behind her. She had a tape recorder with her, which she placed on the table.

"Are you worried?" she asked, sitting down at the table.

Yasmin nodded and sat down opposite. She took the plastic cup that was on the table and drank some water. Her mouth felt like a desert landscape no matter how she tried to elicit more saliva.

"Is it Jacob you're worried about?"

"Yes, I should have called you already when he arrived at the club," she said with tears in her eyes. "Is it his parents sitting out there?"

Reneé nodded as she looked embarrassed.

"Yes, they're sitting in our break room. This Ali we are trying to get hold of

I. Do you think he is the one who picked up Jacob?"

"There were only two people who knew he was with us and that was Ali and his friend Mustafa. I noticed Mustafa's sudden interest in Jacob when they visited us."

"This Mustafa, does he live in Sweden?" asked Reneé.

"No, I think he lives in Turkey. He has visited Sweden on various occasions, but what he is doing here I do not know. Ali was already living in Sweden when my mother and I came here."

"We have looked up Ali Naharaim and his papers seemed to be in order. The same also applies to you and your mother. We tried to call him. We are now trying to track his cell phone to try to find out where he is and has been. We have also tried to track down the taxi without any fruitful results and talked to the taxi owner who was a compatriot of yours, and more concerned about the car than the driver. Do you have any ideas about where he might be staying?" Yasmin shook her head.

"I don't know where Ali is. On the other hand, I have seen a tattoo on Mustafa's arm," she said with some restraint.

"What kind of a tattoo is that?" Yasmin shrugged.

"Does Ali have such a tattoo?" asked Reneé.

"No, not what I've seen."

"You also don't know where Mustafa is staying?" asked Reneé.

"No," Yasmin replied with a determined look.

"You think Jacob might be with Ali and Mustafa? Do you know if there is any form of child recruitment to ISIS or

other warring factions?"

Yasmin shook her head.

"The only thing I noticed was that Mustafa was interested in Jacob's father. He and Ali googled the name and found out information about him."

"What was that?" She did not have time to say more before a heartbreaking scream was heard from outside.

Quick steps could be heard outside in the corridor and seconds later the door went open and in came George looking torn up.

"Damn it! I need help. The bitch runs for hell amok in there, howling like a ... I do not know what, demon. That damn interpreter drew as a payoff with be-nen on the back. But..." George managed to say when Reneé and Yasmin stood up at the same time so that the chairs fell to the floor.

George was left with a resigned face while he thought about reconsidering his career choice again. It was high time for that. When Reneé and Yasmin reached the doorway, Linda stood in front of Yasmin's mother, who was kneeling on the floor, desperately tugging at her clothes. Next to it was Chris like a question mark. Yasmin forced her way in and crouched down next to her mother.

"Mom, mom, what do you see?" she asked in Arabic.

"Boy! I see Jacob. He has left us," stammered the woman with trembling lips.

"What does she say?" exclaimed Linda worriedly.

"What's left? Is he dead?" asked Yasmin horrified.

"No, my girl. He lives with nine other children," the mother replied with some relief, letting go of Linda's clothes.

"What's going on?" asked Reneé as she squeezed in between the doorpost and Linda.

"My mother is a Sierra. She can see and experience what others feel and experience or will experience. She saw and felt the presence of Jacob."

George covered his hands over his face with a resigned frustration.

"Good night. Now we too are being haunted in this damned investigation," he sighed resignedly.

"Lay off, George. Can she see where Jacob is?" asked Reneé, crouching down next to Yasmin.

"Mom. Can you see where Jacob is?"

"I see floral wallpaper and two mattresses in one room. It's a house near the railroad."

"Okay, great. Then we will send two cars to that address," George said cryptically, then shook his head.

Reneé gave him a serious look that told him to shut up. Suddenly, Yasmin's mother grabbed Linda's arm and stared at her with a terrifying look.

"Jacob will travel a long way in a tin box beyond repair. We will lose him," she said in Arabic with trembling lips.

Yasmin stood up and looked at Linda with tearful eyes. Then she helped her mother up from the floor to a chair where she sat down with a deep sigh.

"What did she say?" asked Linda, putting her hand on Yasmin's arm at the same time.

"She said Jacob, my Jacob, will travel far," Yasmin replied with a convincing look.

"What, your Jacob?" Linda managed to say before Chris interrupted her.

"What are you talking about? Jacob is our son," he said firmly.

"He was your son," Yasmin replied, turning her gaze to Chris.

"He's still my son," Linda exclaimed in dismay, nudging Yasmin.

Reneé intervened at once.

"Stop and prove, this is not how we work," she said. "Is your mother absolutely certain that Jacob will be abducted somewhere with other children?"

Yasmin nodded when her mother suddenly stood up and walked over to Linda. She placed her wrinkled hand on her stomach and smiled.

"You're going to get another one," she said in Arabic as she nodded with a smile and patted Linda's gently stomach. She backed away and stared wide-eyed at Yasmin's mother.

"Are you pregnant?" asked Yasmin.

Linda nodded and looked at Chris with a pleading look. Reneé wanted to end the interrogation for today, it did not yield as much as she had hoped for. Instead, there was a lot of speculation that also did not give anything concrete, a floral wall and two sleeping mattresses were the only things to go on. Reneé did not want to reject anything that Yasmin's mother had shown, even though it could be interpreted as superstitious waffle. Nor were there sufficient reasons to put Yasmin and her mother under arrest. It would lead to more obstacles than good, so she offered Yasmin and her mother a ride home and then looked at George a little pleadingly.

Chapter 50

30 SEPTEMBER 2014

During the night, the first real autumn storm had made its entry over Sörmland, Västmanland and Mälardalen, with sometimes harsh, whipping winds. Ali felt the gusts hitting the red bus and occasionally had to hold on to the steering wheel while driving along the E18 towards Buying. He had bought the bus from two young Moroccans whose big construction plans ended abruptly after they were caught with a cargo of marijuana. They were simply robbed of their precious cargo after crossing the Swedish border, which led to them having to sell the car for cheap money.

He turned off from the E18 towards Strängnäs and Katrineholm while the rain poured down again. In addition to the severe weather, there was another alarming thought that plagued his mind. Hadishe. She had not been heard from either on the phone or by text message, something that was unlike her. Could it be Mustafa who had silenced her for good, as he did with that old man at Arlanda? he thought worriedly, creasing his brow with nervousness.

* * *

Flowing cleared the breakfast table and stuffed everything into food in plastic bags from Coop. After that, she began scrubbing the entire kitchen with chlorine and dishwashing liquid.

In the living room, Mustafa had the day's briefing with the children in Arabic. Jacob sat closest to him and tried to figure out what certain often lost words meant in Swedish. He sensed that something positive was going to happen today because the other children smiled and nodded in unison as Mustafa spoke and ended the sentences with a broad smile. The children got up and went to another room while Jacob remained seated to be informed in English of what had been said.

Mustafa began the briefing with how Jacob would be able to start his new life in a dignified way. Then he told me about a journey that was to begin this morning.

"Where are we going?" asked Jacob with a surprised look.

"To my homeland, where Toh welcomes us to his kingdom," Mustafa replied in English.

"But Yasmin!" exclaimed Jacob, horrified.

"She greets you with a big hug. You will be reunited in my homeland and there you will live together," Mustafa said confidently with a smile.

Jacob turned his gaze to the other room where the other children were playing carelessly. He then looked again at Mustafa, who stood in front of him.

"Jacob, do you trust me?" he asked with a sustained smile. "Are you prepared to do anything for Toh?"

Jacob nodded, and Mustafa placed his firsthand his shoulders in a fatherly way.

"Good, you should know that I will be on this journey and protect you. It was a demand from Yasmin."

Jacob hugged him as the unanswered thoughts went around in his head. Owen was standing there with Yasmin waiting for him. The thoughts of mom and dad were there all the time and the questions remained unanswered even there. It was as if Mom and Dad had not even existed.

A car stopped outside. Mustafa walked up to the window and saw a red Toyota Hi Ace bus. He turned to Jacob.

"Now, my friend, let's go," he said, looking at his watch that showed 7:30 a.m.

Chapter 51

30 SEPTEMBER 2014

Breakfast didn't feel like a highlight this morning for Chris and Linda at all. Instead, the feeling grew that the closer Jacob they got, the further away he slipped away from them. It was like two magnets chasing each other. The incident at the police station yesterday was frightening and etched itself in their minds. What did Yasmin mean by claiming Jacob was her child? Obviously, there was no slip of the tongue or language difficulties, but the Syrian woman meant that Jacob was her child. It was hard to absorb considering everything that had happened and it led to even more frustration and inner pain.

Chris looked at the clock that showed a quarter past eight. He wondered if he should contact his brother Owen.

"I'm going to call Owen. We need to get professional help," he said Chris. "I should have called earlier."

"It's half past two at night in Chicago, Chris."

"I need to talk to him before we go to the police."

"I think you should wait a few hours," Linda said, carrying away the coffee mugs.

Chris did not listen but took the cell phone from the table to make a call. Several signals passed before a newly awakened female voice responded.

"Hey," it said in English.

"Hi Paula, sorry I'm calling at such an inopportune time," Chris said apologetically, regretting not waiting until later to call.

"It's okay. Has anything happened?"

"Jacob has disappeared," he said, tears in his eyes.

"Oh God! When did he disappear?" asked Paula, suddenly sounding wide awake.

"A week ago. Is Owen home?"

"No, he's in Iraq and won't be home for two weeks," Paula replied. "Can I do something for you? How is Linda?"

"She's not feeling well. Paula, thank you for your consideration, but I would need advice from my brother."

"I'll ask him to call when he gets in touch on Skype," she promised.

"Thank you, take care and greet the children. May God be with you," Chris said.

"Greet Linda from me and give her a hug. You should not lose hope, it will work out," Paula said and hung up.

Chris put the cell phone on the kitchen table and realized he was dressed in pajamas, so he went off to change. It was time to get ready for today's police interrogation. Whatever that would lead to, he thought.

* * *

Reneé and George were sitting inside the office when Lelle came in and sat down next to George. There were a few ideas to go on about

Jacob's disappearance. Ali Naharaim's car, which had been found the same morning in a garage at Hötorget and salvaged to technical for examination, and Hadishe who seemed to have disappeared without a trace along with the refugee children at Arlanda. The search at her home did not really yield anything, except that DNA and some fingerprints could be recovered.

George took the opportunity to sarcastically remind them that if you found that flowery room by the railway, you would at least have come a long way. There was hope yet was the final line. Reneé looked at him seriously, and then shook his head.

"Joking aside, when would the Sjogren-Lester couple show up?" he asked to tidy up his serious police side. He did not want to annoy Reneé to the point where she would be unbearable to work with for the rest of the day.

"Half past ten," she replied when the phone rang. She replied and received word from the guard that the Sjögren-Lester couple had arrived.

"Lelle, are you going to meet Jacob's parents down at the entrance?" asked Reneé as she hung up the phone. He stood up but turned around at the door.

"I thought about this club Harem that Yasmin works at. Should I check it a little closer?"

George started laughing while looking at his wristwatch and made Reneé show a smile. "Were you thinking of a personal study visit, Lelle?" exclaimed George laughing.

"Imagine grown men becoming like children as soon as women are concerned, especially if are mentioned," Reneé said, rolling her eyes.

"It was just a suggestion because we don't have anything else to go on currently, but okay we give a about it," Lelle said, making a dismissive gesture. "I'll go down and get the parents, Then I'll go to technical and check," he added, feeling a little awkward.

"Wait Lelle. Do so, check the ownership structure and all partners in the company. Then you can check your criminal record," Reneé said.

Lelle nodded and disappeared out the door.

* * *

George was talking on his cell phone inside his office when there was a knock on the door.

"Oh, now comes my visit. We will see if I can come with you some evening. I want to remind you once again; our so-called relationship and contact should stay between us. No more surprises, Moa."

He pushed the conversation away and glanced at the desk to make sure nothing classified was available. He leaned back and shouted at the visitors to enter. The door opened and in came Chris Sjögren-Lester, who at once closed the door behind him. He walked over and greeted George who in turn gestured for him to sit down in front of the desk.

"Good that you could come. You know why you and your wife have been called," George began the conversation.

"No, not really. Just that we were coming here for some supplementation, whatever that entails," Chris replied.

"Exactly. I would like to know a little more about your connection to the Pentecostal church in Knutby, since your wife came to Åhléns with Moa Waldarud."

"We were members of the congregation when we lived in Knutby," Chris replied.

"That means you only have friendly relations with Moa?"

"We had no contact with either the congregation or Moa until Jacob disappeared. We have already explained this to you."

"You have done so. What I am most concerned about is that Jacob does not contact either you or anyone else in your circle of acquaintances, which makes it a little hard for me to believe that this bicycle accident would be the main cause of his disappearance. What has appeared, however, is that he is attracted to grown men, something that you might have thoughts about?" asked George, leaning over the desk with one arm.

"I don't really know what you're after?" said Chris with an uneasy feeling.

"Your son is ten years old. He seeks out men who have sexual relations with him for compensation, right now. This is not a normal pattern of behavior in a ten-year-old boy," George noted. "Would you mind if we took a DNA on you?"

* * *

Reneé noticed how bothered Linda seemed to be by the questions about Moa and the Pentecostal church in Knutby. She had answered briefly that they are not members of that congregation and when the questions then turned to Linda's personal relationship with Moa, the answers were very vague and the explanations were drawn out. Intuitively, Reneé became increasingly suspicious and began asking questions about her relationship with Chris and their sex life in general. Linda's reaction revealed a relentlessly sore spot, but eventually it crept up that her relationship with Chris was strained in connection with Jacob's disappearance. When it concerned the questions about her sex life, she simply refused to answer. Instead, she questioned the issues and their relevance to Jacob's disappearance.

Linda felt a strong discomfort with the intimate questions that were asked. She was reluctantly able to understand the reason for the issues concerning the Pentecostal church and Moa, even for the question of her relationship with Chris there was a grudging acceptance.

Reneé had gotten Linda where she wanted and asked if she had any ideas about why Jacob was referring to grown men. Linda looked at Reneé uncomprehendingly.

"There's a natural reason for that. Jacob was close to his father and Owen. Owen is Chris' brother who resides in the United States."

"We can probably ignore the brother on this issue," Reneé said. "Now for a more sensitive question, have you had any suspicions that your husband may have a sexual attraction to boys?" "Sorry! What did you say now?" exclaimed Linda in horror.

"If your husband has a sexual orientation to underage boys," Reneé reiterated.

Linda stared at her in horror with a gaping mouth.

"First of all, my husband is heterosexual to the core. Sorry... I cannot understand what you are after. This certainly does not lead to you finding Jacob. That you have the nerve to say that my husband has such sexual inclinations, I certainly did not expect. I feel so violated."

"I never said your husband is a pedophile. I asked if you had seen any such tendencies or have any suspicions about it. We are looking for a reason Jacob does not contact you; he chooses instead to stay away. We know that he has suffered traumatic abuse and yet he hears Not by itself, why I wonder? According to the interview with Yasmin, it emerged that she had offered to call you, but Jacob immediately reacted negatively and intended to leave."

"Don't get in touch! Do you have the faintest idea how many times a day my husband and I have asked that question? Are you at all interested in finding our boy? Why did you let Yasmin go?" exclaimed Linda with a frustration that only grew.

* * *

Throughout the morning, Yasmin had been trying to reach Ali via cell phone without success. With anger and a sense of powerlessness, she threw it on the kitchen table. The fact that he did not answer when she called had never happened before, he was far too obsessed with her. That he suddenly chose not to exist in connection with Jacob's disappearance was no coincidence, she noted. She was absolutely convinced that Ali had something to do with it, as did that fucking Mustafa. She was determined to find that coward. She would do everything in her power to find Jacob.

Yasmin took the cell phone and left the kitchen to go to the hall. Inside the toilet, she heard her mother cleaning the bathtub. Yasmin opened the closet, stepped in, and started looking up at the shelves and down on the floor. In the far corner, she found her black leather bag with a shoulder strap. She opened it and started searching with her right hand. Finally, she found what she was looking for, a stiletto knife.

She put on white sports shoes, and then took her jacket and walked out. She would find Ali at any cost, with or without bloodshed.

Chapter 52

30 SEPTEMBER 2014

It was 08:45 in the morning when a Liberia-flagged container ship named King Jacob docked at the port of Arendal in Gothenburg. The hull of the one hundred- and eleven-meter-long ship showed traces of her having been in rough seas before arriving in Gothenburg.

Fifty-five-year-old commander Emrah Okyar was pleased with the crew's performance while scouting over the ship's eighty-two containers. They had arrived on time, despite the storm on the North Sea with strong southwesterly winds against the waters of the Skagerrak. He turned and walked out onto the port side of the dock wing to scout out over the harbor where there was a lot of activity. Emrah saw a blue forty-foot container standing a little separate from the other containers and noted that everything was going according to plan. He went into the command bridge and called for the guard commander to be released and be able to go to his office.

Inside the office cabin, he sat down at his desk and took out a cell phone with a Swedish prepaid card from a desk drawer. He turned on the cell phone and put it on his desk while looking at the ship's clock on the wall, which showed 8:59 Swedish time. At exactly 9.00 a.m., the cell phone rang with a ringing that was a recorded call to prayer.

"Yes," Emrah replied in Turkish, glancing at the door.

"Have you arrived?" asked Mustafa.

"We added 8:45 a.m. Everything seems to be ready."

"Good. Has passed Katrineholm. Have about three hours left."

"Then you have plenty of time. We leave at 15:00," Emrah stated and hung up.

There was a knock on the door and a sailor stepped in with a tray of food. On the tray was a warm little copper cauldron with Turkish coffee and a stainless-steel jug with cream. On a plate next to it were two toasted sandwiches with two fried eggs. The sailor set the tray down on the desk and left without a word. Emrah watched breakfast as he poured a cup of coffee and added two sugar cubes. He tasted it and it was to his satisfaction. Then he took the knife, lifted a little on one of the fried eggs and pushed it aside. It turned out that the yolk was not cooked through and floated out over the plate. Emrah was pleased.

* * *

From Katrineholm the journey went towards North Buying and then south on the E4. Ali drove with all the children and flowing sitting in the back. Jacob preferred to sit in the front seat because of motion sickness, but Ali did not allow that. Instead, he had to sit closest to the side door with a view both forward and side, which should relieve the motion sickness, he said with a sarcastic grin.

At Preemmacken just after Huskvarna, they stopped for lunch. They ate kebab meat with bulgur and a red, spicy sauce that Flowing had prepared. Mustafa also allowed a shorter leg to stretch before continuing the drive.

When about an hour of travel time remained, they had reached Bollebygdmotet along road forty. Ali stopped at a Statoil gas station and flowing walked into the gas station while a dark Mercedes stopped behind them. Mustafa got out of the car and walked over to Ali, who was still sitting in the bus, and cranked down the side window. Mustafa gave him two foil packs of Remeron and Postafen.

Flowing came out of the gas station carrying a plastic bag. At the car, she took out thirteen plastic glasses and lined them up on a table. From the plastic bag she picked up thirteen smaller plastic bottles of orange juice.

Ali got out of the car and discreetly handed over the packs of pills, then grabbed a bottle of orange juice and walked back to the car. Flowing put one Remeron tablet in each drinking glass and half a tablet of Postafen and mixed thoroughly with a plastic knife.

Everything was ready to consume. Mustafa opened the side door and the children got to step out and drink a glass each. Jacob drank from his glass and then found some grains in the glass. He walked up to Mustafa and showed it off. He explained that it was leftovers from the motion sickness tablet that everyone had received to avoid motion sickness and unnecessary stops.

"We don't want to get into trouble like that, do we?" he asked, and Jacob shook his head.

Flowing urged all the children to get in the car. Ali slammed the side door shut and the bus continued on its way towards Gothenburg, closely followed by the black Mercedes.

After a while, Jacob felt how tired he was. He looked around as he yawned and saw that he was not alone. Three of the children had already fallen asleep. His eyelids felt heavier and heavier as he tried to stay awake. After five minutes, all the children were asleep.

Chapter 53

30 SEPTEMBER 2014

EMRAH GUARDED ONE of the rail-going harbor cranes that unloaded the containers. There were forty-five containers to be unloaded before twenty-five new ones could be loaded on board and shipped to Portugal. He let his gaze sweep over the vast port area and stopped at the blue container, one of the twenty-five to be loaded on board.

Two selected sailors went ashore from King Jacob and up to the blue container. They opened the doors and lifted a ramp that was placed in front of it. The 40-foot container was loaded with clothes boxes and some refrigerators and freezers. Outside, about ten boxes were lined up. Now we just had to wait.

Mustafa turned right and could glimpse a bit of the ship's command bridge. In the rearview mirror, he saw that the red bus was close behind. At the quayside, the entire container ship appeared. Mustafa spotted the blue container and stopped the car a little to the side so as not to get in the way.

Ali saw the open container with the driving ramp standing against the doorway. He paused before turning around and looking intently at Flowing and smiling.

"Are you going to stay in the car or are you going to get out?" whispered Ali

"I have orders to stay seated in case anyone wakes up," she replied, showing her loyalty.

Two sailors ran up to the bus, folded in the exterior mirrors and then gave Ali permission to drive into the container. He drove as far in as he could, turned off the engine with the gear in and then applied the handbrake just in case. Now it was just a matter of getting out of the car without making a noise. He looked at Flowing and met her worried gaze. She forced a small smile that showed that everything was okay before he, with some difficulty, forced his way out of the car and closed the car door gently. He had to press himself against the steel wall to get out while both sailors began to load the boxes that were outside.

Mustafa stood and inspected how one of the sailors sealed the container after closing the steel doors. The harbor crane brought down a square steel frame that lay on the roof and locked it before slowly lifting the container, which began to rock lightly in the air.

Jacob woke up sleep drunk as the car rocked, while a heavy thud was heard from above. He looked around. It was like being in a black hole, it was pitch black. Suddenly, he felt the car lift and someone from his left grabbed his hand. He assumed it was Flowing sitting next to him. With a motor sound from outside, Jacob felt the car soar higher and higher, while the grip on his hand tightened. The floating feeling ceased with a thud and Jacob felt a faint swaying sideways.

The car moved with a motor whining sound in the background, then it stopped with some rocking movements. When the rocking then stopped, there was again a motor sound and some thumping sounds. At the same moment, he felt the car slide downward into the darkness. With a metallic thud, it felt as if the car landed on a hard floor. A new metallic sound was heard and a thud, then the engine sound disappeared. Instead, male voices and rapid footsteps were heard.

Jacob felt someone trying to get him to drink from a plastic bottle as he heard Flowing's calmed voice whisper something in Arabic. It tasted like orange juice as he drank three sips, and he felt someone's hand stroke his head. Jacob had time to swallow the last sip when something heavy was suddenly placed on top of the car. Then there were more male voices and someone whistling in the background. Jacob could not keep his eyes open and fell asleep when he thought he heard Mustafa's firm voice somewhere out there in the dark. He had kept his promise, he was there as his protector.

* * *

Inside the cab, Mustafa felt dissatisfied on the bed bunk before throwing the bag onto it. It had to be enough, he had slept on worse surfaces than this. There was a knock on the door, and he opened it carefully. Captain Emrah stood outside with a smile and without saying anything. Mustafa let him in and then looked out into the narrow corridor just in case before the cabin door closed.

"God is great," Emrah said in Arabic as Mustafa went to his bag and picked out a white, well-filled A5 envelope and handed it to Emrah.

"God is greater," Mustafa replied with a smile.

Emrah opened the envelope and found that there were crowns bills in it but did not bother to count before closing the envelope.

"You didn't count," Mustafa said with a small smile.

"I think Toh can count, he has never let me down before," he said with a smile. "We depart at 15:00. We will get pleasant weather and the waves will have settled a bit when we get out onto the open sea. I have to go."

* * *

At three o'clock in the afternoon, Ali could witness how the moorings to King Jacob were unloaded and the ship slowly slipped out of the concrete wharf. He got into the black Mercedes as the ship set off and held out for an oncoming container ship to dock at the dock.

The dockworkers saw the swaying Liberian flag in the stern as the ship passed Kyrkogårdsholmen and Älvsborg Fortress. A view of historic proportions viewed by Emrah with binoculars from the starboard bridge wing.

After passing Galterö at the height of Lilla Rawholmen, the container ship changed its course to a northwesterly direction. The aftermath of the earlier storm was barely noticeable. Against the horizon you could discern a faint haze which could become foggy during the evening.

Mustafa stepped onto the command bridge where Emrah stood with binoculars at the ready, looking out at the horizon. Mustafa stood by and looked out at all the containers lined up on the ship's deck. Then he looked below the bridge and saw the blue container at the bottom of the deck with four containers loaded on top. Emrah lowered the binoculars a little thoughtfully and held it to her chest.

“In two hours, you can open, then we’ll be on the international Waters. I have told the diner to arrange extra meals for the evening. I will let you know when it is time,” he said.

“Thank you,” Mustafa replied with a smile.

* * *

When Jacob woke up, he was leaning against Flowing, who was sitting with a flashlight reading from the Koran. Outside, the screams of seagulls could be heard as the car highlighted a slow rocking motion with cracking sounds. He heard waves sporadically hitting something. He turned around and saw in the dim light of the flashlight that there were more children who had woken up. Where are we? Jacob thought, looking at Flowing with a surprised look.

Chapter 54

1 OCTOBER 2014

TEN KILOMETERS NORTHWEST of the city of Mosul in northern Iraq was the small village of Hatarah. Near the prayer site Hakeem Fers there was a farm centered between two neighboring farms with small-scale animal husbandry. The farm did not make much of a fuss, there were a few cows and chickens grazing along the wall, just like in all the other nearby farms. The village of Hatarah was one of the few places in Iraq that the war had not yet touched.

For Abu Bakr, the village, and the farm he lived in were strategically well. The dwelling house was centrally found between the two side buildings where his elite fighters lived, there were IS fighters dressed as workers to blend in with the surroundings. Not even the black symbol flag was raised, in its place fluttered a sun-bleached Iraqi flag. All to keep the tranquility of the village and thus the safety of Abu Bakr.

Inside a room in the dwelling house, a little girl slept with a sheet and an extra blanket over her. Her dark, semi-curly hair was spread across the pillow. Outside, there was a brief cackle of the chickens pecking around the courtyard. Soon after, a brown-black wooden door to the bedroom opened, and a tall, black-clad person with a covered face mask stepped in. The person kept a firm grip around a sword handle that stuck up above the waist belt. Next to it was a Russian army pistol of the brand Yarygin PYa - 6P35 stabbed.

The face was gently pulled down and a tanned face with a well-groomed beard appeared. Abu Bakr walked over and crouched down next to the girl lying in bed. He looked at her while admiring her hair while she slept. He put his scarred hand over her head and gently caressed her hair. The girl woke up and turned around. She smiled as she stretched and then straightened the blanket.

"Good morning Nassiva. Has my jewel slept well?" asked Abu Bakr, the leader of the Islamic State, as he gave his daughter a kiss on the forehead.

Eleven-year-old Nassiva nodded eagerly, shining like a morning sun with her beautiful brown eyes as she raised her arms to her father.

"Good morning father, when will I receive my gift?"

"Patience my daughter, patience. It is coming," he replied with a smile.

She gave her father a morning hug and whispered, "God is great."

"God is greater," he replied.

INSHA'ALLAH

Printed in the USA
CPSIA information can be obtained
at www.ICGtesting.com
LVHW041238261023
762201LV00001B/149

9 781961 438668